D0893479

DISCARDED

THE SHREWSBURY EDITION OF THE WORKS OF SAMUEL BUTLER. EDITED BY HENRY FESTING JONES AND A. T. BARTHOLOMEW. IN TWENTY VOLUMES. VOLUME SIXTEEN: EREWHON REVISITED

SAMUEL BUTLER AT HOME (1898)

From a photograph by Alfred Emery Cathie

EREWHON REVISITED

by

SAMUEL BUTLER

AMS PRESS
NEW YORK

From the edition of 1925, London & New York
First AMS EDITION published 1968
Manufactured in the United States of America

AMS PRESS, INC.
New York, N.Y. 10003

Contents

Erewhon Revisited

Illustrations

ON RETURNING FROM ITALY AT THE END of October 1923, I found among the letters and parcels which had accumulated during the last week or so of my absence, volumes i and ii of this Shrewsbury Edition of Butler's Works. Of course I left the other things to wait, and took up the first volume which contains Butler's *First Year in Canterbury Settlement.* It opened of its own accord at page 116 and, in accordance with the natural law which provides that if a book does contain a misprint that misprint will be the first thing to spring up out of it into the face of anyone who has had much to do with the preparation of the book, I found myself confronted with the illustration of Butler's Homestead, Mesopotamia, N.Z., and saw that it had been reversed. I seemed to hear all New Zealand rising in an uproar; for I know that in the Colony they are very proud of Butler's Homestead, and would certainly resent its appearing as in a looking-glass.

There was, however, nothing to be done at the moment; and, after glancing through the rest of the volume, and looking cursorily at vol. ii, I turned to my letters. The first I opened was from Sir Joseph Kinsey and runs as follows:

160, Hereford Street, Christchurch, N.Z.
7th September, 1923.

"DEAR SIR, Recently, in going through some old matter on early Canterbury, N.Z., I came across the original water-colour sketches made by the late Sir Julius Haast when exploring the Head Waters of the Rakaia river in 1864–which sketches were reproduced as coloured lithographs in his paper 'Report on the Head Waters of the Rakaia, with illustrations and maps, 1866.'

"Another find was a small water-colour drawing, which Professor Wall of Canterbury College has identified as a sketch of Samuel Butler's hut at Mesopotamia

" The Professor being anxious to obtain a lantern slide to illustrate a lecture he is shortly giving on ' The Upper Rangitata–Butler's country,' I had a photo taken of the sketch.

" I understand you desire to make the new Shrewsbury Edition as complete as possible, and this drawing, being probably the first taken of Butler's historic hut–even before the photo mentioned by the late Mr. J. D. Enys in the *Memoir of Samuel Butler*, vol. i, pp. 103-4, and vol. ii, pp. 103-4–you may be glad to include it with other illustrations on the same subject. I enclose a print herewith.

" I have given my agents, Messrs. Whitcombe & Tombs, Ltd., through their Christchurch house, instructions to secure a copy of the Shrewsbury Edition, and I'm sure it will make a valuable addition to the works I already possess on Butler's writings.

" Yours faithfully,

" JOSEPH KINSEY."

Here was a chance of salvation, and I quoted to myself Mr. Higgs's remark in chapter 4 of *Erewhon*: " As luck would have it, Providence was on my side." The publication of *Erewhon Revisited* in the Shrewsbury Edition of Butler's Works provides an opportunity for me to attempt to avert the fury of New Zealand by introducing into it a reproduction of Sir Joseph Kinsey's photograph. It will thus illustrate the country which provided the scenery for the return of Mr. Higgs to Erewhon, just as it might have been used to illustrate the scenery he saw on his first visit to that country. And I trust that this time the " historic hut " will manage to get itself reproduced the right way round.

Erewhon Revisited is the last book written by Butler and the last of his books to be published in his lifetime. As I have said in the *Memoir* he intended the visit of Mr. Higgs

BUTLER'S HOMESTEAD, MESOPOTAMIA, N.Z.

From an early water-colour drawing

to be the prologue, and the visit of his son, John, was to have been the book; instead of which there was so much to say in the prologue that it became the book, and John's visit had to be confined to an epilogue. He wrote it more rapidly and more easily than any of his other books. This was, no doubt, because he had been contemplating a return to Erewhon nearly ever since the original book had appeared, that is for nearly thirty years, and had made many notes for it, some of which are given in the *Note-Books*. In May or June 1902, when he was on his death-bed in London, he said to me something which appears thus in the Biographical Sketch of his Life (vol. i of the Shrewsbury Edition):

"I am much better to-day. I don't feel at all as though I were going to die. Of course, it will be all wrong if I do get well, for there is my literary position to be considered. First I write *Erewhon*—that is my opening subject; then, after modulating freely through all my other books and the music and so on, I return gracefully to my original key and write *Erewhon Revisited*. Obviously, now is the proper moment to come to a full close, make my bow and retire; but I believe I am getting well, after all. It's very inartistic, but I cannot help it."

This was no doubt a conscious repetition to me of a speech he had made to Fuller Maitland a few weeks earlier in Palermo—a speech which he had in his mind when he added the postscript to the pathetic letter to Mr. and Mrs. Fuller Maitland from Naples of 14th May 1902 on his return from Sicily for the last time. The letter is reproduced in facsimile in the *Memoir*, vol. ii, p. 393, and the postscript is as follows:

"You will not forget the pretty roundness of my literary career! α *Erewhon* ω *Erewhon Revisited*."

In confining himself to *Erewhon* and *Erewhon Revisited* he was overlooking something, and the roundness of his literary career was even prettier than he thought at the time. The return to Erewhon and the reporting of progress there had been actively in his mind for nearly thirty years, as I have said; but that other subject which enters into his pamphlet, *The Evidence for the Resurrection of Jesus Christ as given by the Four Evangelists critically examined*, published in 1865, had also been sleeping there, turning over restlessly now and then and reminding him that here was another matter to be attended to some day, if he lived to do it. He saw in time that this subject would combine in counterpoint with the return to Erewhon. Accordingly the progress reported as having taken place between the two visits of Mr. Higgs shows the effect that one supposed miracle had on the Erewhonians. It shows how it is not the miracle that gives rise to the faith; it is the people's love of mystery that invests the natural event with miraculous attributes. The reader of the second book, who has, of course, read the first, knows that there was nothing miraculous in the ascent of Mr. Higgs in the balloon, nor in the subsequent falling of the rain; the miraculousness was supplied because the people demanded it.

There is also a third subject in the book. He wrote to the *Daily Chronicle* (31st October 1901, *Memoir*, ii, 356-7) when correcting an error into which their reviewer had fallen:

" The name Yram was fixed, quite guilelessly, some thirty years ago, and could not be changed. That she should have had a son by Higgs was an afterthought not contemplated till I began to write *Erewhon Revisited* and saw how useful an ally a son would be to him. Moreover, this afterthought gave occasion for the second leading idea of the book, which so far no reviewer has noticed. I mean the story of a father trying to win the love of a hitherto unknown son, by risking his life in order to show himself worthy of it–and succeeding. The marriage of Strong with Yram was dictated by my inability to see

Dates of Events mentioned
in Erewhon revisited.

1846 about Nov. or December — my father born — (p. 4 of Erewhon)

1868 Say, Augt. 1 or thereabouts, he left England (p. 2 of Erewhon)

" " Nov. or December he reached a colony, whose name is not given. p. 4 (he was a year & 2 mos. at the station [illegible] p. 14.)

1870 after shearing, p. 14 i.e. say, Feb. [for we are to be in the Southern hemisphere] my father starts exploring, and reaches the Statues about Feb. 28. 1870

1870. He was all the time in Erewhon till Dec. 7, on which day he escaped in the balloon.

1871. Sep 29. I am born.

1872 Easter — my father published his book, & supports himself for a time by writing tracts — afterwards takes to drawing pictures on the pavement.

1885. say Nov. my father inherits his uncle's property.

1890. Augt. 1. (say) my father begins to talk of an intended journey

October (1) (say) he quietly disappears.

1890 December 4 (summer in Southern hemisphere)

XIX. xii. 29 Thurs. he reaches the statues. On the evening of that day he falls in with Professors Hanky & Panky

xii 30 Fri Dec. 5. He returns for his European dress.

xii 31 Sat " 6. He again enters Erewhon.

XX i. 1 S. " 7. The twentieth anniversary of his escape in the balloon he goes to Coldharbour, now Sunchildston, gets into trouble, is rescued by Yram and conveyed by her sons to a place of safety.

[illegible] Being able now to travel he is escorted by a son of Yram's, and is left near the statues. He gets down to the wooled and camps.

1891 Feb. 1. He reaches S. Francisco, & sends a telegram. Towards the end of the month he returns home.

1891 Early summer, he dies.

DATES OF EVENTS MENTIONED IN "EREWHON REVISITED"

From the MS. at the British Museum

any other way of saving Yram and of putting her son in a position to help his father."

This, of course, was a return to something earlier than the pamphlet–to the memories of his own home life; it was a dreaming of how it might have been with him, if, like George, he had had a sympathetic father.

*

The full title of the book is *Erewhon Revisited twenty years later, both by the Original Discoverer of the Country and by his Son.* It was published in July 1901, and a second edition appeared in September 1902.

A Chronology for the book was found among Butler's papers after Streatfeild's death; a portion of it is here reproduced in facsimile, in accordance with the statement in the Introduction to *Erewhon* (vol. ii of the Shrewsbury Edition).

1924. H. F. JONES.

POSTSCRIPT

IN 1875 someone gave me a copy of the fifth edition of *Erewhon* (1873). This was before I knew Butler; soon after I made his acquaintance he pasted into the book two leaves of additions in MS. I then lent it to a friend but forgot to which friend, and consequently could not ask for its return. Afterwards, one evening, in my chambers in Holborn, Butler said he wanted to look at *Erewhon*, and I had to confess that I had lost it. He thereupon made me promise never to lend any of his books because he was so liable to want to refer to one or other of them when he was with me. I promised; and, so far as I remember, I have religiously kept that promise.

I said something about this in my *Memoir* of Butler, i, 167-8, but I heard no more of my lost book until it turned up in a sale at Sotheby's on the 28th of October 1924, and fetched £7, paid by Messrs. Spurr and Swift, 123 Pall Mall, S.W.1, for their client, Mr. Joseph Halle Schaffner, of Chicago. I communicated with this gentleman, begging him to let me have a copy of the inserted MS. so that I might see whether, in the *Memoir*, I had correctly stated the substance of it. I was astonished and delighted to receive from him in reply a letter of which the following is a copy:

Hart Schaffner & Marx
Chicago   New York

Chicago December 6 1924.

Mr. Henry Festing Jones,
St. John's College,
Cambridge, England.

"MY DEAR MR. JONES, Spurr & Swift have forwarded to me your letter of November twenty-second and I take pleasure in sending to you under separate cover the copy of the book referred to, to be added to the collection of Butler items at St. John's College.

"No one who has enjoyed the hospitality of Cambridge as I did this summer (Trinity and Caius) and has viewed with delight, at least from the outside, the beauties of St. John's can be other than grateful for an opportunity to show his appreciation of all the beauty that St. John's and Cambridge have added to the world. You will not, I trust, feel that I am presumptuous in exceeding your request in this way. It gives me great pleasure to return this book to its proper home and to add in this way my small tribute to Butler's memory by entrusting the book to the shrine which you have created for him.

"Yours sincerely,

"JOSEPH HALLE SCHAFFNER."

In due course the book arrived, and I am depositing it at St. John's with the letters and documents relating to its recovery. It was particularly graceful of Mr. Schaffner to think of returning it to me, so that I might have the pleasure of handing it on, and I am happy to be able to take this opportunity of thanking him publicly for his sympathetic and generous action.

When I looked into the volume I found that in writing the passage in the *Memoir* I had forgotten that it contained two MS. additions. The longer one was the one I was thinking of; it is inserted between pp. 98 and 99 as a conclusion to chapter 11, "An Erewhonian Trial," and is as follows:

"Other and hardly less extraordinary cases then came on, which I only refrain from describing lest I should try the reader's patience. Thus one poor fellow was indicted for having lost his wife to whom he had been tenderly attached. The defence attempted was that he had never been really fond of her, but it broke down completely, for the neighbours were unanimous in testifying to the affectionate terms on which the couple had lived together; indeed it was all the prisoner could do to avoid bursting into tears as incident after incident came out in evidence against him. The judge told him that nature had evidently [intended] the loss of such a wife to be severely punished, and that the pain which he evidently felt was the natural consequence of his calamity. Whenever nature attached a penalty the previous conduct had been in some way or other immoral, and contrary to her laws; it was necessary therefore that society should mark its sense of the transgression. The prisoner was then ordered to be whipped.

"Another case was that of a youth barely arrived at man's estate, who was accused of having been swindled by some of his nearest relations–among them his own father. The lad, who was undefended, pleaded that he was young, inexperienced, greatly in awe of his father, and wholly without independent professional advice. 'Young man,' replied the judge with great severity, 'your avowal is the most shameless which I ever listened to. People have no right to be young, inexperienced, greatly in awe of their fathers, wholly without independent professional advice, and to have reversionary interests in nice houses; if young people thus outrage the moral sense of their friends they must expect to suffer for it.' He, too, was ordered to be whipped, but more severely than the man who had lost his wife.

"S.B."

Not only had I forgotten that there were two inserted pieces of MS., but it looks as though I had also forgotten all about the trial of the poor man who had lost his wife; for the purpose of the passage in the *Memoir*, however, it was not necessary to say anything about him, whether I actually had forgotten him or not.

In the MS. Butler wrote, "Nature had evidently the loss." The word "evidently" is struck through in pencil and "intended" is substituted, also in pencil; this is either in Butler's handwriting or in mine, I cannot determine which, but I think it is in mine.

If the reader will refer to the opening of chapter 11 in any copy of *Erewhon* dated 1901, or later, he will find that, though the wording is altered, this account of the trials of the man who had lost his wife and of the inexperienced youth with a reversionary interest in a nice house is substantially the same. It was Pauli who made Butler cut out the latter from the original *Erewhon*, lest it might offend Canon Butler, for it would have been recognized at Langar as an allusion to the sale of the Whitehall at Shrewsbury; but Butler restored it in the 1901 edition of *Erewhon*, his father being then dead.

The other inserted passage is about the Italian use of

the word "disgrazia." It occurs in my recovered copy of *Erewhon* between pp. 92 and 93 as the conclusion of chapter 10, "Current Opinions," and is as follows:

"It is possible to detect some traces of the Erewhonian philosophy even in our own country; thus it is common to hear poor people say they are 'very bad,' meaning that they are ill; or that they have a 'bad' hand or arm if they have hurt one or the other. Examples will occur readily to the reader. Among some foreign nations traces of the Erewhonian manner of looking at things may be seen yet more distinctly. The Mahommedans for example send all their female prisoners to hospitals, while the Maories in New Zealand visit any misfortune with a forcible entry into the house of the offender, and the breaking up and burning of all his goods. The Italians go so far as to use the same word for disgrace and misfortune, 'son disgraziato,' meaning simply, 'I have been unfortunate.'"

I do not think that Butler cut this second piece of MS. out of the original *Erewhon*; I think rather that it did not occur to him, while writing the book, that it ought to go in; and that when he inserted it in my copy he was regretting that it had not gone in and intending to include it should a reconsidered version ever be called for. The Italian use of the word "disgrazia" as something to be referred to some day had been in his mind even longer than the Return to Erewhon, for he had first observed it when he was a mere boy, spending the winter of 1843-4 with his family in Rome and Naples. This is his note:

"Signora Capocci (I think her name was) who used to teach us Italian at Naples, told us of a poor dear young friend of hers who had had a great misfortune. Her words impressed me:

"'Povero disgraziato!' she exclaimed, 'Ha ammazzato il suo zio e la sua zia.' (Poor unfortunate fellow! he has murdered his uncle and his aunt.)"

This is quoted in the *Memoir*, i, 26, and I go on to say

that in 1882 he wrote in *Alps and Sanctuaries*: "If an accident does happen they call it a 'disgrazia,' thus confirming the soundness of a philosophy which I put forward in a previous work."

When it came to reconsidering *Erewhon* for the 1901 edition he added, near the opening of chapter 10, "Current Opinions," the illustration about people speaking of having a "bad" arm or finger, and also Signora Capocci's remark about the youth who had had the misfortune to murder his uncle. And he goes on with another illustration which could not have been included in the original *Erewhon* because the incident did not happen until we had been several times in Sicily. This was about the young coachman, Francesco Corona, who once met us on our arrival at Trapani and, apologizing for not having seen us on our recent visits, gave as his reason that he had had "tre anni di militare e due anni di disgrazia" (three years of military service and two years of misfortune)–the latter two years, as we afterwards learned, having been spent in prison for shooting at his father with intent to kill him.

I agree that the story of the recovery of my lost copy of *Erewhon* ought to have been told in this Shrewsbury edition in the Introduction to the volume containing *Erewhon*, but that volume had already appeared a year before the book was sold at Sotheby's, so that my reason for not telling it in its right place resembles Butler's for not recording Francesco Corona's remark in the original edition.

And now something else has happened too late for the introduction to the volume of this edition which contains *A First Year in Canterbury Settlement* where, like Sir Joseph Kinsey's letter, it ought to have been mentioned. I recently received from New Zealand a letter of which the following is a copy:

Introduction to the Shrewsbury Edition

Sale St. Auckland N.Z.
10 December, 1924.

H. Festing Jones Esq.
120 Maida Vale W.

"DEAR SIR, I have long been an admirer of Samuel Butler and have a good collection of his works, including early editions of *Erewhon*, *Life and Habit*, and *The Fair Haven.* I bought your very interesting Life of S.B. about two years ago and was absorbed in reading it. I only regret that you had not more material relating to his life in Canterbury. I recently came across a very rare book–*The Brand Book of Canterbury*, by G. Turner–which gives the brand used by Butler at Mesopotamia. As I do not see any mention of this in your book I think it might interest you to have it.

"Yours truly,

"JOHN KENDERDINE.

"Butler, Samuel. Mesopotamia, Forks of the Rangitata. Registered 26 November 1860.

"From: *Brand Book for Canterbury: containing a fac-simile of every sheep-brand registered in the Province of Canterbury, with the name of the owner or overseer, title of the run, and situation of the Head Station*, etc. By G. Turner Registrar of Brands.–Christchurch: Union Printing Office, 1861. 8°, pp. 30."

When I read this it seemed to me possible that in choosing for his brand a representation of a common kitchen candlestick Butler was thinking of a common tallow candle.

I supposed that on a sheep-station the tallow would be made of mutton-fat and the wick of sheep's wool. But I have had to give up the wool, at any rate at Mesopotamia, because on looking at the *Memoir*, i, 82, I find that among the " Things for the Dray to bring up " from Christchurch to his run, about 1863, one entry is, " Candle wick 20 lbs., £2." So I suppose they bought ready-made cotton wicks; but that is no reason against their using mutton-fat for the tallow. If we had known of this before the Shrewsbury edition began to appear someone might have thought of adopting Butler's candlestick as a badge, so that every one of his books might have been issued branded with the same mark as that borne by every one of his sheep. And each book might have carried as a motto these words: " We are the people of his pasture and the sheep of his hand." This latter suggestion, however, might have been considered irreverent, so it is perhaps just as well that it could not be made.

March 1925. H.F.J.

PREFACE TO THE FIRST EDITION

I FORGET WHEN, BUT NOT VERY LONG AFTER I had published *Erewhon* in 1872, it occurred to me to ask myself what course events in Erewhon would probably take after Mr. Higgs, as I suppose I may now call him, had made his escape in the balloon with Arowhena. Given a people in the conditions supposed to exist in Erewhon, and given the apparently miraculous ascent of a remarkable stranger into the heavens with an earthly bride–what would be the effect on the people generally?

There was no use in trying to solve this problem before, say, twenty years should have given time for Erewhonian developments to assume something like permanent shape, and in 1892 I was too busy with books now published to be able to attend to Erewhon. It was not till the early winter of 1900, *i.e.* as nearly as may be thirty years after the date of Higgs's escape, that I found time to deal with the question above stated, and to answer it, according to my lights, in the book which I now lay before the public.

I have concluded, I believe rightly, that the events described in chapter 24 of *Erewhon* would give rise to such a cataclysmic change in the old Erewhonian opinions as would result in the development of a new religion. Now the development of all new religions follows much the same general course. In all cases the times are more or less out of joint–older faiths are losing their hold upon the masses. At such times, let a personality appear, strong in itself, and made to seem still stronger by association with some supposed transcendent miracle, and it will be easy to raise a Lo here! that will attract many followers. If there be a single great, and apparently well-authenticated, miracle, others will accrete round it; then, in all religions that have so originated, there will follow temples, priests, rites, sincere believers, and unscrupulous exploiters of public credulity. To chronicle the events that followed Higgs's balloon ascent without showing that they were much as they have been under like conditions in other places, would be to hold the mirror up to something very wide of nature.

Analogy, however, between courses of events is one thing–historic parallelisms abound; analogy between the main actors in events is a very different one, and one, moreover, of which few examples can be found. The development of the new ideas in Erewhon is a familiar one, but there is no more likeness between Higgs and the founder of any other religion, than there is between Jesus Christ and Mahomet. He is a typical middle-class Englishman, deeply tainted with priggishness in his earlier years, but in great part freed from it by the sweet uses of adversity.

If I may be allowed for a moment to speak about myself, I would say that I have never ceased to profess myself a member of the more advanced wing of the English Broad Church. What those who belong to this wing believe, I believe. What they reject, I reject. No two people think absolutely alike on any subject, but when I converse with advanced Broad Churchmen I find myself in substantial harmony with them. I believe–and should be very sorry if I did not believe–that, *mutatis mutandis*, such men will find the advice given on pp. 277-281 and 287-291[1] of this book much what, under the supposed circumstances, they would themselves give.

Lastly, I should express my great obligations to Mr. R. A. Streatfeild of the British Museum, who, in the absence from England of my friend Mr. H. Festing Jones, has kindly supervised the corrections of my book as it passed through the press.

1st May 1901. SAMUEL BUTLER.

[1] [Shrewsbury Edition, pp. 218-221 and 227-229.]

Erewhon Revisited

CHAPTER ONE: UPS AND DOWNS OF FORTUNE, MY FATHER STARTS FOR EREWHON

BEFORE TELLING THE STORY OF MY father's second visit to the remarkable country which he discovered now some thirty years since, I should perhaps say a few words about his career between the publication of his book in 1872, and his death in the early summer of 1891. I shall thus touch briefly on the causes that occasioned his failure to maintain that hold on the public which he had apparently secured at first.

His book, as the reader may perhaps know, was published anonymously, and my poor father used to ascribe the acclamation with which it was received, to the fact that no one knew who it might not have been written by. *Omne ignotum pro magnifico*, and during its month of anonymity the book was a frequent topic of appreciative comment in good literary circles. Almost coincidently with the discovery that he was a mere nobody, people began to feel that their admiration had been too hastily bestowed, and before long opinion turned all the more seriously against him for this very reason. The subscription, to which the Lord Mayor had at first given his cordial support, was curtly announced as closed before it had been opened a week; it had met with so little success that I will not specify the amount eventually handed over, not without protest, to my father; small, however, as it was, he narrowly escaped being prosecuted for trying to obtain money under false pretences.

The Geographical Society, which had for a few days received him with open arms, was among the first to turn upon him—not, so far as I can ascertain, on account of the mystery in which he had enshrouded the exact whereabouts of Erewhon, nor yet by reason of its being persistently alleged that he was subject to frequent attacks of alcoholic poisoning – but through his own want of tact, and a highly-strung nervous state, which led him to attach too much importance to his own discoveries, and not enough to those of other people. This, at least, was my father's version of the matter, as I heard it from his own lips in the later years of his life.

"I was still very young," he said to me, "and my mind was more or less unhinged by the strangeness and peril of my adventures." Be this as it may, I fear there is no doubt that he was injudicious; and an ounce of judgement is worth a pound of discovery.

Hence, in a surprisingly short time, he found himself dropped even by those who had taken him up most warmly, and had done most to find him that employment as a writer of religious tracts on which his livelihood was then dependent. The discredit, however, into which my father fell, had the effect of deterring any considerable number of people from trying to rediscover Erewhon, and thus caused it to remain as unknown to geographers in general as though it had never been found. A few shepherds and cadets at up-country stations had, indeed, tried to follow in my father's footsteps, during the time when his book was still being taken seriously; but they had most of them returned, unable to face the difficulties that had opposed them. Some few, however, had not returned, and though search was made for them, their bodies had not been found. When he reached Erewhon on his second visit, my father learned that others had attempted to visit the country more recently – probably quite independently of his own book; and before he had himself been in it many hours he gathered what the fate of these poor fellows doubtless was.

Another reason that made it more easy for Erewhon to remain unknown, was the fact that the more mountainous districts, though repeatedly prospected for gold, had been pronounced non-auriferous, and as there was no sheep or cattle country, save a few river-bed flats, above the upper gorges of any of the rivers, and no game to tempt the sportsman, there was nothing to induce people to penetrate into the fastnesses of the great snowy range. No more, therefore, being heard of Erewhon, my father's book came to be regarded as a mere work of fiction, and I have heard quite recently of its having been seen on a second-hand bookstall, marked "*6d.* very readable."

Though there was no truth in the stories about my father's being subject to attacks of alcoholic poisoning, yet, during the first few years after his return to England, his occasional fits of ungovernable excitement gave some colour to the opinion that much of what he said he had seen and done might be only subjectively true. I refer more particularly to his interview with Chowbok in the wool-shed, and his highly coloured description of the statues on the top of the pass leading into Erewhon. These were soon set down as forgeries of delirium, and it was maliciously urged, that though in his book he had only admitted having taken "two or three bottles of brandy" with him, he had probably taken at least a dozen; and that if on the night before he reached the statues he had "only four ounces of brandy" left, he must have been drinking heavily for the preceding fortnight or three weeks. Those who read the following pages will, I think, reject all idea that my father was in a state of delirium, not without surprise that any one should have ever entertained it.

It was Chowbok who, if he did not originate these calumnies, did much to disseminate and gain credence for them. He remained in England for some years, and never tired of doing what he could to disparage my father. The cunning creature had ingratiated himself with our leading religious societies, especially with the more evangelical among them. Whatever doubt there might be about his sincerity, there was none about his colour, and a coloured convert in those days was more than Exeter Hall could resist. Chowbok saw that there was no room for him and for my father, and declared my poor father's story to be almost wholly false. It was true, he said, that he and my father had explored the head-waters of the river described in his book, but he denied that my father had gone on without him, and he named the river as one distant by many thousands of miles from the one it really was. He said that after about a fortnight he had returned in company with my father, who by that time had become incapacitated for further travel. At this point he would shrug his shoulders, look mysterious, and thus say "alcoholic poisoning" even more effectively than if he had uttered the words themselves. For a man's tongue lies often in his shoulders.

Readers of my father's book will remember that Chowbok had given a very different version when he had returned to his employer's station; but time and distance afford cover under which falsehood can often do truth to death securely.

I never understood why my father did not bring my mother forward to confirm his story. He may have done so while I was too young to know anything about it. But when people have made up their minds, they are impatient of further evidence; my mother, moreover, was of a very retiring disposition. The Italians say:

> "Chi lontano va ammogliare
> Sarà ingannato, o vorrà ingannare."

"If a man goes far afield for a wife, he will be deceived—or means deceiving." The proverb is as true for women as for men, and my mother was never quite happy in her new surroundings. Wilfully deceived she assuredly was not, but she could not accustom herself to English modes of thought; indeed she never even nearly mastered our language; my father always talked with her in Erewhonian, and so did I, for as a child she had taught me to do so, and I was as fluent with her language as with my father's. In this respect she often told me I could pass myself off anywhere in Erewhon as a native; I shared also her personal appearance, for though not wholly unlike my father, I had taken more closely after my mother. In mind, if I may venture to say so, I believe I was more like my father.

I may as well here inform the reader that I was born at the end of September 1871, and was christened John, after my grandfather. From what I have said above he will readily believe that my earliest experiences were somewhat squalid. Memories of childhood rush vividly upon me when I pass through a low London alley, and catch the faint sickly smell that pervades it–half paraffin, half black-currants, but wholly something very different. I have a fancy that we lived in Blackmoor Street, off Drury Lane. My father, when first I knew of his doing anything at all, supported my mother and myself by drawing pictures with coloured chalks upon the pavement; I used sometimes to watch him, and marvel at the skill with which he represented fogs, floods, and fires. These three "f's," he would say, were his three best friends, for they were easy to do and brought in halfpence freely. The return of the dove to the ark was his favourite subject. Such a little ark, on such a hazy morning, and such a little pigeon–the rest of the picture being cheap sky, and still cheaper sea; nothing, I have often heard him say, was more popular than this with his clients. He held it to be his masterpiece, but would add with some naïveté that he considered himself a public benefactor for carrying it out in such perishable fashion. "At any rate," he would say, "no one can bequeath one of my many replicas to the nation."

I never knew how much my father earned by his profession, but it must have been something considerable, for we always had enough to eat and drink; I imagine that he did better than many a struggling artist with more ambitious aims. He was strictly temperate during all the time that I knew anything about him, but he was not a teetotaler; I never saw any of the fits of nervous excitement which in his earlier years had done so much to wreck him. In the evenings, and on days when the state of the pavement did not permit him to work, he took great pains with my education, which he could very well do, for as a boy he had been in the sixth form of one of our foremost public schools. I found him a patient, kindly instructor, while to my mother he was a model husband. Whatever others may have said about him, I can never think of him without very affectionate respect.

Things went on quietly enough, as above indicated, till I was about fourteen, when by a freak of fortune my father became suddenly affluent. A brother of his father's had emigrated to Australia in 1851, and had amassed great wealth. We knew of his existence, but there had been no intercourse between him and my father, and we did not even know that he was rich and unmarried. He died intestate towards the end of 1885, and my father was the only relative he had, except, of course, myself, for both my father's sisters had died young, and without leaving children.

The solicitor through whom the news reached us was, happily, a man of the highest integrity, and also very sensible and kind. He was a Mr. Alfred Emery Cathie, of 15 Clifford's Inn, E.C., and my father placed himself unreservedly in his hands. I was at once sent to a first-rate school, and such pains had my father taken with me that I was placed in a higher form than might have been expected considering my age. The way in which he had taught me had prevented my feeling any dislike for study; I therefore stuck fairly well to my books, while not neglecting the games which are so important a part of healthy education. Everything went well with me, both as regards masters and school-fellows; nevertheless, I was declared to be of a highly nervous and imaginative temperament, and the school doctor more than once urged our headmaster not to push me forward too rapidly–for which I have ever since held myself his debtor.

Early in 1890, I being then home from Oxford (where I had been entered in the preceding year), my mother died; not so much from active illness, as from what was in reality a kind of *maladie du pays*. All along she had felt herself an exile, and though she had borne up wonderfully during my father's long struggle with adversity, she began to break as soon as prosperity had removed the necessity for exertion on her own part.

My father could never divest himself of the feeling that he had wrecked her life by inducing her to share her lot with his own; to say that he was stricken with remorse on losing her is not enough; he had been so stricken almost from the first year of his marriage; on her death he was haunted by the wrong he accused himself–as it seems to me very unjustly–of having done her, for it was neither his fault nor hers–it was Ate.

His unrest soon assumed the form of a burning desire to revisit the country in which he and my mother had been happier together than perhaps they ever again were. I had often heard him betray a hankering after a return to Erewhon, disguised so that no one should recognize him; but as long as my mother lived he would not leave her. When death had taken her from him, he so evidently stood in need of a complete change of scene, that even those friends who had most strongly dissuaded him from what they deemed a madcap enterprise, thought it better to leave him to himself. It would have mattered little how much they tried to dissuade him, for before long his passionate longing for the journey became so overmastering that nothing short of restraint in prison or a madhouse could have stayed his going; but we were not easy about him.

" He had better go," said Mr. Cathie to me, when I was at home for the Easter vacation, " and get it over. He is not well, but he is still in the prime of life; doubtless he will come back with renewed health and will settle down to a quiet home life again."

This, however, was not said till it had become plain that in a few days my father would be on his way. He had made a new will, and left an ample power of attorney with Mr. Cathie–or, as we always called him, Alfred–who was to supply me with whatever money I wanted; he had put all other matters in order in case anything should happen to prevent his ever returning, and he set out on 1st October 1890 more composed and cheerful than I had seen him for some time past.

I had not realized how serious the danger to my father would be if he were recognized while he was in Erewhon, for I am ashamed to say that I had not yet read his book. I had heard over and over again of his flight with my mother in the balloon, and had long since read his few opening chapters, but I had found, as a boy naturally would, that the succeeding pages were a little dull, and soon put the book aside. My father, indeed, repeatedly urged me not to read it, for he said there was much in it–more especially in the earlier chapters, which I had alone found interesting–that he would gladly cancel if he could. " But there ! " he had said with a laugh, " what does it matter ? "

He had hardly left, before I read his book from end

to end, and, on having done so, not only appreciated the risks that he would have to run, but was struck with the wide difference between his character as he had himself portrayed it, and the estimate I had formed of it from personal knowledge. When, on his return, he detailed to me his adventures, the account he gave of what he had said and done corresponded with my own ideas concerning him; but I doubt not the reader will see that the twenty years between his first and second visit had modified him even more than so long an interval might be expected to do.

I heard from him repeatedly during the first two months of his absence, and was surprised to find that he had stayed for a week or ten days at more than one place of call on his outward journey. On 26th November he wrote from the port whence he was to start for Erewhon, seemingly in good health and spirits; and on 27th December 1890 he telegraphed for a hundred pounds to be wired out to him at this same port. This puzzled both Mr. Cathie and myself, for the interval between 26th November and 27th December seemed too short to admit of his having paid his visit to Erewhon and returned; as, moreover, he had added the words, "Coming home," we rather hoped that he had abandoned his intention of going there.

We were also surprised at his wanting so much money, for he had taken a hundred pounds in gold, which, from some fancy, he had stowed in a small silver jewel-box that he had given my mother not long before she died. He had also taken a hundred pounds worth of gold nuggets, which he had intended to sell in Erewhon so as to provide himself with money when he got there.

I should explain that these nuggets would be worth in Erewhon fully ten times as much as they would in Europe, owing to the great scarcity of gold in that country. The Erewhonian coinage is entirely silver–

which is abundant, and worth much what it is in England–or copper, which is also plentiful; but what we should call five pounds' worth of silver money would not buy more than one of our half-sovereigns in gold.

He had put his nuggets into ten brown holland bags, and he had had secret pockets made for the old Erewhonian dress which he had worn when he escaped, so that he need never have more than one bag of nuggets accessible at a time. He was not likely, therefore, to have been robbed. His passage to the port above referred to had been paid before he started, and it seemed impossible that a man of his very inexpensive habits should have spent two hundred pounds in a single month–for the nuggets would be immediately convertible in an English colony. There was nothing, however, to be done but to cable out the money and wait my father's arrival.

Returning for a moment to my father's old Erewhonian dress, I should say that he had preserved it simply as a memento and without any idea that he should again want it. It was not the court dress that had been provided for him on the occasion of his visit to the king and queen, but the everyday clothing that he had been ordered to wear when he was put in prison, though his English coat, waistcoat, and trousers had been allowed to remain in his own possession. These, I had seen from his book, had been presented by him to the queen (with the exception of two buttons, which he had given to Yram as a keepsake), and had been preserved by her displayed upon a wooden dummy. The dress in which he escaped had been soiled during the hours that he and my mother had been in the sea, and had also suffered from neglect during the years of his poverty; but he wished to pass himself off as a common peasant or working man, so he preferred to have it set in order as might best be done, rather than copied.

So cautious was he in the matter of dress that he took with him the boots he had worn on leaving Erewhon, lest the foreign make of his English boots should arouse suspicion. They were nearly new, and when he had had them softened and well greased, he found he could still wear them quite comfortably.

But to return. He reached home late at night one day at the beginning of February, and a glance was enough to show that he was an altered man.

"What is the matter?" said I, shocked at his appearance. "Did you go to Erewhon, and were you ill-treated there?"

"I went to Erewhon," he said, "and I was not ill-treated there, but I have been so shaken that I fear I shall quite lose my reason. Do not ask me more now. I will tell you all about it to-morrow. Let me have something to eat, and go to bed."

When we met at breakfast next morning, he greeted me with all his usual warmth of affection, but he was still taciturn. "I will begin to tell you about it," he said, "after breakfast. Where is your dear mother? How was it that I have . . ."

Then of a sudden his memory returned, and he burst into tears.

I now saw, to my horror, that his mind was gone. When he recovered, he said: "It has all come back again, but at times now I am a blank, and every week am more and more so. I daresay I shall be sensible now for several hours. We will go into the study after breakfast, and I will talk to you as long as I can do so."

Let the reader spare me, and let me spare the reader any description of what we both of us felt.

When we were in the study, my father said, "My dearest boy, get pen and paper and take notes of what I tell you. It will be all disjointed; one day I shall remember this, and another that, but there will not be many more days on which I shall remember anything at all. I cannot write a coherent page. You, when I am gone, can piece what I tell you together, and tell it as I should have told it if I had been still sound. But do not publish it yet; it might do harm to those dear good people. Take the notes now, and arrange them the sooner the better, for you may want to ask me questions, and I shall not be here much longer. Let publishing wait till you are confident that publication can do no harm; and above all, say nothing to betray the whereabouts of Erewhon, beyond admitting (which I fear I have already done) that it is in the Southern hemisphere."

These instructions I have religiously obeyed. For the first days after his return, my father had few attacks of loss of memory, and I was in hopes that his former health of mind would return when he found himself in his old surroundings. During these days he poured forth the story of his adventures so fast, that if I had not had a fancy for acquiring shorthand, I should not have been able to keep pace with him. I repeatedly urged him not to overtax his strength, but he was oppressed by the fear that if he did not speak at once, he might never be able to tell me all he had to say; I had, therefore, to submit, though seeing plainly enough that he was only hastening the complete paralysis which he so greatly feared.

Sometimes his narrative would be coherent for pages together, and he could answer any questions without hesitation; at others, he was now here and now there, and if I tried to keep him to the order of events he would say that he had forgotten intermediate incidents, but that they would probably come back to him, and I should perhaps be able to put them in their proper places.

After about ten days he seemed satisfied that I had got all the facts, and that with the help of the pamphlets which he had brought with him I should be able to make out a connected story. "Remember," he said, "that I thought I was quite well so long as I was in Erewhon, and do not let me appear as anything else."

When he had fully delivered himself, he seemed easier in his mind, but before a month had passed he became completely paralysed, and though he lingered till the beginning of June, he was seldom more than dimly conscious of what was going on around him.

His death robbed me of one who had been a very kind and upright elder brother rather than a father; and so strongly have I felt his influence still present, living and working, as I believe for better within me, that I did not hesitate to copy the epitaph which he saw in the Musical Bank at Fairmead,[1] and to have it inscribed on the very simple monument which he desired should alone mark his grave.

*

The foregoing was written in the summer of 1891; what I now add should be dated 3rd December 1900. If, in the course of my work, I have misrepresented my father, as I fear I may have sometimes done, I would ask my readers to remember that no man can tell another's story without some involuntary misrepresentation both of facts and characters. They will, of course, see that *Erewhon Revisited* is written by one who has far less literary skill than the author of *Erewhon*; but again I would ask indulgence on the score of youth, and the fact that this is my first book. It was written nearly ten years ago, *i.e.* in the months from March to August 1891, but for reasons already given it could not then be made public. I have now received permission, and therefore publish the following chapters exactly or very nearly exactly, as they were left when I had finished editing my father's diaries, and the notes I took down

[1] See chapter 10.

from his own mouth—with the exception, of course, of these last few lines, hurriedly written as I am on the point of leaving England; of the additions I made in 1892, on returning from my own three hours' stay in Erewhon; and of the Postscript.

CHAPTER TWO: TO THE FOOT OF THE PASS INTO EREWHON

WHEN MY FATHER REACHED THE colony for which he had left England some twenty-two years previously, he bought a horse, and started up country on the evening of the day after his arrival, which was, as I have said, on one of the last days of November 1890. He had taken an English saddle with him, and a couple of roomy and strongly made saddle-bags. In these he packed his money, his nuggets, some tea, sugar, tobacco, salt, a flask of brandy, matches, and as many ship's biscuits as he thought he was likely to want; he took no meat, for he could supply himself from some accommodation-house or sheep-station, when nearing the point after which he would have to begin camping out. He rolled his Erewhonian dress and small toilet necessaries inside a warm red blanket, and strapped the roll on to the front part of his saddle. On to other D's, with which his saddle was amply provided, he strapped his Erewhonian boots, a tin pannikin, and a billy that would hold about a quart. I should, perhaps, explain to English readers that a billy is a tin can, the name for which (doubtless of French Canadian origin) is derived from the words *faire bouillir*. He also took with him a pair of hobbles and a small hatchet.

He spent three whole days in riding across the plains, and was struck with the very small signs of change that he could detect, but the fall in wool, and the failure, so far, to establish a frozen meat trade, had prevented any material development of the resources of the country. When he had got to the front ranges, he followed up the river next to the north of the one that he had explored years ago, and from the head waters of which he had been led to discover the only practicable pass into Erewhon. He did this, partly to avoid the terribly dangerous descent on to the bed of the more northern river, and partly to escape being seen by shepherds or bullock-drivers who might remember him.

If he had attempted to get through the gorge of this river in 1870, he would have found it impassable; but a few river-bed flats had been discovered above the gorge, on which there was now a shepherd's hut, and on the discovery of these flats a narrow horse track had been made from one end of the gorge to the other.

He was hospitably entertained at the shepherd's hut just mentioned, which he reached on Monday, 1st December. He told the shepherd in charge of it that he had come to see if he could find traces of a large wingless bird, whose existence had been reported as having been discovered among the extreme head waters of the river.

"Be careful, sir," said the shepherd; "the river is very dangerous; several people–one only about a year ago–have left this hut, and though their horses and their camps have been found, their bodies have not. When a great fresh comes down, it would carry a body out to sea in twenty-four hours."

He evidently had no idea that there was a pass through the ranges up the river, which might explain the disappearance of an explorer.

Next day my father began to ascend the river. There was so much tangled growth still unburnt wherever there was room for it to grow, and so much swamp, that my father had to keep almost entirely to the river-bed–and here there was a good deal of quicksand. The stones also were often large for some distance together, and he had to cross and recross streams of the river more than once, so that though he travelled all day with the exception of a couple of hours for dinner, he had not made more than some five and twenty miles when he reached a suitable camping ground, where he unsaddled his horse, hobbled him, and turned him out to feed. The grass was beginning to seed, so that though it was none too plentiful, what there was of it made excellent feed.

He lit his fire, made himself some tea, ate his cold mutton and biscuits, and lit his pipe, exactly as he had done twenty years before. There was the clear starlit sky, the rushing river, and the stunted trees on the mountain-side; the woodhens cried, and the "more-pork" hooted out her two monotonous notes exactly as they had done years since; one moment, and time had so flown backwards that youth came bounding back to him with the return of his youth's surroundings; the next, and the intervening twenty years–most of them grim ones–rose up mockingly before him, and the buoyancy of hope yielded to the despondency of admitted failure. By and by buoyancy reasserted itself, and, soothed by the peace and beauty of the night, he wrapped himself up in his blanket and dropped off into a dreamless slumber.

Next morning, *i.e.*, 3rd December, he rose soon after dawn, bathed in a backwater of the river, got his breakfast, found his horse on the river-bed, and started as soon as he had duly packed and loaded. He had now to cross streams of the river and recross them more often than on the preceding day, and this, though his horse took well to the water, required care; for he was anxious not to wet his saddle-bags, and it was only by crossing at the wide, smooth, water above a rapid, and by picking places where the river ran in two or three streams, that he could find fords where his practised eye told him that the water would not be above his horse's belly–for the river was of great volume. Fortunately, there had been a late fall of snow on the higher ranges, and the river was, for the summer season, low.

Towards evening, having travelled, so far as he could guess, some twenty or five and twenty miles (for he had made another mid day halt), he reached the place, which he easily recognized, as that where he had camped before crossing to the pass that led into Erewhon. It was the last piece of ground that could be called a flat (though it was in reality only the sloping delta of a stream that descended from the pass) before reaching a large glacier that had encroached on the river-bed, which it traversed at right angles for a considerable distance.

Here he again camped, hobbled his horse, and turned him adrift, hoping that he might again find him some two or three months hence, for there was a good deal of sweet grass here and there, with sow-thistle and anise; and the coarse tussock grass would be in full seed shortly, which alone would keep him going for as long a time as my father expected to be away. Little did he think that he should want him again so shortly.

Having attended to his horse, he got his supper, and while smoking his pipe congratulated himself on the way in which something had smoothed away all the obstacles that had so nearly baffled him on his earlier journey. Was he being lured on to his destruction by some malicious fiend, or befriended by one who had compassion on him and wished him well? His naturally sanguine temperament inclined him to adopt the friendly spirit theory, in the peace of which he again laid himself down to rest, and slept soundly from dark till dawn.

In the morning, though the water was somewhat icy, he again bathed, and then put on his Erewhonian boots and dress. He stowed his European clothes, with some difficulty, into his saddle-bags. Herein also he left his case full of English sovereigns, his spare pipes, his purse, which contained two pounds in gold and seven or eight shillings, part of his stock of tobacco, and whatever provision was left him, except the meat—which he left for sundry hawks and parrots that were eyeing his proceedings apparently without fear of man. His nuggets he concealed in the secret pockets of which I have already spoken, keeping one bag alone accessible.

He had had his hair and beard cut short on shipboard

the day before he landed. These he now dyed with a dye that he had brought from England, and which in a few minutes turned them very nearly black. He also stained his face and hands deep brown. He hung his saddle and bridle, his English boots, and his saddle-bags on the highest bough that he could reach, and made them fairly fast with strips of flax leaf, for there was some stunted flax growing on the ground where he had camped. He feared that, do what he might, they would not escape the inquisitive thievishness of the parrots, whose strong beaks could easily cut leather; but he could do nothing more. It occurs to me, though my father never told me so, that it was perhaps with a view to these birds that he had chosen to put his English sovereigns into a metal box, with a clasp to it which would defy them.

He made a roll of his blanket, and slung it over his shoulder; he also took his pipe, tobacco, a little tea, a few ship's biscuits, and his billy and pannikin; matches and salt go without saying. When he had thus ordered everything as nearly to his satisfaction as he could, he looked at his watch for the last time, as he believed, till many weeks should have gone by, and found it to be about seven o'clock. Remembering what trouble it had got him into years before, he took down his saddle-bags, reopened them, and put the watch inside. He then set himself to climb the mountain side, towards the saddle on which he had seen the statues.

CHAPTER THREE: MY FATHER WHILE CAMPING IS ACCOSTED BY PROFESSORS HANKY AND PANKY

MY FATHER FOUND THE ASCENT MORE fatiguing than he remembered it to have been. The climb, he said, was steady, and took him between four and five hours, as near as he could guess, now that he had no watch; but it offered nothing that could be called a difficulty, and the water-course that came down from the saddle was a sufficient guide; once or twice there were waterfalls, but they did not seriously delay him.

After he had climbed some three thousand feet, he began to be on the alert for some sound of ghostly chanting from the statues; but he heard nothing, and toiled on till he came to a sprinkling of fresh snow–part of the fall which he had observed on the preceding day as having whitened the higher mountains; he knew, therefore, that he must now be nearing the saddle. The snow grew rapidly deeper, and by the time he reached the statues the ground was covered to a depth of two or three inches.

He found the statues smaller than he had expected. He had said in his book–written many months after he had seen them–that they were about six times the size of life, but he now thought that four or five times would have been enough to say. Their mouths were much clogged with snow, so that even though there had been a strong wind (which there was not) they would not have chanted. In other respects he found them not less mysteriously impressive than at first. He walked two or three times all round them, and then went on.

The snow did not continue far down, but before long my father entered a thick bank of cloud, and had to feel his way cautiously along the stream that descended from the pass. It was some two hours before he emerged into clear air, and found himself on the level bed of an old lake now grassed over. He had quite forgotten this feature of the descent—perhaps the clouds had hung over it; he was overjoyed, however, to find that the flat ground abounded with a kind of quail, larger than ours, and hardly, if at all, smaller than a partridge. The abundance of these quails surprised him, for he did not remember them as plentiful anywhere on the Erewhonian side of the mountains.

The Erewhonian quail, like its now nearly, if not quite, extinct New Zealand congener, can take three successive flights of a few yards each, but then becomes exhausted; hence quails are only found on ground that is never burned, and where there are no wild animals to molest them; the cats and dogs that accompany European civilization soon exterminate them; my father, therefore, felt safe in concluding that he was still far from any village. Moreover he could see no sheep or goats' dung; and this surprised him, for he thought he had found signs of pasturage much higher than this. Doubtless, he said to himself, when he wrote his book he had forgotten how long the descent had been. But it was odd, for the grass was good feed enough, and ought, he considered, to have been well stocked.

Tired with his climb, during which he had not rested to take food, but had eaten biscuits as he walked, he gave himself a good long rest, and when refreshed, he ran down a couple of dozen quails, some of which he meant to eat when he camped for the night, while the others would help him out of a difficulty which had been troubling him for some time.

What was he to say when people asked him, as they were sure to do, how he was living? And how was he to get enough Erewhonian money to keep him going till he could find some safe means of selling a few of his nuggets? He had had a little Erewhonian money when he went up in the balloon, but had thrown it over, with everything else except the clothes he wore and his MSS., when the balloon was nearing the water. He had nothing with him that he dared offer for sale, and though he had plenty of gold, was in reality penniless.

When, therefore, he saw the quails, he again felt as though some friendly spirit was smoothing his way before him. What more easy than to sell them at Coldharbour (for so the name of the town in which he had been imprisoned should be translated), where he knew they were a delicacy, and would fetch him the value of an English shilling apiece?

It took him between two and three hours to catch two dozen. When he had thus got what he considered a sufficient stock, he tied their legs together with rushes, and ran a stout stick through the whole lot. Soon afterwards he came upon a wood of stunted pines, which, though there was not much undergrowth, nevertheless afforded considerable shelter and enabled him to gather wood enough to make himself a good fire. This was acceptable, for though the days were long, it was now evening, and as soon as the sun had gone the air became crisp and frosty.

Here he resolved to pass the night. He chose a part where the trees were thickest, lit his fire, plucked and cleaned four quails, filled his billy with water from the stream hard by, made tea in his pannikin, grilled two of his birds on the embers, ate them, and when he had done all this, he lit his pipe and began to think things over.

" So far so good," said he to himself; but hardly had the words passed through his mind before he was startled by the sound of voices, still at some distance, but evidently drawing towards him.

He instantly gathered up his billy, pannikin, tea, biscuits, and blanket, all of which he had determined to discard and hide on the following morning; everything that could betray him he carried full speed into the wood some few yards off, in the direction opposite to that from which the voices were coming, but he let his quails lie where they were, and put his pipe and tobacco in his pocket.

The voices drew nearer and nearer, and it was all my father could do to get back and sit down innocently by his fire, before he could hear what was being said.

"Thank goodness," said one of the speakers (of course in the Erewhonian language), "we seem to be finding somebody at last. I hope it is not some poacher; we had better be careful."

"Nonsense!" said the other. "It must be one of the rangers. No one would dare to light a fire while poaching on the King's preserves. What o'clock do you make it?"

"Half after nine." And the watch was still in the speaker's hand as he emerged from darkness into the glowing light of the fire. My father glanced at it, and saw that it was exactly like the one he had worn on entering Erewhon nearly twenty years previously.

The watch, however, was a very small matter; the dress of these two men (for there were only two) was far more disconcerting. They were not in the Erewhonian costume. The one was dressed like an Englishman or would-be Englishman, while the other was wearing the same kind of clothes but turned the wrong way round, so that when his face was towards my father his body seemed to have its back towards him, and *vice versa*. The man's head, in fact, appeared to have been screwed right round; and yet it was plain that if he were stripped he would be found built like other people.

What could it all mean? The men were about fifty years old. They were well-to-do people, well clad, well fed, and were felt instinctively by my father to belong to the academic classes. That one of them should be dressed like a sensible Englishman dismayed my father as much as that the other should have a watch, and look as if he had just broken out of Bedlam, or as King Dagobert must have looked if he had worn all his clothes as he is said to have worn his breeches. Both wore their clothes so easily–for he who wore them reversed had evidently been measured with a view to this absurd fashion–that it was plain their dress was habitual.

My father was alarmed as well as astounded, for he saw that what little plan of campaign he had formed must be reconstructed, and he had no idea in what direction his next move should be taken; but he was a ready man, and knew that when people have taken any idea into their heads, a little confirmation will fix it. A first idea is like a strong seedling; it will grow if it can.

In less time than it will have taken the reader to get through the last foregoing paragraphs, my father took up the cue furnished him by the second speaker.

"Yes," said he, going boldly up to this gentleman, "I am one of the rangers, and it is my duty to ask you what you are doing here upon the King's preserves."

"Quite so, my man," was the rejoinder. "We have been to see the statues at the head of the pass, and have a permit from the Mayor of Sunch'ston to enter upon the preserves. We lost ourselves in the thick fog, both going and coming back."

My father inwardly blessed the fog. He did not catch the name of the town, but presently found that it was commonly pronounced as I have written it.

"Be pleased to show it me," said my father in his politest manner. On this a document was handed to him.

I will here explain that I shall translate the names of men and places, as well as the substance of the document; and I shall translate all names in future. Indeed I have just done so in the case of Sunch'ston. As an example, let me explain that the true Erewhonian names for Hanky and Panky, to whom the reader will be immediately introduced, are Sukoh and Sukop–names too cacophonous to be read with pleasure by the English public. I must ask the reader to believe that in all cases I am doing my best to give the spirit of the original name.

I would also express my regret that my father did not either uniformly keep to the true Erewhonian names, as in the cases of Senoj, Nosnibor, Ydgrun, Thims, etc.–names which occur constantly in Erewhon–or else invariably invent a name, as he did whenever he considered the true name impossible. My poor mother's name, for example, was really Nna Haras, and Mahaina's Enaj Ysteb, which he dared not face. He, therefore, gave these characters the first names that euphony suggested, without any attempt at translation. Rightly or wrongly, I have determined to keep consistently to translation for all names not used in my father's book; and throughout, whether as regards names or conversations, I shall translate with the freedom without which no translation rises above construe level.

Let me now return to the permit. The earlier part of the document was printed, and ran as follows:

" Extracts from the Act for the afforesting of certain lands lying between the town of Sunchildston, formerly called Coldharbour, and the mountains which bound the kingdom of Erewhon, passed in the year Three, being the eighth year of the reign of his Most Gracious Majesty King Well-beloved the Twenty-Second.

" Whereas it is expedient to prevent any of his Majesty's subjects from trying to cross over into unknown lands beyond the mountains, and in like manner to protect his Majesty's kingdom from intrusion on the part of foreign devils, it is hereby enacted that certain lands, more particularly described hereafter, shall be afforested and set apart as a hunting-ground for his Majesty's private use.

" It is also enacted that the Rangers and Under-rangers

shall be required to immediately kill without parley any foreign devil whom they may encounter coming from the other side of the mountains. They are to weight the body, and throw it into the Blue Pool under the waterfall shown on the plan hereto annexed; but on pain of imprisonment for life they shall not reserve to their own use any article belonging to the deceased. Neither shall they divulge what they have done to any one save the Head Ranger, who shall report the circumstances of the case fully and minutely to his Majesty.

"As regards any of his Majesty's subjects who may be taken while trespassing on his Majesty's preserves without a special permit signed by the Mayor of Sunchildston, or any who may be convicted of poaching on the said preserves, the Rangers shall forthwith arrest them and bring them before the Mayor of Sunchildston, who shall enquire into their antecedents, and punish them with such term of imprisonment, with hard labour, as he may think fit, provided that no such term be of less duration than twelve calendar months.

"For the further provisions of the said Act, those whom it may concern are referred to the Act in full, a copy of which may be seen at the official residence of the Mayor of Sunchildston."

Then followed in MS. "XIX. xii. 29. Permit Professor Hanky, Royal Professor of Worldly Wisdom at Bridgeford, seat of learning, city of the people who are above suspicion, and Professor Panky, Royal Professor of Unworldly Wisdom in the said city, or either of them" [here the MS. ended, the rest of the permit being in print] "to pass freely during the space of forty-eight hours from the date hereof, over the King's preserves, provided, under pain of imprisonment with hard labour for twelve months, that they do not kill, nor cause to be killed, nor eat, if another have killed, any one or more of his Majesty's quails."

The signature was such a scrawl that my father could not read it, but underneath was printed, "Mayor of Sunchildston, formerly called Coldharbour."

What a mass of information did not my father gather as he read, but what a far greater mass did he not see that he must get hold of ere he could reconstruct his plans intelligently.

"The year three," indeed; and XIX. xii. 29, in Roman and Arabic characters! There were no such characters when he was in Erewhon before. It flashed upon him that he had repeatedly shown them to the Nosnibors, and had once even written them down. It could not be that . . . No, it was impossible; and yet there was the European dress, aimed at by the one Professor, and attained by the other. Again "XIX." what was that? "xii." might do for December, but it was now the 4th of December not the 29th. "Afforested" too? Then that was why he had seen no sheep tracks. And how about the quails he had so innocently killed? What would have happened if he had tried to sell them in Coldharbour? What other like fatal error might he not ignorantly commit? And why had Coldharbour become Sunchildston?

These thoughts raced through my poor father's brain as he slowly perused the paper handed to him by the Professors. To give himself time he feigned to be a poor scholar, but when he had delayed as long as he dared, he returned it to the one who had given it him. Without changing a muscle he said:

"Your permit, sir, is quite regular. You can either stay here the night or go on to Sunchildston as you think fit. May I ask which of you two gentlemen is Professor Hanky, and which Professor Panky?"

"My name is Panky," said the one who had the watch, who wore his clothes reversed, and who had thought my father might be a poacher.

" And mine Hanky," said the other.

" What do you think, Panky," he added, turning to his brother Professor, " had we not better stay here till sunrise? We are both of us tired, and this fellow can make us a good fire. It is very dark, and there will be no moon this two hours. We are hungry, but we can hold out till we get to Sunchildston; it cannot be more than eight or nine miles further down."

Panky assented, but then, turning sharply to my father, he said, " My man, what are you doing in the forbidden dress? Why are you not in ranger's uniform, and what is the meaning of all those quails? " For his seedling idea that my father was in reality a poacher was doing its best to grow.

Quick as thought my father answered, " The Head Ranger sent me a message this morning to deliver him three dozen quails at Sunchildston by to-morrow afternoon. As for the dress, we can run the quails down quicker in it, and he says nothing to us so long as we only wear out old clothes and put on our uniforms before we near the town. My uniform is in the ranger's shelter an hour and a half higher up the valley."

" See what comes," said Panky, " of having a whipper-snapper not yet twenty years old in the responsible post of Head Ranger. As for this fellow, he may be speaking the truth, but I distrust him."

" The man is all right, Panky," said Hanky, " and seems to be a decent fellow enough." Then to my father, " How many brace have you got? " And he looked at them a little wistfully.

" I have been at it all day, sir, and I have only got eight brace. I must run down ten more brace to-morrow."

" I see, I see." Then, turning to Panky, he said, " Of course, they are wanted for the Mayor's banquet on Sunday. By the way, we have not yet received our invitation; I suppose we shall find it when we get back to Sunchildston."

"Sunday, Sunday, Sunday!" groaned my father inwardly; but he changed not a muscle of his face, and said stolidly to Professor Hanky, "I think you must be right, sir; but there was nothing said about it to me. I was only told to bring the birds."

Thus tenderly did he water the Professor's second seedling. But Panky had his seedling too, and, Cain-like, was jealous that Hanky's should flourish while his own was withering.

"And what, pray, my man," he said somewhat peremptorily to my father, "are those two plucked quails doing? Were you to deliver them plucked? And what bird did those bones belong to which I see lying by the fire with the flesh all eaten off them? Are the under-rangers allowed not only to wear the forbidden dress but to eat the King's quails as well?"

The form in which the question was asked gave my father his cue. He laughed heartily, and said, "Why, sir, those plucked birds are landrails, not quails, and those bones are landrail bones. Look at this thigh-bone; was there ever a quail with such a bone as that?"

I cannot say whether or no Professor Panky was really deceived by the sweet effrontery with which my father proffered him the bone. If he was taken in, his answer was dictated simply by a donnish unwillingness to allow any one to be better informed on any subject than he was himself.

My father, when I suggested this to him, would not hear of it. "Oh no," he said; "the man knew well enough that I was lying." However this may be, the Professor's manner changed.

"You are right," he said, "I thought they were landrail bones, but was not sure till I had one in my hand. I see, too, that the plucked birds are landrails, but there is little light, and I have not often seen them without their feathers."

"I think," said my father to me, "that Hanky knew

what his friend meant, for he said, 'Panky, I am very hungry.'"

"Oh, Hanky, Hanky," said the other, modulating his harsh voice till it was quite pleasant, "don't corrupt the poor man."

"Panky, drop that; we are not at Bridgeford now; I am very hungry, and I believe half those birds are not quails but landrails."

My father saw he was safe. He said, "Perhaps some of them might prove to be so, sir, under certain circumstances. I am a poor man, sir."

"Come, come," said Hanky; and he slipped a sum equal to about half a crown into my father's hand.

"I do not know what you mean, sir," said my father, "and if I did, half a crown would not be nearly enough."

"Hanky," said Panky, "you must get this fellow to give you lessons."

CHAPTER FOUR: MY FATHER OVERHEARS MORE OF HANKY AND PANKY'S CONVERSATION

MY FATHER, SCHOOLED UNDER ADversity, knew that it was never well to press advantage too far. He took the equivalent of five shillings for three brace, which was somewhat less than the birds would have been worth when things were as he had known them. Moreover, he consented to take a shilling's worth of Musical Bank money, which (as he has explained in his book) has no appreciable value outside these banks. He did this because he knew that it would be respectable to be seen carrying a little Musical Bank money, and also because he wished to give some of it to the British Museum, where he knew that this curious coinage was unrepresented. But the coins struck him as being much thinner and smaller than he had remembered them.

It was Panky, not Hanky, who had given him the Musical Bank money. Panky was the greater humbug of the two, for he would humbug even himself–a thing, by the way, not very hard to do; and yet he was the less successful humbug, for he could humbug no one who was worth humbugging–not for long. Hanky's occasional frankness put people off their guard. He was the mere common, superficial, perfunctory Professor, who, being a Professor, would of course profess, but would not lie more than was in the bond; he was log-rolled and log-rolling, but still, in a robust wolfish fashion, human.

Panky, on the other hand, was hardly human; he had thrown himself so earnestly into his work, that he had become a living lie. If he had had to play the part of Othello he would have blacked himself all over, and very likely smothered his Desdemona in good earnest. Hanky would hardly have blacked himself behind the ears, and his Desdemona would have been quite safe.

Philosophers are like quails in the respect that they

can take two or three flights of imagination, but rarely more without an interval of repose. The Professors had imagined my father to be a poacher and a ranger; they had imagined the quails to be wanted for Sunday's banquet; they had imagined that they imagined (at least Panky had) that they were about to eat landrails; they were now exhausted, and cowered down into the grass of their ordinary conversation, paying no more attention to my father than if he had been a log. He, poor man, drank in every word they said, while seemingly intent on nothing but his quails, each one of which he cut up with a knife borrowed from Hanky. Two had been plucked already, so he laid these at once upon the clear embers.

" I do not know what we are to do with ourselves," said Hanky, " till Sunday. To-day is Thursday–it is the twenty-ninth, is it not ? Yes, of course it is–Sunday is the first. Besides, it is on our permit. To-morrow we can rest; what, I wonder, can we do on Saturday ? But the others will be here then, and we can tell them about the statues."

" Yes, but mind you do not blurt out anything about the landrails."

" I think we may tell Dr. Downie."

" Tell nobody," said Panky.

They then talked about the statues, concerning which it was plain that nothing was known. But my father soon broke in upon their conversation with the first instalment of quails, which a few minutes had sufficed to cook.

" What a delicious bird a quail is," said Hanky.

" Landrail, Hanky, landrail," said the other reproachfully.

Having finished the first birds in a very few minutes they returned to the statues.

" Old Mrs. Nosnibor," said Panky, " says the Sunchild told her they were symbolic of ten tribes who had incurred the displeasure of the sun, his father."

I make no comment on my father's feelings.

"Of the sun! his fiddlesticks' ends," retorted Hanky. "He never called the sun his father. Besides, from all I have heard about him, I take it he was a precious idiot."

"O Hanky, Hanky! you will wreck the whole thing if you ever allow yourself to talk in that way."

"You are more likely to wreck it yourself, Panky, by never doing so. People like being deceived, but they like also to have an inkling of their own deception, and you never inkle them."

"The Queen," said Panky, returning to the statues, "sticks to it that . . ."

"Here comes another bird," interrupted Hanky; "never mind about the Queen."

The bird was soon eaten, whereon Panky again took up his parable about the Queen.

"The Queen says they are connected with the cult of the ancient Goddess Kiss-me-quick."

"What if they are? But the Queen sees Kiss-me-quick in everything. Another quail, if you please, Mr. Ranger."

My father brought up another bird almost directly. Silence while it was being eaten.

"Talking of the Sunchild," said Panky; "did you ever see him?"

"Never set eyes on him, and hope I never shall."

And so on till the last bird was eaten.

"Fellow," said Panky, "fetch some more wood; the fire is nearly dead."

"I can find no more, sir," said my father, who was afraid lest some genuine ranger might be attracted by the light, and was determined to let it go out as soon as he had done cooking.

"Never mind," said Hanky, "the moon will be up soon."

"And now, Hanky," said Panky, "tell me what you propose to say on Sunday. I suppose you have pretty well made up your mind about it by this time."

"Pretty nearly. I shall keep it much on the usual lines. I shall dwell upon the benighted state from which the Sunchild rescued us, and shall show how the Musical Banks, by at once taking up the movement, have been the blessed means of its now almost universal success. I shall talk about the immortal glory shed upon Sunch'-ston by the Sunchild's residence in the prison, and wind up with the Sunchild Evidence Society, and an earnest appeal for funds to endow the canonries required for the due service of the temple."

"Temple! what temple?" groaned my father inwardly.

"And what are you going to do about the four black and white horses?"

"Stick to them, of course–unless I make them six."

"I really do not see why they might not have been horses."

"I dare say you do not," returned the other drily, "but they were black and white storks, and you know that as well as I do. Still, they have caught on, and they are in the altar-piece, prancing and curveting magnificently, so I shall trot them out."

"Altar-piece! Altar-piece!" again groaned my father inwardly.

He need not have groaned, for when he came to see the so-called altar-piece he found that the table above which it was placed had nothing in common with the altar in a Christian church. It was a mere table, on which were placed two bowls full of Musical Bank coins; two cashiers, who sat on either side of it, dispensed a few of these to all comers, while there was a box in front of it wherein people deposited coin of the realm according to their will or ability. The idea of sacrifice was not contemplated, and the position of the table, as well as the name given to it, was an instance of the way in which the Erewhonians had caught names and practices from my father, without understanding what they either were or meant. So, again, when Professor Hanky had spoken of canonries, he had none but the vaguest idea of what a canonry is.

I may add further that as a boy my father had had his Bible well drilled into him, and never forgot it. Hence biblical passages and expressions had been often in his mouth, as the effect of mere unconscious cerebration. The Erewhonians had caught many of these, sometimes corrupting them so that they were hardly recognizable. Things that he remembered having said were continually meeting him during the few days of his second visit, and it shocked him deeply to meet some gross travesty of his own words, or of words more sacred than his own, and yet to be unable to correct it. " I wonder," he said to me, " that no one has ever hit on this as a punishment for the damned in Hades."

Let me now return to Professor Hanky, whom I fear that I have left too long.

" And of course," he continued, " I shall say all sorts of pretty things about the Mayoress–for I suppose we must not even think of her as Yram now."

" The Mayoress," replied Panky, " is a very dangerous woman; see how she stood out about the way in which the Sunchild had worn his clothes before they gave him the then Erewhonian dress. Besides, she is a sceptic at heart, and so is that precious son of hers."

" She was quite right," said Hanky, with something of a snort. " She brought him his dinner while he was still wearing the clothes he came in, and if men do not notice how a man wears his clothes, women do. Besides, there are many living who saw him wear them."

" Perhaps," said Panky, " but we should never have

talked the King over if we had not humoured him on this point. Yram nearly wrecked us by her obstinacy. If we had not frightened her, and if your study, Hanky, had not happened to have been burned . . ."

"Come, come, Panky, no more of that."

"Of course I do not doubt that it was an accident; nevertheless if your study had not been accidentally burned, on the very night the clothes were entrusted to you for earnest, patient, careful, scientific investigation–and Yram very nearly burned too–we should never have carried it through. See what work we had to get the King to allow the way in which the clothes were worn to be a matter of opinion, not dogma. What a pity it is that the clothes were not burned before the King's tailor had copied them."

Hanky laughed heartily enough. "Yes," he said, "it was touch and go. Why, I wonder, could not the Queen have put the clothes on a dummy that would show back from front? As soon as it was brought into the council chamber the King jumped to a conclusion, and we had to bundle both dummy and Yram out of the royal presence, for neither she nor the King would budge an inch."

Even Panky smiled. "What could we do? The common people almost worship Yram; and so does her husband, though her fair-haired eldest son was born barely seven months after marriage. The people in these parts like to think that the Sunchild's blood is in the country, and yet they swear through thick and thin that he is the Mayor's duly begotten offspring–Faugh! Do you think they would have stood his being jobbed into the rangership by any one else but Yram?"

My father's feelings may be imagined, but I will not here interrupt the Professors.

"Well, well," said Hanky; "for men must rob and women must job so long as the world goes on. I did the best I could. The King would never have embraced Sunchildism if I had not told him he was right; then, when satisfied that we agreed with him, he yielded to popular prejudice and allowed the question to remain open. One of his Royal Professors was to wear the clothes one way, and the other the other."

"My way of wearing them," said Panky, "is much the most convenient."

"Not a bit of it," said Hanky warmly. On this the two Professors fell out, and the discussion grew so hot that my father interfered by advising them not to talk so loud lest another ranger should hear them. "You know," he said, "there are a good many landrail bones lying about, and it might be awkward."

The Professors hushed at once. "By the way," said Panky, after a pause, "it is very strange about those footprints in the snow. The man had evidently walked round the statues two or three times, as though they were strange to him, and he had certainly come from the other side."

"It was one of the rangers," said Hanky impatiently, "who had gone a little beyond the statues, and come back again."

"Then we should have seen his footprints as he went. I am glad I measured them."

"There is nothing in it; but what were your measurements?"

"Eleven inches by four and a half; nails on the soles; one nail missing on the right foot and two on the left." Then, turning to my father quickly, he said, "My man, allow me to have a look at your boots."

"Nonsense, Panky, nonsense!"

Now my father by this time was wondering whether he should not set upon these two men, kill them if he could, and make the best of his way back, but he had still a card to play.

"Certainly, sir," said he, "but I should tell you that they are not my boots."

He took off his right boot and handed it to Panky.

"Exactly so! Eleven inches by four and a half, and one nail missing. And now, Mr. Ranger, will you be good enough to explain how you became possessed of that boot. You need not show me the other." And he spoke like an examiner who was confident that he could floor his examinee in *viva voce*.

"You know our orders," answered my father, "you have seen them on your permit. I met one of those foreign devils from the other side, of whom we have had more than one lately; he came from out of the clouds that hang higher up, and as he had no permit and could not speak a word of our language, I gripped him, flung him, and strangled him. Thus far I was only obeying orders, but seeing how much better his boots were than mine, and finding that they would fit me, I resolved to keep them. You may be sure I should not have done so if I had known there was snow on the top of the pass."

"He could not invent that," said Hanky; "it is plain he has not been up to the statues."

Panky was staggered. "And of course," said he ironically, "you took nothing from this poor wretch except his boots."

"Sir," said my father, "I will make a clean breast of everything. I flung his body, his clothes, and my own old boots into the pool; but I kept his blanket, some things he used for cooking, and some strange stuff that looks like dried leaves, as well as a small bag of something which I believe is gold. I thought I could sell the lot to some dealer in curiosities who would ask no questions."

"And what, pray, have you done with all these things?"

"They are here, sir." And as he spoke he dived into

the wood, returning with the blanket, billy, pannikin, tea, and the little bag of nuggets, which he had kept accessible.

" This is very strange," said Hanky, who was beginning to be afraid of my father when he learned that he sometimes killed people.

Here the Professors talked hurriedly to one another in a tongue which my father could not understand, but which he felt sure was the hypothetical language of which he has spoken in his book.

Presently Hanky said to my father quite civilly, " And what, my good man, do you propose to do with all these things? I should tell you at once that what you take to be gold is nothing of the kind; it is a base metal, hardly, if at all, worth more than copper."

" I have had enough of them; to-morrow morning I shall take them with me to the Blue Pool, and drop them into it."

" It is a pity you should do that," said Hanky musingly: " the things are interesting as curiosities, and–and–and–what will you take for them? "

" I could not do it, sir," answered my father. " I would not do it, no, not for—" and he named a sum equivalent to about five pounds of our money. For he wanted Erewhonian money, and thought it worth his while to sacrifice his ten pounds' worth of nuggets in order to get a supply of current coin.

Hanky tried to beat him down, assuring him that no curiosity dealer would give half as much, and my father so far yielded as to take £4, 10*s*. in silver, which, as I have already explained, would not be worth more than half a sovereign in gold. At this figure a bargain was struck, and the Professors paid up without offering him a single Musical Bank coin. They wanted to include the boots in the purchase, but here my father stood out.

But he could not stand out as regards another matter,

which caused him some anxiety. Panky insisted that my father should give them a receipt for the money, and there was an altercation between the Professors on this point, much longer than I can here find space to give. Hanky argued that a receipt was useless, inasmuch as it would be ruin to my father ever to refer to the subject again. Panky, however, was anxious, not lest my father should again claim the money, but (though he did not say so outright) lest Hanky should claim the whole purchase as his own. In the end Panky, for a wonder, carried the day, and a receipt was drawn up to the effect that the undersigned acknowledged to have received from Professors Hanky and Panky the sum of £4, 10*s.* (I translate the amount), as joint purchasers of certain pieces of yellow ore, a blanket, and sundry articles found without an owner in the King's preserves. This paper was dated, as the permit had been, XIX. xii. 29.

My father, generally so ready, was at his wits' end for a name, and could think of none but Mr. Nosnibor's. Happily, remembering that this gentleman had also been called Senoj–a name common enough in Erewhon–he signed himself "Senoj, Under-ranger."

Panky was now satisfied. "We will put it in the bag," he said, "with the pieces of yellow ore."

"Put it where you like," said Hanky contemptuously; and into the bag it was put.

When all was now concluded, my father laughingly said, "If you have dealt unfairly by me, I forgive you. My motto is, 'Forgive us our trespasses, as we forgive them that trespass against us.'"

"Repeat those last words," said Panky eagerly. My father was alarmed at his manner, but thought it safer to repeat them.

"You hear that, Hanky? I am convinced; I have not another word to say. The man is a true Erewhonian; he has our corrupt reading of the Sunchild's prayer."

" Please explain."

" Why, can you not see ? " said Panky, who was by way of being great at conjectural emendations. " Can you not see how impossible it is for the Sunchild, or any of the people to whom he declared (as we now know provisionally) that he belonged, could have made the forgiveness of his own sins depend on the readiness with which he forgave other people ? No man in his senses would dream of such a thing. It would be asking a supposed all-powerful being not to forgive his sins at all, or at best to forgive them imperfectly. No; Yram got it wrong. She mistook ' but do not ' for ' as we.' The sound of the words is very much alike; the correct reading should obviously be, ' Forgive us our trespasses, but do not forgive them that trespass against us.' This makes sense, and turns an impossible prayer into one that goes straight to the heart of every one of us." Then, turning to my father, he said, " You can see this, my man, can you not, as soon as it is pointed out to you ? "

My father said that he saw it now, but had always heard the words as he had himself spoken them.

" Of course you have, my good fellow, and it is because of this that I know they never can have reached you except from an Erewhonian source."

Hanky smiled, snorted, and muttered in an undertone, " I shall begin to think that this fellow is a foreign devil after all."

" And now, gentlemen," said my father, " the moon is risen. I must be after the quails at daybreak; I will therefore go to the ranger's shelter " (a shelter, by the way, which existed only in my father's invention), " and get a couple of hours' sleep, so as to be both close to the quail-ground and fresh for running. You are so near the boundary of the preserves that you will not want your permit further; no one will meet you, and should any one do so, you need only give your names and say that you have made a mistake. You will have to give it up to-morrow at the Ranger's office; it will save you trouble if I collect it now, and give it up when I deliver my quails.

"As regards the curiosities, hide them as you best can outside the limits. I recommend you to carry them at once out of the forest, and rest beyond the limits rather than here. You can then recover them whenever, and in whatever way, you may find convenient. But I hope you will say nothing about any foreign devil's having come over on to this side. Any whisper to this effect unsettles people's minds, and they are too much unsettled already; hence our orders to kill any one from over there at once, and to tell no one but the Head Ranger. I was forced by you, gentlemen, to disobey these orders in self-defence; I must trust your generosity to keep what I have told you secret. I shall, of course, report it to the Head Ranger. And now, if you think proper, you can give me up your permit."

All this was so plausible that the Professors gave up their permit without a word but thanks. They bundled their curiosities hurriedly into "the poor foreign devil's" blanket, reserving a more careful packing till they were out of the preserves. They wished my father a very good night, and all success with his quails in the morning; they thanked him again for the care he had taken of them in the matter of the landrails, and Panky even went so far as to give him a few Musical Bank coins, which he gratefully accepted. They then started off in the direction of Sunch'ston.

My father gathered up the remaining quails, some of which he meant to eat in the morning, while the others he would throw away as soon as he could find a safe place. He turned towards the mountains, but before he had gone a dozen yards he heard a voice, which he recognized as Panky's, shouting after him, and saying:

" Mind you do not forget the true reading of the Sunchild's prayer."

" You are an old fool," shouted my father in English, knowing that he could hardly be heard, still less understood, and thankful to relieve his feelings.

CHAPTER FIVE: MY FATHER MEETS A SON, OF WHOSE EXISTENCE HE WAS IGNORANT, AND STRIKES A BARGAIN WITH HIM

THE INCIDENTS RECORDED IN THE LAST two chapters had occupied about two hours, so that it was nearly midnight before my father could begin to retrace his steps and make towards the camp that he had left that morning. This was necessary, for he could not go any further in a costume that he now knew to be forbidden. At this hour no ranger was likely to meet him before he reached the statues, and by making a push for it he could return in time to cross the limits of the preserves before the Professors' permit had expired. If challenged, he must brazen it out that he was one or other of the persons therein named.

Fatigued though he was, he reached the statues, as near as he could guess, at about three in the morning. What little wind there had been was warm, so that the tracks, which the Professors must have seen shortly after he had made them, had disappeared. The statues looked very weird in the moonlight but they were not chanting.

While ascending, he pieced together the information he had picked up from the Professors. Plainly, the Sunchild, or child of the sun, was none other than himself, and the new name of Coldharbour was doubtless intended to commemorate the fact that this was the first town he had reached in Erewhon. Plainly, also, he was supposed to be of superhuman origin–his flight in the balloon having been not unnaturally believed to be miraculous. The Erewhonians had for centuries been effacing all knowledge of their former culture; archaeologists, indeed, could still glean a little from museums, and from volumes hard to come by, and still harder to understand; but archaeologists were few, and even though they had made researches (which they may or may not have done), their labours had never reached the masses. What wonder, then, that the mushroom spawn of myth, ever present in an atmosphere highly charged with ignorance, had germinated in a soil so favourably prepared for its reception?

He saw it all now. It was twenty years next Sunday since he and my mother had eloped. That was the meaning of XIX. xii. 29. They had made a new era, dating from the day of his return to the palace of the sun with a bride who was doubtless to unite the Erewhonian nature with that of the sun. The New Year, then, would date from Sunday, 7th December, which would therefore become XX. i. 1. The Thursday, now nearly if not quite over, being only two days distant from the end of a month of thirty-one days, which was also the last of the year, would be XIX. xii. 29, as on the Professors' permit.

I should like to explain here what will appear more clearly on a later page–I mean, that the Erewhonians, according to their new system, do not believe the sun to be a god except as regards this world and his other planets. My father had told them a little about astronomy, and had assured them that all the fixed stars were suns like our own, with planets revolving round them, which were probably tenanted by intelligent living beings, however unlike they might be to ourselves. From this they evolved the theory that the sun was the ruler of this planetary system, and that he must be personified, as they had personified the air-god, the gods of time and space, hope, justice, and the other deities mentioned in my father's book. They retain their old belief in the actual existence of these gods, but they now make them all subordinate to the sun. The nearest approach they make to our own conception of God is to say that He is the ruler over all the suns throughout the universe–the suns being to Him much as our planets and their denizens are to our own sun. They deny that He takes more interest in one sun and its system than in another.

All the suns with their attendant planets are supposed to be equally His children, and He deputes to each sun the supervision and protection of its own system. Hence they say that though we may pray to the air-god, etc., and even to the sun, we must not pray to God. We may be thankful to Him for watching over the suns, but we must not go further.

Going back to my father's reflections he perceived that the Erewhonians had not only adopted our calendar, as he had repeatedly explained it to the Nosnibors, but had taken our week as well, and were making Sunday a high day, just as we do. Next Sunday, in commemoration of the twentieth year after his ascent, they were about to dedicate a temple to him; in this there was to be a picture showing himself and his earthly bride on their heavenward journey, in a chariot drawn by four black and white horses–which, however, Professor Hanky had positively affirmed to have been only storks.

Here I interrupted my father. "But were there," I said, "any storks?"

"Yes," he answered. "As soon as I heard Hanky's words I remembered that a flight of some four or five of the large storks so common in Erewhon during the summer months had been wheeling high aloft in one of those aerial dances that so much delight them. I had quite forgotten it, but it came back to me at once that these creatures, attracted doubtless by what they took to be an unknown kind of bird, swooped down towards the balloon and circled round it like so many satellites to a heavenly body. I was fearful lest they should strike at it with their long and formidable beaks, in which case all would have been soon over; either they were afraid, or they had satisfied their curiosity–at any rate, they let us alone; but they kept with us till we were well away from the capital. Strange, how completely this incident had escaped me."

Father and Son

I return to my father's thoughts as he made his way back to his old camp.

As for the reversed position of Professor Panky's clothes, he remembered having given his own old ones to the Queen, and having thought that she might have got a better dummy on which to display them than the headless scarecrow, which, however, he supposed was all her ladies-in-waiting could lay their hands on at the moment. If that dummy had never been replaced, it was perhaps not very strange that the King could not at the first glance tell back from front, and if he did not guess right at first, there was little chance of his changing, for his first ideas were apt to be his last. But he must find out more about this.

Then how about the watch? Had their views about machinery also changed? Or was there an exception made about any machine that he had himself carried?

Yram too. She must have been married not long after she and he had parted. So she was now wife to the Mayor, and was evidently able to have things pretty much her own way in Sunch'ston, as he supposed he must now call it. Thank heaven she was prosperous! It was interesting to know that she was at heart a sceptic, as was also her light-haired son, now Head Ranger. And that son? Just twenty years of age! Born seven months after marriage! Then the Mayor doubtless had light hair too; but why did not those wretches say in which month Yram was married? If she had married soon after he had left, this was why he had not been sent for or written to. Pray heaven it was so. As for current gossip, people would talk, and if the lad was well begotten, what could it matter to them whose son he was? "But," thought my father, "I am glad I did not meet him on my way down. I had rather have been killed by some one else."

Hanky and Panky again. He remembered Bridgeford

as the town where the Colleges of Unreason had been most rife; he had visited it, but he had forgotten that it was called "The city of the people who are above suspicion." Its Professors were evidently going to muster in great force on Sunday; if two of them had robbed him, he could forgive them, for the information he had gleaned from them had furnished him with a *pied à terre*. Moreover, he had got as much Erewhonian money as he should want, for he had resolved to retrace his steps immediately after seeing the temple dedicated to himself. He knew the danger he should run in returning over the preserves without a permit, but his curiosity was so great that he resolved to risk it.

Soon after he had passed the statues he began to descend, and it being now broad day, he did so by leaps and bounds, for the ground was not precipitous. He reached his old camp soon after five–this, at any rate, was the hour at which he set his watch on finding that it had run down during his absence. There was now no reason why he should not take it with him, so he put it in his pocket. The parrots had attacked his saddle-bags, saddle, and bridle, as they were sure to do, but they had not got inside the bags. He took out his English clothes and put them on–stowing his bags of gold in various pockets, but keeping his Erewhonian money in the one that was most accessible. He put his Erewhonian dress back into the saddle-bags, intending to keep it as a curiosity; he also refreshed the dye upon his hands, face, and hair; he lit himself a fire, made tea, cooked and ate two brace of quails, which he had plucked while walking so as to save time, and then flung himself on to the ground to snatch an hour's very necessary rest. When he woke he found he had slept two hours, not one, which was perhaps as well, and by eight he began to reascend the pass.

He reached the statues about noon, for he allowed

himself not a moment's rest. This time there was a stiffish wind, and they were chanting lustily. He passed them with all speed, and had nearly reached the place where he had caught the quails, when he saw a man in a dress which he guessed at once to be a ranger's, but which, strangely enough, seeing that he was in the King's employ, was not reversed. My father's heart beat fast; he got out his permit and held it open in his hand, then with a smiling face he went towards the Ranger, who was standing his ground.

"I believe you are the Head Ranger," said my father, who saw that he was still smooth-faced and had light hair. "I am Professor Panky, and here is my permit. My brother Professor has been prevented from coming with me, and, as you see, I am alone."

My father had preferred to pass himself off as Panky, for he had rather gathered that Hanky was the better known man of the two.

While the youth was scrutinizing the permit, evidently with suspicion, my father took stock of him, and saw his own past self in him too plainly–knowing all he knew–to doubt whose son he was. He had the greatest difficulty in hiding his emotion, for the lad was indeed one of whom any father might be proud. He longed to be able to embrace him and claim him for what he was, but this, as he well knew, might not be. The tears again welled into his eyes when he told me of the struggle with himself that he had then had.

"Don't be jealous, my dearest boy," he said to me. "I love you quite as dearly as I love him, or better, but he was sprung upon me so suddenly, and dazzled me with his comely debonair face, so full of youth, and health, and frankness. Did you see him, he would go straight to your heart, for he is wonderfully like you in spite of your taking so much after your poor mother."

I was not jealous; on the contrary, I longed to see this youth, and find in him such a brother as I had often wished to have. But let me return to my father's story.

The young man, after examining the permit, declared it to be in form, and returned it to my father, but he eyed him with polite disfavour.

" I suppose," he said, " you have come up, as so many are doing, from Bridgeford, and all over the country, to the dedication on Sunday."

" Yes," said my father. " Bless me ! " he added, " what a wind you have up here ! How it makes one's eyes water, to be sure; " but he spoke with a cluck in his throat which no wind that blows can cause.

" Have you met any suspicious characters between here and the statues ? " asked the youth. " I came across the ashes of a fire lower down; there had been three men sitting for some time round it, and they had all been eating quails. Here are some of the bones and feathers, which I shall keep. They had not been gone more than a couple of hours, for the ashes were still warm; they are getting bolder and bolder–who would have thought they would dare to light a fire ? I suppose you have not met any one; but if you have seen a single person, let me know."

My father said quite truly that he had met no one. He then laughingly asked how the youth had been able to discover as much as he had.

" There were three well-marked forms, and three separate lots of quail bones hidden in the ashes. One man had done all the plucking. This is strange, but I dare say I shall get at it later."

After a little further conversation the Ranger said he was now going down to Sunch'ston, and, though somewhat curtly, proposed that he and my father should walk together.

" By all means," answered my father.

Before they had gone more than a few hundred yards his companion said, " If you will come with me a little to the left, I can show you the Blue Pool."

To avoid the precipitous ground over which the stream here fell, they had diverged to the right, where they had found a smoother descent; returning now to the stream, which was about to enter on a level stretch for some distance, they found themselves on the brink of a rocky basin, of no great size, but very blue, and evidently deep.

" This," said the Ranger, " is where our orders tell us to fling any foreign devil who comes over from the other side. I have only been Head Ranger about nine months, and have not yet had to face this horrid duty; but," and here he smiled, " when I first caught sight of you I thought I should have to make a beginning. I was very glad when I saw you had a permit."

" And how many skeletons do you suppose are lying at the bottom of this pool ? "

" I believe not more than seven or eight in all. There were three or four about eighteen years ago, and about the same number of late years; one man was flung here only about three months before I was appointed. I have the full list, with dates, down in my office, but the rangers never let people in Sunch'ston know when they have Blue-Pooled any one; it would unsettle men's minds, and some of them would be coming up here in the dark to drag the pool, and see whether they could find anything on the body."

My father was glad to turn away from this most repulsive place. After a time he said, " And what do you good people hereabouts think of next Sunday's grand doings ? "

Bearing in mind what he had gleaned from the Professors about the Ranger's opinions, my father gave a slightly ironical turn to his pronunciation of the words "grand doings." The youth glanced at him with a quick penetrative look, and laughed as he said, "The doings will be grand enough."

"What a fine temple they have built," said my father. "I have not yet seen the picture, but they say the four black and white horses are magnificently painted. I saw the Sunchild ascend, but I saw no horses in the sky, nor anything like horses."

The youth was much interested. "Did you really see him ascend?" he asked; "and what, pray, do you think it all was?"

"Whatever it was, there were no horses."

"But there must have been, for, as you of course know, they have lately found some droppings from one of them, which have been miraculously preserved, and they are going to show them next Sunday in a gold reliquary."

"I know," said my father, who, however, was learning the fact for the first time. "I have not yet seen this precious relic, but I think they might have found something less unpleasant."

"Perhaps they would if they could," replied the youth, laughing, "but there was nothing else that the horses could leave. It is only a number of curiously rounded stones, and not at all like what they say it is."

"Well, well," continued my father, "but relic or no relic, there are many who, while they fully recognize the value of the Sunchild's teaching, dislike these cock and bull stories as blasphemy against God's most blessed gift of reason. There are many in Bridgeford who hate this story of the horses."

The youth was now quite reassured. "So there are here, sir," he said warmly, "and who hate the Sunchild too. If there is such a hell as he used to talk about to my mother we doubt not but that he will be cast into its deepest fires. See how he has turned us all upside down. But we dare not say what we think. There is no courage left in Erewhon."

Then waxing calmer he said, "It is you Bridgeford people and your Musical Banks that have done it all. The Musical Bank Managers saw that the people were falling away from them. Finding that the vulgar believed this foreign devil Higgs–for he gave this name to my mother when he was in prison–finding that— But you know all this as well as I do. How can you Bridgeford Professors pretend to believe about these horses, and about the Sunchild's being son to the sun, when all the time you know there is no truth in it?"

"My son–for considering the difference in our ages I may be allowed to call you so–we at Bridgeford are much like you at Sunch'ston; we dare not always say what we think. Nor would it be wise to do so, when we should not be listened to. This fire must burn itself out, for it has got such hold that nothing can either stay or turn it. Even though Higgs himself were to return and tell it from the house-tops that he was a mortal–ay, and a very common one–he would be killed, but not believed."

"Let him come; let him show himself, speak out and die, if the people choose to kill him. In that case I would forgive him, accept him for my father, as silly people sometimes say he is, and honour him to my dying day."

"Would that be a bargain?" said my father, smiling in spite of emotion so strong that he could hardly bring the words out of his mouth.

"Yes, it would," said the youth doggedly.

"Then let me shake hands with you on his behalf, and let us change the conversation."

He took my father's hand, doubtfully and somewhat disdainfully, but he did not refuse it.

CHAPTER SIX: FURTHER CONVERSATION BETWEEN FATHER AND SON, THE PROFESSORS' HOARD

IT IS ONE THING TO DESIRE A CONVERSAtion to be changed, and another to change it. After some little silence my father said, "And may I ask what name your mother gave you?"

"My name," he answered, laughing, "is George, and I wish it were some other, for it is the first name of that arch-impostor Higgs. I hate it as I hate the man who owned it."

My father said nothing, but he hid his face in his hands.

"Sir," said the other, "I fear you are in some distress."

"You remind me," replied my father, "of a son who was stolen from me when he was a child. I searched for him during many years, and at last fell in with him by accident, to find him all the heart of father could wish. But alas! he did not take kindly to me as I to him, and after two days he left me; nor shall I ever again see him."

"Then, sir, had I not better leave you?"

"No, stay with me till your road takes you elsewhere; for though I cannot see my son, you are so like him that I could almost fancy he is with me. And now–for I shall show no more weakness–you say your mother knew the Sunchild, as I am used to call him. Tell me what kind of a man she found him."

"She liked him well enough in spite of his being a little silly. She does not believe he ever called himself child of the sun. He used to say he had a father in heaven to whom he prayed, and who could hear him; but he said that all of us, my mother as much as he, have this unseen father. My mother does not believe he meant doing us any harm, but only that he wanted to get himself and Mrs. Nosnibor's younger daughter out of the country. As for there having been anything supernatural about the balloon, she will have none of it; she says that it was some machine which he knew how to make, but which we have lost the art of making, as we have of many another.

"This is what she says amongst ourselves, but in public she confirms all that the Musical Bank Managers say about him. She is afraid of them. You know, perhaps, that Professor Hanky, whose name I see on your permit, tried to burn her alive?"

"Thank heaven!" thought my father, "that I am Panky;" but aloud he said, "Oh, horrible! horrible! I cannot believe this even of Hanky."

"He denies it, and we say we believe him; he was most kind and attentive to my mother during all the rest of her stay in Bridgeford. He and she parted excellent friends, but I know what she thinks. I shall be sure to see him while he is in Sunch'ston, I shall have to be civil to him but it makes me sick to think of it."

"When shall you see him?" said my father, who was alarmed at learning that Hanky and the Ranger were likely to meet. Who could tell but that he might see Panky too?

"I have been away from home a fortnight, and shall not be back till late on Saturday night. I do not suppose I shall see him before Sunday."

"That will do," thought my father, who at that moment deemed that nothing would matter to him much when Sunday was over. Then, turning to the Ranger, he said, "I gather, then, that your mother does not think so badly of the Sunchild after all?"

"She laughs at him sometimes, but if any of us boys and girls say a word against him we get snapped up directly. My mother turns every one round her finger. Her word is law in Sunch'ston; every one obeys her; she has faced more than one mob, and quelled them when my father could not do so."

"I can believe all you say of her. What other children has she besides yourself?"

"We are four sons, of whom the youngest is now fourteen, and three daughters."

"May all health and happiness attend her and you, and all of you, henceforth and for ever," and my father involuntarily bared his head as he spoke.

"Sir," said the youth, impressed by the fervency of my father's manner, "I thank you, but you do not talk as Bridgeford Professors generally do, so far as I have seen or heard them. Why do you wish us all well so very heartily? Is it because you think I am like your son, or is there some other reason?"

"It is not my son alone that you resemble," said my father tremulously, for he knew he was going too far. He carried it off by adding, "You resemble all who love truth and hate lies, as I do."

"Then, sir," said the youth gravely, "you much belie your reputation. And now I must leave you for another part of the preserves, where I think it likely that last night's poachers may now be, and where I shall pass the night in watching for them. You may want your permit for a few miles further, so I will not take it. Neither need you give it up at Sunch'ston. It is dated, and will be useless after this evening."

With this he strode off into the forest, bowing politely but somewhat coldly, and without encouraging my father's half proffered hand.

My father turned sad and unsatisfied away.

"It serves me right," he said to himself; "he ought never to have been my son; and yet, if such men can be brought by hook or by crook into the world, surely the world should not ask questions about the bringing. How cheerless everything looks now that he has left me."

*

By this time it was three o'clock, and in another few

minutes my father came upon the ashes of the fire beside which he and the Professors had supped on the preceding evening. It was only some eighteen hours since they had come upon him, and yet what an age it seemed! It was well the Ranger had left him, for though my father, of course, would have known nothing about either fire or poachers, it might have led to further falsehood, and by this time he had become exhausted—not to say, for the time being, sick of lies altogether.

He trudged slowly on, without meeting a soul, until he came upon some stones that evidently marked the limits of the preserves. When he had got a mile or so beyond these, he struck a narrow and not much frequented path, which he was sure would lead him towards Sunch'ston, and soon afterwards, seeing a huge old chestnut tree some thirty or forty yards from the path itself, he made towards it and flung himself on the ground beneath its branches. There were abundant signs that he was nearing farm lands and homesteads, but there was no one about, and if any one saw him there was nothing in his appearance to arouse suspicion.

He determined, therefore, to rest here till hunger should wake him, and drive him into Sunch'ston, which, however, he did not wish to reach till dusk if he could help it. He meant to buy a valise and a few toilet necessaries before the shops should close, and then engage a bedroom at the least frequented inn he could find that looked fairly clean and comfortable.

He slept till nearly six, and on waking gathered his thoughts together. He could not shake his newly found son from out of them, but there was no good in dwelling upon him now, and he turned his thoughts to the Professors. How, he wondered, were they getting on, and what had they done with the things they had bought from him?

"How delightful it would be," he said to himself,

"if I could find where they have hidden their hoard, and hide it somewhere else."

He tried to project his mind into those of the Professors, as though they were a team of straying bullocks whose probable action he must determine before he set out to look for them.

On reflection, he concluded that the hidden property was not likely to be far from the spot on which he now was. The Professors would wait till they had got some way down towards Sunch'ston, so as to have readier access to their property when they wanted to remove it; but when they came upon a path and other signs that inhabited dwellings could not be far distant, they would begin to look out for a hiding-place. And they would take pretty well the first that came. "Why, bless my heart," he exclaimed, "this tree is hollow; I wonder whether—" and on looking up he saw an innocent little strip of the very tough fibrous leaf commonly used while green as string, or even rope, by the Erewhonians. The plant that makes this leaf is so like the ubiquitous New Zealand *Phormium tenax*, or flax, as it is there called, that I shall speak of it as flax in future, as indeed I have already done without explanation on an earlier page; for this plant grows on both sides of the great range. The piece of flax, then, which my father caught sight of was fastened, at no great height from the ground, round the branch of a strong sucker that had grown from the roots of the chestnut tree, and going thence for a couple of feet or so towards the place where the parent tree became hollow, it disappeared into the cavity below. My father had little difficulty in swarming the sucker till he reached the bough on to which the flax was tied, and soon found himself hauling up something from the bottom of the tree. In less time than it takes to tell the tale he saw his own familiar red blanket begin to show above the broken edge of the hollow, and in another second there was a clinkum-clankum as the bundle fell upon the ground. This was caused by the billy and the pannikin, which were wrapped inside the blanket. As for the blanket, it had been tied tightly at both ends, as well as at several points between, and my father inwardly complimented the Professors on the neatness with which they had packed and hidden their purchase. " But," he said to himself with a laugh, " I think one of them must have got on the other's back to reach that bough."

" Of course," thought he, " they will have taken the nuggets with them." And yet he had seemed to hear a dumping as well as a clinkum-clankum. He undid the blanket, carefully untying every knot and keeping the flax. When he had unrolled it, he found to his very pleasurable surprise that the pannikin was inside the billy, and the nuggets with the receipt inside the pannikin. The paper containing the tea having been torn, was wrapped up in a handkerchief marked with Hanky's name.

" Down, conscience, down ! " he exclaimed as he transferred the nuggets, receipt, and handkerchief to his own pocket. " Eye of my soul that you are ! if you offend me I must pluck you out." His conscience feared him and said nothing. As for the tea, he left it in its torn paper.

He then put the billy, pannikin, and tea, back again inside the blanket, which he tied neatly up, tie for tie with the Professors' own flax, leaving no sign of any disturbance. He again swarmed the sucker, till he reached the bough to which the blanket and its contents had been made fast, and having attached the bundle, he dropped it back into the hollow of the tree. He did everything quite leisurely, for the Professors would be sure to wait till nightfall before coming to fetch their property away.

" If I take nothing but the nuggets," he argued, " each of the Professors will suspect the other of having conjured them into his own pocket while the bundle was being made up. As for the handkerchief, they must think what they like; but it will puzzle Hanky to know why Panky should have been so anxious for a receipt, if he meant stealing the nuggets. Let them muddle it out their own way."

Reflecting further, he concluded, perhaps rightly, that they had left the nuggets where he had found them, because neither could trust the other not to filch a few, if he had them in his own possession, and they could not make a nice division without a pair of scales. " At any rate," he said to himself, " there will be a pretty quarrel when they find them gone."

Thus charitably did he brood over things that were not to happen. The discovery of the Professors' hoard had refreshed him almost as much as his sleep had done, and it being now past seven, he lit his pipe–which, however, he smoked as furtively as he had done when he was a boy at school, for he knew not whether smoking had yet become an Erewhonian virtue or no–and walked briskly on towards Sunch'ston.

CHAPTER SEVEN: SIGNS OF THE NEW ORDER OF THINGS CATCH MY FATHER'S EYE ON EVERY SIDE

HE HAD NOT GONE FAR BEFORE A turn in the path–now rapidly widening–showed him two high towers, seemingly some two miles off; these he felt sure must be at Sunch'ston, he therefore stepped out, lest he should find the shops shut before he got there.

On his former visit he had seen little of the town, for he was in prison during his whole stay. He had had a glimpse of it on being brought there by the people of the village where he had spent his first night in Erewhon –a village which he had seen at some little distance on his right hand, but which it would have been out of his way to visit, even if he had wished to do so; and he had seen the Museum of old machines, but on leaving the prison he had been blindfolded. Nevertheless he felt sure that if the towers had been there he should have seen them, and rightly guessed that they must belong to the temple which was to be dedicated to himself on Sunday.

When he had passed through the suburbs he found himself in the main street. Space will not allow me to dwell on more than a few of the things which caught his eye, and assured him that the change in Erewhonian habits and opinions had been even more cataclysmic than he had already divined. The first important building that he came to proclaimed itself as the College of Spiritual Athletics, and in the window of a shop that was evidently affiliated to the college he saw an announcement that moral try-your-strengths, suitable for every kind of ordinary temptation, would be provided on the shortest notice. Some of those that aimed at the more common kinds of temptation were kept in stock, but these consisted chiefly of trials to the temper. On dropping, for example, a penny into a slot, you could have a jet of fine pepper, flour, or brickdust, whichever you might prefer, thrown on to your face, and thus discover whether your composure stood in need of further development or no. My father gathered this from the writing that was pasted on to the try-your-strength, but he had no time to go inside the shop and test either the machine or his own temper. Other temptations to irritability required the agency of living people, or at any rate living beings. Crying children, screaming parrots, a spiteful monkey, might be hired on ridiculously easy terms. He saw one advertisement, nicely framed, which ran as follows:

" Mrs. Tantrums, Nagger, certificated by the College of Spiritual Athletics. Terms for ordinary nagging, two shillings and sixpence per hour. Hysterics extra."

Then followed a series of testimonials–for example:

" Dear Mrs. Tantrums,–I have for years been tortured with a husband of unusually peevish, irritable temper, who made my life so intolerable that I sometimes answered him in a way that led to his using personal violence towards me. After taking a course of twelve sittings from you, I found my husband's temper comparatively angelic, and we have ever since lived together in complete harmony."

Another was from a husband:

" Mr. — presents his compliments to Mrs. Tantrums, and begs to assure her that her extra special hysterics have so far surpassed anything his wife can do, as to render him callous to those attacks which he had formerly found so distressing."

There were many others of a like purport, but time did not permit my father to do more than glance at them. He contented himself with the two following, of which the first ran :

" He did try it at last. A little correction of the right kind taken at the right moment is invaluable. No more swearing. No more bad language of any kind. A lamb-like temper ensured in about twenty minutes, by a single dose of one of our spiritual indigestion tabloids. In cases of all the more ordinary moral ailments, from simple lying to homicidal mania, in cases again of tendency to hatred, malice, and uncharitableness; of atrophy or hypertrophy of the conscience, of costiveness or diarrhoea of the sympathetic instincts, etc., etc., our spiritual indigestion tabloids will afford unfailing and immediate relief.

" *N.B.*–A bottle or two of our Sunchild Cordial will assist the operation of the tabloids."

The second and last that I can give was as follows:

" All else is useless. If you wish to be a social success, make yourself a good listener. There is no short cut to this. A would-be listener must learn the rudiments of his art and go through the mill like other people. If he would develop a power of suffering fools gladly, he must begin by suffering them without the gladness. Professor Proser, ex-straightener, certificated bore, pragmatic or coruscating, with or without anecdotes, attends pupils at their own houses. Terms moderate.

" Mrs. Proser, whose success as a professional mind-dresser is so well-known that lengthened advertisement is unnecessary, prepares ladies or gentlemen with appropriate remarks to be made at dinner-parties or at-homes. Mrs. P. keeps herself well up to date with all the latest scandals."

" Poor, poor, straighteners ! " said my father to himself. " Alas ! that it should have been my fate to ruin you–for I suppose your occupation is gone."

Tearing himself away from the College of Spiritual Athletics and its affiliated shop, he passed on a few doors, only to find himself looking in at what was neither more nor less than a chemist's shop. In the window there were advertisements which showed that the practice of medicine was now legal, but my father could not stay to copy a single one of the fantastic announcements that a hurried glance revealed to him.

It was also plain here, as from the shop already more fully described, that the edicts against machines had been repealed, for there were physical try-your-strengths, as in the other shop there had been moral ones, and such machines under the old law would not have been tolerated for a moment.

My father made his purchases just as the last shops were closing. He noticed that almost all of them were full of articles labelled " Dedication." There was Dedication gingerbread, stamped with a moulded representation of the new temple; there were Dedication syrups, Dedication pocket-handkerchiefs, also showing the temple, and in one corner giving a highly idealized portrait of my father himself. The chariot and the horses figured largely, and in the confectioners' shops there were models of the newly discovered relic–made, so my father thought, with a little heap of cherries or strawberries, smothered in chocolate. Outside one tailor's shop he saw a flaring advertisement which can only be translated, " Try our Dedication trousers, price ten shillings and sixpence."

Presently he passed the new temple, but it was too dark for him to do more than see that it was a vast fane, and must have cost an untold amount of money. At every turn he found himself more and more shocked, as he realized more and more fully the mischief he had already occasioned, and the certainty that this was small as compared with that which would grow up hereafter.

" What," he said to me, very coherently and quietly, " was I to do? I had struck a bargain with that dear fellow, though he knew not what I meant, to the effect that I should try to undo the harm I had done, by standing up before the people on Sunday and saying who I was. True, they would not believe me. They would look at my hair and see it black, whereas it should be very light. On this they would look no further, but very likely tear me in pieces then and there. Suppose that the authorities held a *post-mortem* examination, and that many who knew me (let alone that all my measurements and marks were recorded twenty years ago) identified the body as mine: would those in power admit that I was the Sunchild? Not they. The interests vested in my being now in the palace of the sun are too great to allow of my having been torn to pieces in Sunch'ston, no matter how truly I had been torn; the whole thing would be hushed up, and the utmost that could come of it would be a heresy which would in time be crushed.

"On the other hand, what business have I with 'would be' or 'would not be?' Should I not speak out, come what may, when I see a whole people being led astray by those who are merely exploiting them for their own ends? Though I could do but little, ought I not to do that little? What did that good fellow's instinct–so straight from heaven, so true, so healthy–tell him? What did my own instinct answer? What would the conscience of any honourable man answer? Who can doubt?

"And yet, is there not reason? and is it not God-given as much as instinct? I remember having heard an anthem in my young days, 'O where shall wisdom be found? the deep saith it is not in me.' As the singers kept on repeating the question, I kept on saying sorrowfully to myself–'Ah, where, where, where?' and when the triumphant answer came, 'The fear of the Lord, that is wisdom, and to depart from evil is understanding,' I shrunk ashamed into myself for not having foreseen it. In later life, when I have tried to use this answer as a light by which I could walk, I found it served but to the raising of another question, 'What is the fear of the Lord, and what is evil in this particular case?' And my easy method with spiritual dilemmas proved to be but a case of *ignotum per ignotius*.

"If Satan himself is at times transformed into an angel of light, are not angels of light sometimes transformed into the likeness of Satan? If the devil is not so black as he is painted, is God always so white? And is there not another place in which it is said, 'The fear of the Lord is the beginning of wisdom,' as though it were not the last word upon the subject? If a man should not do evil that good may come, so neither should he do good that evil may come; and though it were good for me to speak out, should I not do better by refraining?

"Such were the lawless and uncertain thoughts that tortured me very cruelly, so that I did what I had not done for many a long year–I prayed for guidance. 'Show me Thy will, O Lord,' I cried in great distress, 'and strengthen me to do it when Thou hast shown it me.' But there was no answer. Instinct tore me one way and reason another. Whereon I settled that I would obey the reason with which God had endowed me, unless the instinct He had also given me should thrash it out of me. I could get no further than this, that the Lord hath mercy on whom He will have mercy, and whom He willeth He hardeneth; and again I prayed that I might be among those on whom He would show His mercy.

"This was the strongest internal conflict that I ever remember to have felt, and it was at the end of it that I perceived the first, but as yet very faint, symptoms of that sickness from which I shall not recover. Whether this be a token of mercy or no, my Father which is in heaven knows, but I know not."

From what my father afterwards told me, I do not think the above reflections had engrossed him for more than three or four minutes; the giddiness which had for some seconds compelled him to lay hold of the first thing he could catch at in order to avoid falling, passed away without leaving a trace behind it, and his path seemed to become comfortably clear before him. He settled it that the proper thing to do would be to buy some food, start back at once while his permit was still valid, help himself to the property which he had sold the Professors, leaving the Erewhonians to wrestle as they best might with the lot that it had pleased Heaven to send them.

This, however, was too heroic a course. He was tired, and wanted a night's rest in a bed; he was hungry, and wanted a substantial meal; he was curious, moreover, to see the temple dedicated to himself, and hear Hanky's sermon; there was also this further difficulty, he should have to take what he had sold the Professors without returning them their £4, 10*s*., for he could not do without his blanket, etc.; and even if he left a bag of nuggets made fast to the sucker, he must either place it where it could be seen so easily that it would very likely get stolen, or hide it so cleverly that the Professors would never find it. He therefore compromised by concluding that he would sup and sleep in Sunch'ston, get through the morrow as he best could without attracting attention, deepen the stain on his face and hair, and rely on the change so made in his appearance to prevent his being recognized at the dedication of the temple. He would do nothing to disillusion the people–to do this would only be making bad worse. As soon as the service was over, he would set out towards the preserves, and, when it was well dark, make for the statues. He hoped that on such a great day the rangers might be many of them in Sunch'ston; if there were any about, he must trust the moonless night and his own quick eyes and ears to get him through the preserves safely.

The shops were by this time closed, but the keepers of a few stalls were trying by lamplight to sell the wares they had not yet got rid of. One of these was a bookstall, and, running his eye over some of the volumes, my father saw one entitled:

"The Sayings of the Sunchild during his stay in Erewhon, to which is added a true account of his return to the palace of the sun with his Erewhonian bride. This is the only version authorized by the Presidents and Vice-Presidents of the Musical Banks; all other versions being imperfect and inaccurate."–Bridgeford, XVIII, 150 pp. 8vo. Price 3*s.*

The reader will understand that I am giving the prices as nearly as I can in their English equivalents. Another title was:

"The Sacrament of Divorce: an Occasional Sermon preached by Dr. Gurgoyle, President of the Musical Banks for the Province of Sunch'ston." 8vo, 16 pp. 6*d.*

Other titles ran:

"Counsels of Imperfection." 8vo, 20 pp. 6*d.*

"Hygiene; or, How to Diagnose your Doctor." 8vo, 10 pp. 3*d.*

"The Physics of Vicarious Existence, by Dr. Gurgoyle, President of the Musical Banks for the Province of Sunch'ston." 8vo, 20 pp. 6*d.*

There were many other books whose titles would probably have attracted my father as much as those that I have given, but he was too tired and hungry to look at more. Finding that he could buy all the foregoing for 4*s.* 9*d.*, he bought them and stuffed them into the valise that he had just bought. His purchases in all had now amounted to a little over £1, 10*s.* (silver), leaving him about £3 (silver), including the money for which he had sold the quails, to carry him on till Sunday afternoon. He intended to spend say £2 (silver), and keep the rest of the money in order to give it to the British Museum.

He now began to search for an inn, and walked about the less fashionable parts of the town till he found an unpretending tavern, which he thought would suit him. Here, on importunity, he was given a servant's room at the top of the house, all others being engaged by visitors who had come for the dedication. He ordered a meal, of which he stood in great need, and having eaten it, he retired early for the night. But he smoked a pipe surreptitiously up the chimney before he got into bed.

Meanwhile other things were happening, of which, happily for his repose, he was still ignorant, and which he did not learn till a few days later. Not to depart from chronological order I will deal with them in my next chapter.

CHAPTER EIGHT: YRAM, NOW MAYORESS, GIVES A DINNER-PARTY, IN THE COURSE OF WHICH SHE IS DISQUIETED BY WHAT SHE LEARNS FROM PROFESSOR HANKY, SHE SENDS FOR HER SON GEORGE AND QUESTIONS HIM

THE PROFESSORS, RETURNING TO THEIR hotel early on the Friday morning, found a note from the Mayoress urging them to be her guests during the remainder of their visit, and to meet other friends at dinner on this same evening. They accepted, and then went to bed; for they had passed the night under the tree in which they had hidden their purchase, and, as may be imagined, had slept but little. They rested all day, and transferred themselves and their belongings to the Mayor's house in time to dress for dinner.

When they came down into the drawing-room they found a brilliant company assembled, chiefly Musical-Bankical like themselves. There was Dr. Downie, Professor of Logomachy, and perhaps the most subtle dialectician in Erewhon. He could say nothing in more words than any man of his generation. His text-book "On the Art of Obscuring Issues" had passed through ten or twelve editions, and was in the hands of all aspirants for academic distinction. He had earned a high reputation for sobriety of judgement by resolutely refusing to have definite views on any subject; so safe a man was he considered, that while still quite young he had been appointed to the lucrative post of Thinker in Ordinary to the Royal Family. There was Mr. Principal Crank, with his sister Mrs. Quack; Professors Gabb and Bawl, with their wives and two or three erudite daughters.

Old Mrs. Humdrum (of whom more anon) was there of course, with her venerable white hair and rich black satin dress, looking the very ideal of all that a stately old dowager ought to be. In society she was commonly known as Ydgrun, so perfectly did she correspond with the conception of this strange goddess formed by the

Erewhonians. She was one of those who had visited my father when he was in prison twenty years earlier. When he told me that she was now called Ydgrun, he said, " I am sure that the Erinyes were only Mrs. Humdrums, and that they were delightful people when you came to know them. I do not believe they did the awful things we say they did. I think, but am not quite sure, that they let Orestes off; but even though they had not pardoned him, I doubt whether they would have done anything more dreadful to him than issue a *mot d'ordre* that he was not to be asked to any more afternoon teas. This, however, would be downright torture to some people. At any rate," he continued, " be it the Erinyes, or Mrs. Grundy, or Ydgrun, in all times and places it is woman who decides whether society is to condone an offence or no."

Among the most attractive ladies present was one for whose Erewhonian name I can find no English equivalent, and whom I must therefore call Miss La Frime. She was Lady President of the principal establishment for the higher education of young ladies, and so celebrated was she, that pupils flocked to her from all parts of the surrounding country. Her primer (written for the Erewhonian Arts and Science Series) on the Art of Man-killing, was the most complete thing of the kind that had yet been done; but ill-natured people had been heard to say that she had killed all her own admirers so effectually that not one of them had ever lived to marry her. According to Erewhonian custom the successful marriages of the pupils are inscribed yearly on the oak panelling of the college refectory, and a reprint from these in pamphlet form accompanies all the prospectuses that are sent out to parents. It was alleged that no other ladies' seminary in Erewhon could show such a brilliant record during all the years of Miss La Frime's presidency. Many other guests of less note were there, but the lions of the evening were the two Professors whom we have already met with, and more particularly Hanky, who took the Mayoress in to dinner. Panky, of course, wore his clothes reversed, as did Principal Crank and Professor Gabb; the others were dressed English fashion.

Everything hung upon the hostess, for the host was little more than a still handsome figure-head. He had been remarkable for his good looks as a young man, and Strong is the nearest approach I can get to a translation of his Erewhonian name. His face inspired confidence at once, but he was a man of few words, and had little of that grace which in his wife set every one instantly at his or her ease. He knew that all would go well so long as he left everything to her, and kept himself as far as might be in the background.

Before dinner was announced there was the usual buzz of conversation, chiefly occupied with salutations, good wishes for Sunday's weather, and admiration for the extreme beauty of the Mayoress's three daughters, the two elder of whom were already out; while the third, though only thirteen, might have passed for a year or two older. Their mother was so much engrossed with receiving her guests that it was not till they were all at table that she was able to ask Hanky what he thought of the statues, which she had heard that he and Professor Panky had been to see. She was told how much interested he had been with them, and how unable he had been to form any theory as to their date or object. He then added, appealing to Panky, who was on the Mayoress's left hand, "But we had rather a strange adventure on our way down, had we not, Panky? We got lost, and were benighted in the forest. Happily we fell in with one of the rangers who had lit a fire."

"Do I understand, then," said Yram, as I suppose we may as well call her, "that you were out all last night?

How tired you must be! But I hope you had enough provisions with you?"

"Indeed we were out all night. We stayed by the ranger's fire till midnight, and then tried to find our way down, but we gave it up soon after we had got out of the forest, and then waited under a large chestnut tree till four or five this morning. As for food, we had not so much as a mouthful from about three in the afternoon till we got to our inn early this morning."

"Oh, you poor, poor people! how tired you must be."

"No; we made a good breakfast as soon as we got in, and then went to bed, where we stayed till it was time for us to come to your house."

Here Panky gave his friend a significant look, as much as to say that he had said enough.

This set Hanky on at once. "Strange to say, the ranger was wearing the old Erewhonian dress. It did me good to see it again after all these years. It seems your son lets his men wear what few of the old clothes they may still have, so long as they keep well away from the town. But fancy how carefully these poor fellows husband them; why, it must be seventeen years since the dress was forbidden!"

We all of us have skeletons, large or small, in some cupboard of our lives, but a well regulated skeleton that will stay in its cupboard quietly does not much matter. There are skeletons, however, which can never be quite trusted not to open the cupboard door at some awkward moment, go down stairs, ring the hall-door bell, with grinning face announce themselves as the skeleton, and ask whether the master or mistress is at home. This kind of skeleton, though no bigger than a rabbit, will sometimes loom large as that of a dinotherium. My father was Yram's skeleton. True, he was a mere skeleton of a skeleton, for the chances were thousands to one that he and my mother had perished long years ago; and even though he rang at the bell, there was no harm that he either could or would now do to her or hers; still, so long as she did not certainly know that he was dead, or otherwise precluded from returning, she could not be sure that he would not one day come back by the way that he would alone know; and she had rather he should not do so.

Hence, on hearing from Professor Hanky that a man had been seen between the statues and Sunch'ston wearing the old Erewhonian dress, she was disquieted and perplexed. The excuse he had evidently made to the Professors aggravated her uneasiness, for it was an obvious attempt to escape from an unexpected difficulty. There could be no truth in it. Her son would as soon think of wearing the old dress himself as of letting his men do so; and as for having old clothes still to wear out after seventeen years, no one but a Bridgeford Professor would accept this. She saw, therefore, that she must keep her wits about her, and lead her guests on to tell her as much as they could be induced to do.

"My son," she said innocently, "is always considerate to his men, and that is why they are so devoted to him. I wonder which of them it was? In what part of the preserves did you fall in with him?"

Hanky described the place, and gave the best idea he could of my father's appearance.

"Of course he was swarthy like the rest of us?"

"I saw nothing remarkable about him, except that his eyes were blue and his eyelashes nearly white, which, as you know, is rare in Erewhon. Indeed, I do not remember ever before to have seen a man with dark hair and complexion but light eyelashes. Nature is always doing something unusual."

"I have no doubt," said Yram, "that he was the man they call Blacksheep, but I never noticed this peculiarity in him. If he was Blacksheep, I am afraid you must have found him none too civil; he is a rough diamond, and you would hardly be able to understand his uncouth Sunch'ston dialect."

"On the contrary, he was most kind and thoughtful—even so far as to take our permit from us, and thus save us the trouble of giving it up at your son's office. As for his dialect, his grammar was often at fault, but we could quite understand him."

"I am glad to hear he behaved better than I could have expected. Did he say in what part of the preserves he had been?"

"He had been catching quails between the place where we saw him and the statues; he was to deliver three dozen to your son this afternoon for the Mayor's banquet on Sunday."

This was worse and worse. She had urged her son to provide her with a supply of quails for Sunday's banquet, but he had begged her not to insist on having them. There was no close time for them in Erewhon, but he set his face against their being seen at table in spring and summer. During the winter, when any great occasion arose, he had allowed a few brace to be provided.

"I asked my son to let me have some," said Yram, who was now on full scent. She laughed genially as she added, "Can you throw any light upon the question whether I am likely to get my three dozen? I have had no news as yet."

"The man had taken a good many; we saw them but did not count them. He started about midnight for the ranger's shelter, where he said he should sleep till day-break, so as to make up his full tale betimes."

Yram had heard her son complain that there were no shelters on the preserves, and state his intention of having some built before the winter. Here too, then, the man's story must be false. She changed the conversation for the moment, but quietly told a servant to send high and low in search of her son, and if he could be found, to bid him come to her at once. She then returned to her previous subject.

"And did not this heartless wretch, knowing how hungry you must both be, let you have a quail or two as an act of pardonable charity?"

"My dear Mayoress, how can you ask such a question? We knew you would want all you could get; moreover, our permit threatened us with all sorts of horrors if we so much as ate a single quail. I assure you we never even allowed a thought of eating one of them to cross our minds."

"Then," said Yram to herself, "they gorged upon them." What could she think? A man who wore the old dress, and therefore who had almost certainly been in Erewhon, but had been many years away from it; who spoke the language well, but whose grammar was defective–hence, again, one who had spent some time in Erewhon; who knew nothing of the afforesting law now long since enacted, for how else would he have dared to light a fire and be seen with quails in his possession; an adroit liar, who on gleaning information from the Professors had hazarded an excuse for immediately retracing his steps; a man, too, with blue eyes and light eyelashes. What did it matter about his hair being dark and his complexion swarthy–Higgs was far too clever to attempt a second visit to Erewhon without dyeing his hair and staining his face and hands. And he had got their permit out of the Professors before he left them; clearly, then, he meant coming back, and coming back at once before the permit had expired. How could she doubt? My father, she felt sure, must by this time be in Sunch'ston. He would go back to change his clothes, which would not be very far down on the other side the pass, for he would not put on his old Erewhonian dress till he was on the point of entering Erewhon; and he would hide his English dress rather than throw it away, for he would want it when he went back again. It would be quite possible, then, for him to get through the forest before the permit was void, and he would be sure to go on to Sunch'ston for the night.

She chatted unconcernedly, now with one guest now with another, while they in their turn chatted unconcernedly with one another.

Miss La Frime to Mrs. Humdrum: " You know how he got his professorship? No? I thought every one knew that. The question the candidates had to answer was, whether it was wiser during a long stay at a hotel to tip the servants pretty early, or to wait till the stay was ended. All the other candidates took one side or the other, and argued their case in full. Hanky sent in three lines to the effect that the proper thing to do would be to promise at the beginning, and go away without giving. The King, with whom the appointment rested, was so much pleased with this answer that he gave Hanky the professorship without so much as looking . . ."

Professor Gabb to Mrs. Humdrum: " Oh no, I can assure you there is no truth in it. What happened was this. There was the usual crowd, and the people cheered Professor after Professor, as he stood before them in the great Bridgeford theatre and satisfied them that a lump of butter which had been put into his mouth would not melt in it. When Hanky's turn came he was taken suddenly unwell, and had to leave the theatre, on which there was a report in the house that the butter had melted; this was at once stopped by the return of the Professor. Another piece of butter was put into his mouth, and on being taken out after the usual time, was found to show no signs of having . . ."

Miss Bawl to Mr. Principal Crank: . . . " The Manager was so tall, you know, and then there was that little mite of an assistant manager—it *was* so funny. For the assistant manager's voice was ever so much louder than the . . ."

Mrs. Bawl to Professor Gabb: . . . "Live for art! If I had to choose whether I would lose either art or science, I have not the smallest hesitation in saying that I would lose . . ."

The Mayor and Dr. Downie: . . . "That you are to be canonized at the close of the year along with Professors Hanky and Panky?"

"I believe it is his Majesty's intention that the Professors and myself are to head the list of the Sunchild's Saints, but we have all of us got to . . ."

And so on, and so on, buzz, buzz, buzz, over the whole table. Presently Yram turned to Hanky and said:

"By the way, Professor, you must have found it very cold up at the statues, did you not? But I suppose the snow is all gone by this time?"

"Yes, it was cold, and though the winter's snow is melted, there had been a recent fall. Strange to say, we saw fresh footprints in it, as of some one who had come up from the other side. But thereon hangs a tale, about which I believe I should say nothing."

"Then say nothing, my dear Professor," said Yram with a frank smile. "Above all," she added quietly and gravely, "say nothing to the Mayor, nor to my son, till after Sunday. Even a whisper of some one coming over from the other side disquiets them, and they have enough on hand for the moment."

Panky, who had been growing more and more restive at his friend's outspokenness, but who had encouraged it more than once by vainly trying to check it, was relieved at hearing his hostess do for him what he could not do for himself. As for Yram, she had got enough out of the Professor to be now fully dissatisfied, and mentally informed them that they might leave the witness-box. During the rest of dinner she let the subject of their adventure severely alone.

It seemed to her as though dinner was never going to end; but in the course of time it did so, and presently the ladies withdrew. As they were entering the drawing-room a servant told her that her son had been found more easily than was expected, and was now in his own room dressing.

"Tell him," she said, "to stay there till I come, which I will do directly."

She remained for a few minutes with her guests, and then, excusing herself quietly to Mrs. Humdrum, she stepped out and hastened to her son's room. She told him that Professors Hanky and Panky were staying in the house, and that during dinner they had told her something he ought to know, but which there was no time to tell him until her guests were gone. "I had rather," she said, "tell you about it before you see the Professors, for if you see them the whole thing will be reopened, and you are sure to let them see how much more there is in it than they suspect. I want everything hushed up for the moment; do not, therefore, join us. Have dinner sent to you in your father's study. I will come to you about midnight."

"But, my dear mother," said George, "I have seen Panky already. I walked down with him a good long way this afternoon."

Yram had not expected this, but she kept her countenance. "How did you know," said she, "that he was Professor Panky? Did he tell you so?"

"Certainly he did. He showed me his permit, which was made out in favour of Professors Hanky and Panky, or either of them. He said Hanky had been unable to come with him, and that he was himself Professor Panky."

Yram again smiled very sweetly. "Then, my dear boy," she said, "I am all the more anxious that you should not see him now. See nobody but the servants and your brothers, and wait till I can enlighten you. I must not stay another moment; but tell me this much, have you seen any signs of poachers lately?"

"Yes; there were three last night."

"In what part of the preserves?"

Her son described the place.

"You are sure they had been killing quails?"

"Yes, and eating them–two on one side of a fire they had lit, and one on the other; this last man had done all the plucking."

"Good!"

She kissed him with more than even her usual tenderness, and returned to the drawing-room.

During the rest of the evening she was engaged in earnest conversation with Mrs. Humdrum, leaving her other guests to her daughters and to themselves. Mrs. Humdrum had been her closest friend for many years, and carried more weight than any one else in Sunch'ston, except, perhaps, Yram herself. "Tell him everything," she said to Yram at the close of their conversation; "we all dote upon him; trust him frankly, as you trusted your husband before you let him marry you. No lies, no reserve, no tears, and all will come right. As for me, command me," and the good old lady rose to take her leave with as kind a look on her face as ever irradiated saint or angel. "I go early," she added, "for the others will go when they see me do so, and the sooner you are alone the better."

By half an hour before midnight her guests had gone. Hanky and Panky were given to understand that they must still be tired, and had getter go to bed. So was the Mayor; so were her sons and daughters, except of course George, who was waiting for her with some anxiety, for he had seen that she had something serious to tell him. Then she went down into the study. Her son embraced her as she entered, and moved an easy chair for her, but she would not have it.

"No; I will have an upright one." Then, sitting composedly down on the one her son placed for her, she said:

"And now to business. But let me first tell you that the Mayor was told, twenty years ago, all the more important part of what you will now hear. He does not yet know what has happened within the last few hours, but either you or I will tell him to-morrow."

CHAPTER NINE: INTERVIEW BETWEEN YRAM AND HER SON

"WHAT DID YOU THINK OF PANKY?"

"I could not make him out. If he had not been a Bridgeford Professor I might have liked him; but you know how we all of us distrust those people."

"Where did you meet him?"

"About two hours lower down than the statues."

"At what o'clock?"

"It might be between two and half-past."

"I suppose he did not say that at that hour he was in bed at his hotel in Sunch'ston. Hardly! Tell me what passed between you."

"He had his permit open before we were within speaking distance. I think he feared I should attack him without making sure whether he was a foreign devil or no. I have told you he said he was Professor Panky."

"I suppose he had a dark complexion and black hair like the rest of us?"

"Dark complexion and hair purplish rather than black. I was surprised to see that his eyelashes were as light as my own, and his eyes were blue like mine–but you will have noticed this at dinner."

"No, my dear, I did not, and I think I should have done so if it had been there to notice."

"Oh, but it was so indeed."

"Perhaps. Was there anything strange about his way of talking?"

"A little about his grammar, but these Bridgeford Professors have often risen from the ranks. His pronunciation was nearly like yours and mine."

"Was his manner friendly?"

"Very; more so than I could understand at first. I had not, however, been with him long before I saw tears in his eyes, and when I asked him whether he was in distress, he said I reminded him of a son whom he had lost and had found after many years, only to lose him almost immediately for ever. Hence his cordiality towards me."

"Then," said Yram half hysterically to herself, "he knew who you were. Now, how, I wonder, did he find that out?" All vestige of doubt as to who the man might be had now left her.

"Certainly he knew who I was. He spoke about you more than once, and wished us every kind of prosperity, baring his head reverently as he spoke."

"Poor fellow! Did he say anything about Higgs?"

"A good deal, and I was surprised to find he thought about it all much as we do. But when I said that if I could go down into the hell of which Higgs used to talk to you while he was in prison, I should expect to find him in its hottest fires, he did not like it."

"Possibly not, my dear. Did you tell him how the other boys, when you were at school, used sometimes to say you were son to this man Higgs, and that the people of Sunch'ston used to say so also, till the Mayor trounced two or three people so roundly that they held their tongues for the future?"

"Not all that, but I said that silly people had believed me to be the Sunchild's son, and what a disgrace I should hold it to be son to such an impostor."

"What did he say to this?"

"He asked whether I should feel the disgrace less if Higgs were to undo the mischief he had caused by coming back and showing himself to the people for what he was. But he said it would be no use for him to do so, inasmuch as people would kill him but would not believe him."

"And you said?"

"Let him come back, speak out, and chance what might befall him. In that case, I should honour him, father or no father."

"And he?"

" He asked if that would be a bargain; and when I said it would, he grasped me warmly by the hand on Higgs's behalf–though what it could matter to him passes my comprehension."

" But he saw that even though Higgs were to show himself and say who he was, it would mean death to himself and no good to any one else ? "

" Perfectly."

" Then he can have meant nothing by shaking hands with you. It was an idle jest. And now for your poachers. You do not know who they were ? I will tell you. The two who sat on the one side the fire were Professors Hanky and Panky from the City of the People who are above Suspicion."

" No," said George vehemently. " Impossible."

" Yes, my dear boy, quite possible, and whether possible or impossible, assuredly true."

" And the third man ? "

" The third man was dressed in the old costume. He was in possession of several brace of birds. The Professors vowed they had not eaten any—"

" Oh yes, but they had," blurted out George.

" Of course they had, my dear; and a good thing too. Let us return to the man in the old costume."

" That is puzzling. Who did he say he was ? "

" He said he was one of your men; that you had instructed him to provide you with three dozen quails for Sunday; and that you let your men wear the old costume if they had any of it left, provided—"

This was too much for George; he started to his feet. " What, my dearest mother, does all this mean ? You have been playing with me all through. What is coming ? "

" A very little more, and you shall hear. This man stayed with the Professors till nearly midnight, and then left them on the plea that he would finish the night in the Ranger's shelter—"

"Ranger's shelter, indeed! Why—"

"Hush, my darling boy, be patient with me. He said he must be up betimes, to run down the rest of the quails you had ordered him to bring you. But before leaving the Professors he beguiled them into giving him up their permit."

"Then," said George, striding about the room with his face flushed and his eyes flashing, "he was the man with whom I walked down this afternoon."

"Exactly so."

"And he must have changed his dress?"

"Exactly so."

"But where and how?"

"At some place not very far down on the other side the range, where he had hidden his old clothes."

"And who, in the name of all that we hold most sacred, do you take him to have been–for I see you know more than you have yet told me?"

"My son, he was Higgs the Sunchild, father to that boy whom I love next to my husband more dearly than any one in the whole world."

She folded her arms about him for a second, without kissing him, and left him. "And now," she said, the moment she had closed the door–"and now I may cry."

*

She did not cry for long, and having removed all trace of tears as far as might be, she returned to her son outwardly composed and cheerful. "Shall I say more now," she said, seeing how grave he looked, "or shall I leave you, and talk further with you to-morrow?"

"Now–now–now!"

"Good! A little before Higgs came here, the Mayor, as he now is, poor, handsome, generous to a fault so far as he had the wherewithal, was adored by all the women of his own rank in Sunch'ston. Report said that he had adored many of them in return, but after having known me for a very few days, he asked me to marry him, protesting that he was a changed man. I liked him, as every one else did, but I was not in love with him, and said so; he said he would give me as much time as I chose, if I would not point-blank refuse him; and so the matter was left.

"Within a week or so Higgs was brought to the prison, and he had not been there long before I found, or thought I found, that I liked him better than I liked Strong. I was a fool–but there! As for Higgs, he liked, but did not love me. If I had let him alone he would have done the like by me; and let each other alone we did, till the day before he was taken down to the capital. On that day, whether through his fault or mine I know not–we neither of us meant it–it was as though Nature, my dear, was determined that you should not slip through her fingers–well, on that day we took it into our heads that we were broken-hearted lovers–the rest followed. And how, my dearest boy, as I look upon you, can I feign repentance?

"My husband, who never saw Higgs, and knew nothing about him except the too little that I told him, pressed his suit, and about a month after Higgs had gone, having recovered from my passing infatuation for him, I took kindly to the Mayor and accepted him, without telling him what I ought to have told him–but the words stuck in my throat. I had not been engaged to him many days before I found that there was something which I should not be able to hide much longer.

"You know, my dear, that my mother had been long dead, and I never had a sister or any near kinswoman.

At my wits' end who I should consult, instinct drew me to Mrs. Humdrum, then a woman of about five-and-forty. She was a grand lady, while I was about the rank of one of my own housemaids. I had no claim on her; I went to her as a lost dog looks into the faces of people on a road, and singles out the one who will most surely help him. I had had a good look at her once as she was putting on her gloves, and I liked the way she did it. I marvel at my own boldness. At any rate, I asked to see her, and told her my story exactly as I have now told it to you.

"'You have no mother?' she said, when she had heard all.

"'No.'

"'Then, my dear, I will mother you myself. Higgs is out of the question, so Strong must marry you at once. We will tell him everything, and I, on your behalf, will insist upon it that the engagement is at an end. I hear good reports of him, and if we are fair towards him he will be generous towards us. Besides, I believe he is so much in love with you that he would sell his soul to get you. Send him to me. I can deal with him better than you can.'"

"And what," said George, "did my father, as I shall always call him, say to all this?"

"Truth bred chivalry in him at once. 'I will marry her,' he said, with hardly a moment's hesitation, 'but it will be better that I should not be put on any lower footing than Higgs was. I ought not to be denied anything that has been allowed to him. If I am trusted, I can trust myself to trust and think no evil either of Higgs or her. They were pestered beyond endurance, as I have been ere now. If I am held at arm's length till I am fast bound, I shall marry Yram just the same, but I doubt whether she and I shall ever be quite happy.'

"'Come to my house this evening,' said Mrs. Humdrum, 'and you will find Yram there.' He came, he found me, and within a fortnight we were man and wife."

"How much does not all this explain," said George, smiling but very gravely. "And you are going to ask me to forgive you for robbing me of such a father."

"He has forgiven me, my dear, for robbing him of such a son. He never reproached me. From that day to this he has never given me a harsh word or even syllable. When you were born he took to you at once, as, indeed, who could help doing? for you were the sweetest child both in looks and temper that it is possible to conceive. Your having light hair and eyes made things more difficult; for this, and your being born, almost to the day, nine months after Higgs had left us, made people talk–but your father kept their tongues within bounds. They talk still, but they liked what little they saw of Higgs, they like the Mayor and me, and they like you the best of all; so they please themselves by having the thing both ways. Though, therefore, you are son to the Mayor, Higgs cast some miraculous spell upon me before he left, whereby my son should be in some measure his as well as the Mayor's. It was this miraculous spell that caused you to be born two months too soon, and we called you by Higgs's first name as though to show that we took that view of the matter ourselves.

"Mrs. Humdrum, however, was very positive that there was no spell at all. She had repeatedly heard her father say that the Mayor's grandfather was light-haired and blue-eyed, and that every third generation in that family a light-haired son was born. The people believe this too. Nobody disbelieves Mrs. Humdrum, but they like the miracle best, so that is how it has been settled.

"I never knew whether Mrs. Humdrum told her husband, but I think she must; for a place was found almost immediately for my husband in Mr. Humdrum's business. He made himself useful; after a few years he was taken into partnership, and on Mr. Humdrum's death became head of the firm. Between ourselves, he says laughingly that all his success in life was due to Higgs and me."

"I shall give Mrs. Humdrum a double dose of kissing," said George thoughtfully, "next time I see her."

"Oh, do, do; she will so like it. And now, my darling boy, tell your poor mother whether or no you can forgive her."

He clasped her in his arms, and kissed her again and again, but for a time he could find no utterance. Presently he smiled, and said, "Of course I do, but it is you who should forgive me, for was it not all my fault?"

When Yram, too, had become more calm, she said, "It is late, and we have no time to lose. Higgs's coming at this time is mere accident; if he had had news from Erewhon he would have known much that he did not know. I cannot guess why he has come–probably through mere curiosity, but he will hear or have heard–yes, you and he talked about it–of the temple; being here, he will want to see the dedication. From what you have told me I feel sure that he will not make a fool of himself by saying who he is, but in spite of his disguise he may be recognized. I do not doubt that he is now in Sunch'ston; therefore, to-morrow morning scour the town to find him. Tell him he is discovered, tell him you know from me that he is your father, and that I wish to see him with all good-will towards him. He will come. We will then talk to him, and show him that he must go back at once. You can escort him to the statues; after passing them he will be safe. He will give you no trouble, but if he does, arrest him on a charge of poaching, and take him to the gaol, where we must do the best we can with him–but he will give you none. We need say nothing to the Professors. No one but ourselves will know of his having been here."

On this she again embraced her son and left him. If two photographs could have been taken of her, one as she opened the door and looked fondly back on George, and the other as she closed it behind her, the second portrait would have seemed taken ten years later than the first.

As for George, he went gravely but not unhappily to his own room. "So that ready, plausible fellow," he muttered to himself, "was my own father. At any rate, I am not son to a fool–and he liked me."

CHAPTER TEN: MY FATHER, FEARING RECOGNITION AT SUNCH'STON, BETAKES HIMSELF TO THE NEIGHBOURING TOWN OF FAIRMEAD

I WILL NOW RETURN TO MY FATHER. Whether from fatigue or over-excitement, he slept only by fits and starts, and when awake he could not rid himself of the idea that, in spite of his disguise, he might be recognized, either at his inn or in the town, by some one of the many who had seen him when he was in prison. In this case there was no knowing what might happen, but at best, discovery would probably prevent his seeing the temple dedicated to himself, and hearing Professor Hanky's sermon, which he was particularly anxious to do.

So strongly did he feel the real or fancied danger he should incur by spending Saturday in Sunch'ston, that he rose as soon as he heard any one stirring, and having paid his bill, walked quietly out of the house, without saying where he was going.

There was a town about ten miles off, not so important as Sunch'ston, but having some 10,000 inhabitants; he resolved to find accommodation there for the day and night, and to walk over to Sunch'ston in time for the dedication ceremony, which he had found, on inquiry, would begin at eleven o'clock.

The country between Sunch'ston and Fairmead, as the town just referred to was named, was still mountainous, and being well wooded as well as well watered, abounded in views of singular beauty; but I have no time to dwell on the enthusiasm with which my father described them to me. The road took him at right angles to the main road down the valley from Sunch'ston to the capital, and this was one reason why he had chosen Fairmead rather than Clearwater, which was the next town lower down on the main road. He did not, indeed, anticipate that any one would want to find him, but whoever might so want would be more likely to go straight down the valley than to turn aside towards Fairmead.

On reaching this place, he found it pretty full of people, for Saturday was market-day. There was a considerable open space in the middle of the town, with an arcade running round three sides of it, while the fourth was completely taken up by the venerable Musical Bank of the city, a building which had weathered the storms of more than five centuries. On the outside of the wall, abutting on the market-place, were three wooden *sedilia*, in which the Mayor and two coadjutors sate weekly on market-days to give advice, redress grievances, and, if necessary (which it very seldom was) to administer correction.

My father was much interested in watching the proceedings in a case which he found on inquiry to be not infrequent. A man was complaining to the Mayor that his daughter, a lovely child of eight years old, had none of the faults common to children of her age, and, in fact, seemed absolutely deficient in immoral sense. She never told lies, had never stolen so much as a lollipop, never showed any recalcitrancy about saying her prayers, and by her incessant obedience had filled her poor father and mother with the gravest anxiety as regards her future well-being. He feared it would be necessary to send her to a deformatory.

"I have generally found," said the Mayor, gravely but kindly, "that the fault in these distressing cases lies rather with the parent than the children. Does the child never break anything by accident?"

"Yes," said the father.

"And you have duly punished her for it?"

"Alas! sir, I fear I only told her she was a naughty girl, and must not do it again."

"Then how can you expect your child to learn those petty arts of deception without which she must fall an easy prey to any one who wishes to deceive her? How can she detect lying in other people unless she has had some experience of it in her own practice? How, again, can she learn when it will be well for her to lie, and when to refrain from doing so, unless she has made many a mistake on a small scale while at an age when mistakes do not greatly matter? The Sunchild (and here he reverently raised his hat), as you may read in chapter thirty-one of his Sayings, has left us a touching tale of a little boy, who, having cut down an apple tree in his father's garden, lamented his inability to tell a lie. Some commentators, indeed, have held that the evidence was so strongly against the boy that no lie would have been of any use to him, and that his perception of this fact was all that he intended to convey; but the best authorities take his simple words, 'I cannot tell a lie,' in their most natural sense, as being his expression of regret at the way in which his education had been neglected. If that case had come before me, I should have punished the boy's father, unless he could show that the best authorities are mistaken (as indeed they too generally are), and that under more favourable circumstances the boy would have been able to lie, and would have lied accordingly.

"There is no occasion for you to send your child to a deformatory. I am always averse to extreme measures when I can avoid them. Moreover, in a deformatory she would be almost certain to fall in with characters as intractable as her own. Take her home and whip her next time she so much as pulls about the salt. If you will do this whenever you get a chance, I have every hope that you will have no occasion to come to me again."

"Very well, sir," said the father, "I will do my best, but the child is so instinctively truthful that I am afraid whipping will be of little use."

There were other cases, none of them serious, which in the old days would have been treated by a straightener. My father had already surmised that the straighteners had become extinct as a class, having been superseded by the Managers and Cashiers of the Musical Banks, but this became more apparent as he listened to the cases that next came on. These were dealt with quite reasonably, except that the magistrate always ordered an emetic and a strong purge in addition to the rest of his sentence, as holding that all diseases of the moral sense spring from impurities within the body, which must be cleansed before there could be any hope of spiritual improvement. If any devils were found in what passed from the prisoner's body, he was to be brought up again; for in this case the rest of the sentence might very possibly be remitted.

When the Mayor and his coadjutors had done sitting, my father strolled round the Musical Bank and entered it by the main entrance, which was at the top of a flight of steps that went down on to the principal street of the town. How strange it is that, no matter how gross a superstition may have polluted it, a holy place, if hallowed by long veneration, remains always holy. Look at Delphi. What a fraud it was, and yet how hallowed it must ever remain. But letting this pass, Musical Banks, especially when of great age, always fascinated my father, and being now tired with his walk, he sat down on one of the many rush-bottomed seats, and (for there was no service at this hour) gave free rein to meditation.

How peaceful it all was with its droning old-world smell of ancestor, dry rot, and stale incense. As the clouds came and went, the grey-green, cobweb-chastened light ebbed and flowed over the walls and ceiling; to watch the fitfulness of its streams was a sufficient occupation. A hen laid an egg outside and began to cackle–it was an event of magnitude; a peasant sharpening his scythe, a blacksmith hammering at his anvil, the clack of a wooden shoe upon the pavement, the boom of a bumble-bee, the dripping of the fountain, all these things, with such concert as they kept, invited the dewy-feathered sleep that visited him, and held him for the best part of an hour.

My father has said that the Erewhonians never put up monuments or write epitaphs for their dead, and this he believed to be still true; but it was not so always, and on waking his eye was caught by a monument of great beauty, which bore a date of about 1550 of our era. It was to an old lady, who must have been very lovable if the sweet smiling face of her recumbent figure was as faithful to the original as its strongly marked individuality suggested. I need not give the earlier part of her epitaph, which was conventional enough, but my father was so struck with the concluding lines, that he copied them into the note-book which he always carried in his pocket. They ran:

I FALL ASLEEP
IN THE FULL AND CERTAIN HOPE
THAT MY SLUMBER SHALL NOT BE BROKEN
AND THAT
THOUGH I BE ALL-FORGETTING
YET SHALL I NOT BE ALL-FORGOTTEN
BUT CONTINUE THAT LIFE
IN THE THOUGHTS AND DEEDS OF THOSE I LOVED
INTO WHICH
WHILE THE POWER TO STRIVE WAS YET VOUCHSAFED ME
I FONDLY STROVE TO ENTER

My father deplored his inability to do justice to the subtle tenderness of the original, but the above was the nearest he could get to it.

How different this from the opinions concerning a future state which he had tried to set before the Erewhonians some twenty years earlier. It all came back to him, as the storks had done, now that he was again in an Erewhonian environment, and he particularly remembered how one youth had inveighed against our European notions of heaven and hell with a contemptuous flippancy that nothing but youth and ignorance could even palliate.

" Sir," he had said to my father, " your heaven will not attract me unless I can take my clothes and my luggage. Yes; and I must lose my luggage and find it again. On arriving, I must be told that it has unfortunately been taken to a wrong circle, and that there may be some difficulty in recovering it–or it shall have been sent up to mansion number five hundred thousand millions nine hundred thousand forty six thousand eight hundred and eleven, whereas it should have gone to four hundred thousand millions, etc., etc.; and am I sure that I addressed it rightly? Then, when I am just getting cross enough to run some risk of being turned out, the luggage shall make its appearance, hat-box, umbrella, rug, golf-sticks, bicycle, and everything else all quite correct, and in my delight I shall tip the angel double and realize that I am enjoying myself.

" Or I must have asked what I could have for breakfast, and be told I could have boiled eggs, or eggs and bacon, or filleted plaice. 'Filleted plaice,' I shall exclaim, 'no! not that. Have you any red mullets?' And the angel will say, 'Why no, sir, the gulf has been so rough that there has hardly any fish come in this three days, and there has been such a run on it that we have nothing left but plaice.'

" 'Well, well,' I shall say, 'have you any kidneys?'

" 'You can have one kidney, sir,' will be the answer.

" 'One kidney, indeed, and you call this heaven! At any rate you will have sausages?'

" 'Then the angel will say, 'We shall have some after Sunday, sir, but we are quite out of them at present.'

" And I shall say, somewhat sulkily, ' Then I suppose I must have eggs and bacon.'

" But in the morning there will come up a red mullet, beautifully cooked, a couple of kidneys and three sausages browned to a turn, and seasoned with just so much sage and thyme as will savour without overwhelming them; and I shall eat everything. It shall then transpire that the angel knew about the luggage, and what I was to have for breakfast, all the time, but wanted to give me the pleasure of finding things turn out better than I had expected. Heaven would be a dull place without such occasional petty false alarms as these."

I have no business to leave my father's story, but the mouth of the ox that treadeth out the corn should not be so closely muzzled that he cannot sometimes filch a mouthful for himself; and when I had copied out the foregoing somewhat irreverent paragraphs, which I took down (with no important addition or alteration) from my father's lips, I could not refrain from making a few reflections of my own, which I will ask the reader's forbearance if I lay before him.

Let heaven and hell alone, but think of Hades, with Tantalus, Sisyphus, Tityus, and all the rest of them. How futile were the attempts of the old Greeks and Romans to lay before us any plausible conception of eternal torture. What were the Danaids doing but that which each one of us has to do during his or her whole life? What are our bodies if not sieves that we are for ever trying to fill, but which we must refill continually without hope of being able to keep them full for long together? Do we mind this? Not so long as we can get the wherewithal to fill them; and the Danaids never seem to have run short of water. They would probably ere long take to clearing out any obstruction in their sieves if they found them getting choked. What could it matter to them whether the sieves got full or no? They were not paid for filling them.

Sisyphus, again! Can any one believe that he would go on rolling that stone year after year and seeing it roll down again unless he liked seeing it? We are not told that there was a dragon which attacked him whenever he tried to shirk. If he had greatly cared about getting his load over the last pinch, experience would have shown him some way of doing so. The probability is that he got to enjoy the downward rush of his stone, and very likely amused himself by so timing it as to cause the greatest scare to the greatest number of the shades that were below.

What though Tantalus found the water shun him and the fruits fly from him when he tried to seize them? The writer of the Odyssey gives us no hint that he was dying of thirst or hunger. The pores of his skin would absorb enough water to prevent the first, and we may be sure that he got fruit enough, one way or another, to keep him going.

Tityus, as an effort after the conception of an eternity of torture, is not successful. What could an eagle matter on the liver of a man whose body covered nine acres? Before long he would find it an agreeable stimulant. If, then, the greatest minds of antiquity could invent nothing that should carry better conviction of eternal torture, is it likely that the conviction can be carried at all?

Methought I saw Jove sitting on the topmost ridges of Olympus and confessing failure to Minerva. "I see, my dear," he said, "that there is no use in trying to make people very happy or very miserable for long together. Pain, if it does not soon kill, consists not so much in present suffering as in the still recent memory of a time when there was less, and in the fear that there will soon be more; and so happiness lies less in immediate pleasure than in lively recollection of a worse time and lively hope of better."

As for the young gentleman above referred to, my father met him with the assurance that there had been several cases in which living people had been caught up into heaven or carried down into hell, and been allowed to return to earth and report what they had seen; while to others visions had been vouchsafed so clearly that thousands of authentic pictures had been painted of both states. All incentive to good conduct, he had then alleged, was found to be at once removed from those who doubted the fidelity of these pictures.

This at least was what he had then said, but I hardly think he would have said it at the time of which I am now writing. As he continued to sit in the Musical Bank, he took from his valise the pamphlet "On the Physics of Vicarious Existence," by Dr. Gurgoyle, which he had bought on the preceding evening, doubtless being led to choose this particular work by the tenor of the old lady's epitaph.

The second title he found to run, "Being Strictures on Certain Heresies concerning a Future State that have been Engrafted on the Sunchild's Teaching."

My father shuddered as he read this title. "How long," he said to himself, "will it be before they are at one another's throats?"

On reading the pamphlet, he found it added little to what the epitaph had already conveyed; but it interested him, as showing that, however cataclysmic a change of national opinions may appear to be, people will find means of bringing the new into more or less conformity with the old.

Here it is a mere truism to say that many continue to live a vicarious life long after they have ceased to be aware of living. This view is as old as the *non omnis moriar* of Horace, and we may be sure some thousands of years older. It is only, therefore, with much diffidence that I have decided to give a *résumé* of opinions many of which those whom I alone wish to please will have laid to heart from their youth upwards. In brief, Dr. Gurgoyle's contention comes to little more than saying that the quick are more dead, and the dead more quick, than we commonly think. To be alive, according to him, is only to be unable to understand how dead one is, and to be dead is only to be invincibly ignorant concerning our own livingness–for the dead would be as living as the living if we could only get them to believe it.

CHAPTER ELEVEN: PRESIDENT GURGOYLE'S PAMPHLET "ON THE PHYSICS OF VICARIOUS EXISTENCE"

BELIEF, LIKE ANY OTHER MOVING BODY, follows the path of least resistance, and this path had led Dr. Gurgoyle to the conviction, real or feigned, that my father was son to the sun, probably by the moon, and that his ascent into the sky with an earthly bride was due to the sun's interference with the laws of nature. Nevertheless he was looked upon as more or less of a survival, and was deemed lukewarm, if not heretical, by those who seemed to be the pillars of the new system.

My father soon found that not even Panky could manipulate his teaching more freely than the Doctor had done. My father had taught that when a man was dead there was an end of him, until he should rise again in the flesh at the last day, to enter into eternity either of happiness or misery. He had, indeed, often talked of the immortality which some achieve even in this world; but he had cheapened this, declaring it to be an unsubstantial mockery, that could give no such comfort in the hour of death as was unquestionably given by belief in heaven and hell.

Dr. Gurgoyle, however, had an equal horror, on the one hand, of anything involving resumption of life by the body when it was once dead, and on the other, of the view that life ended with the change which we call death. He did not, indeed, pretend that he could do much to take away the sting from death, nor would he do this if he could, for if men did not fear death unduly, they would often court it unduly. Death can only be belauded at the cost of belittling life; but he held that a reasonable assurance of fair fame after death is a truer consolation to the dying, a truer comfort to surviving friends, and a more real incentive to good conduct in this life, than any of the consolations or incentives falsely fathered upon the Sunchild.

He began by setting aside every saying ascribed, however truly, to my father, if it made against his views, and by putting his own glosses on all that he could gloze into an appearance of being in his favour. I will pass over his attempt to combat the rapidly spreading belief in a heaven and hell such as we accept, and will only summarize his contention that, of our two lives–namely, the one we live in our own persons, and that other life which we live in other people both before our reputed death and after it–the second is as essential a factor of our complete life as the first is, and sometimes more so.

Life, he urged, lies not in bodily organs, but in the power to use them, and in the use that is made of them–that is to say, in the work they do. As the essence of a factory is not in the building wherein the work is done, nor yet in the implements used in turning it out, but in the will-power of the master and in the goods he makes; so the true life of a man is in his will and work, not in his body. "Those," he argued, "who make the life of a man reside within his body, are like one who should mistake the carpenter's tool-box for the carpenter."

He maintained that this had been my father's teaching, for which my father heartily trusts that he may be forgiven.

He went on to say that our will-power is not wholly limited to the working of its own special system of organs, but under certain conditions can work and be worked upon by other will-powers like itself: so that if, for example, A's will-power has got such hold on B's as to be able, through B, to work B's mechanism, what seems to have been B's action will in reality have been more A's than B's, and this in the same real sense as though the physical action had been effected through A's own mechanical system–A, in fact, will have been living in B. The universally admitted maxim that he who does this or that by the hand of an agent does it himself, shows that the foregoing view is only a roundabout way of stating what common sense treats as a matter of course.

Hence, though A's individual will-power must be held to cease when the tools it works with are destroyed or out of gear, yet, so long as any survivors were so possessed by it while it was still efficient, or, again, become so impressed by its operation on them through work that he has left, as to act in obedience to his will-power rather than their own, A has a certain amount of *bona fide* life still remaining. His vicarious life is not affected by the dissolution of his body; and in many cases the sum total of a man's vicarious action and of its outcome exceeds to an almost infinite extent the sum total of those actions and works that were effected through the mechanism of his own physical organs. In these cases his vicarious life is more truly his life than any that he lived in his own person.

"True," continued the Doctor, "while living in his own person, a man knows, or thinks he knows, what he is doing, whereas we have no reason to suppose such knowledge on the part of one whose body is already dust; but the consciousness of the doer has less to do with the livingness of the deed than people generally admit. We know nothing of the power that sets our heart beating, nor yet of the beating itself so long as it is normal. We know nothing of our breathing or of our digestion, of the all-important work we achieved as embryos, nor of our growth from infancy to manhood. No one will say that these were not actions of a living agent, but the more normal, the healthier, and thus the more truly living, the agent is, the less he will know or have known of his own action. The part of our bodily life that enters into our consciousness is very small as compared with that of which we have no consciousness. What completer proof can we have that livingness consists in deed rather than in consciousness of deed?

" The foregoing remarks are not intended to apply so much to vicarious action in virtue, we will say, of a settlement, or testamentary disposition that cannot be set aside. Such action is apt to be too unintelligent, too far from variation and quick change to rank as true vicarious action; indeed it is not rarely found to effect the very opposite of what the person who made the settlement or will desired. They are meant to apply to that more intelligent and versatile action engendered by affectionate remembrance. Nevertheless, even the compulsory vicarious action taken in consequence of a will, and indeed the very name ' will ' itself, shows that though we cannot take either flesh or money with us, we can leave our will-power behind us in very efficient operation.

" This vicarious life (on which I have insisted, I fear at unnecessary length, for it is so obvious that none can have failed to realize it) is lived by every one of us before death as well as after it, and is little less important to us than that of which we are to some extent conscious in our own persons. A man, we will say, has written a book which delights or displeases thousands of whom he knows nothing, and who know nothing of him. The book, we will suppose, has considerable, or at any rate some influence on the action of these people. Let us suppose the writer fast asleep while others are enjoying his work, and acting in consequence of it, perhaps at long distances from him. Which is his truest life–the one he is leading in them, or that equally unconscious life residing in his own sleeping body ? Can there be a doubt that the vicarious life is the more efficient ?

" Or when we are waking, how powerfully does not the life we are living in others pain or delight us, according as others think ill or well of us ? How truly do we not recognize it as part of our own existence, and how great an influence does not the fear of a present hell in men's bad thoughts, and the hope of a present heaven in their good ones, influence our own conduct? Have we not here a true heaven and a true hell, as compared with the efficiency of which these gross material ones so falsely engrafted on to the Sunchild's teaching are but as the flint implements of a prehistoric race? 'If a man,' said the Sunchild, 'fear not man, whom he hath seen, neither will he fear God, whom he hath not seen.'"

My father again assures me that he never said this. Returning to Dr. Gurgoyle, he continued:

"It may be urged that on a man's death one of the great factors of his life is so annihilated that no kind of true life can be any further conceded to him. For to live is to be influenced, as well as to influence; and when a man is dead how can he be influenced? He can haunt, but he cannot any more be haunted. He can come to us, but we cannot go to him. On ceasing, therefore, to be impressionable, so great a part of that wherein his life consisted is removed, that no true life can be conceded to him.

"I do not pretend that a man is as fully alive after his so-called death as before it. He is not. All I contend for is, that a considerable amount of efficient life still remains to some of us, and that a little life remains to all of us, after what we commonly regard as the complete cessation of life. In answer, then, to those who have just urged that the destruction of one of the two great factors of life destroys life altogether, I reply that the same must hold good as regards death.

"If to live is to be influenced and to influence, and if a man cannot be held as living when he can no longer be influenced, surely to die is to be no longer able either to influence or be influenced, and a man cannot be held dead until both these two factors of death are present. If failure of the power to be influenced vitiates life, presence of the power to influence vitiates death. And no one will deny that a man can influence for many a long year after he is vulgarly reputed as dead.

"It seems, then, that there is no such thing as either absolute life without any alloy of death, nor absolute death without any alloy of life, until, that is to say, all posthumous power to influence has faded away. And this, perhaps, is what the Sunchild meant by saying that in the midst of life we are in death, and so also that in the midst of death we are in life.

"And there is this, too. No man can influence fully until he can no more be influenced–that is to say, till after his so-called death. Till then, his 'he' is still unsettled. We know not what other influences may not be brought to bear upon him that may change the character of the influence he will exert on ourselves. Therefore, he is not fully living till he is no longer living. He is an incomplete work, which cannot have full effect till finished. And as for his vicarious life–which we have seen to be very real–this can be, and is, influenced by just appreciation, undue praise or calumny, and is subject, it may be, to secular vicissitudes of good and evil fortune.

"If this is not true, let us have no more talk about the immortality of great men and women. The Sunchild was never weary of talking to us (as we then sometimes thought, a little tediously) about a great poet of that nation to which it pleased him to feign that he belonged. How plainly can we not now see that his words were spoken for our learning–for the enforcement of that true view of heaven and hell on which I am feebly trying to insist? The poet's name, he said, was Shakespeare. Whilst he was alive, very few people understood his greatness; whereas now, after some three hundred years, he is deemed the greatest poet that the world has ever known. 'Can this man,' he asked, 'be said to have been truly born till many a long year after he had been reputed as truly dead? While he was in the flesh, was he more than a mere embryo growing towards birth into that life of the world to come in which he now shines so gloriously? What a small thing was that flesh and blood life, of which he was alone conscious, as compared with that fleshless life which he lives but knows not in the lives of millions, and which, had it ever been fully revealed even to his imagination, we may be sure that he could not have reached?'

"These were the Sunchild's words, as repeated to me by one of his chosen friends while he was yet amongst us. Which, then, of this man's two lives should we deem best worth having, if we could choose one or other, but not both? The felt or the unfelt? Who would not go cheerfully to block or stake if he knew that by doing so he could win such life as this poet lives, though he also knew that on having won it he could know no more about it? Does not this prove that in our heart of hearts we deem an unfelt life, in the heaven of men's loving thoughts, to be better worth having than any we can reasonably hope for and still feel?

"And the converse of this is true; many a man has unhesitatingly laid down his felt life to escape unfelt infamy in the hell of men's hatred and contempt. As body is the sacrament, or outward and visible sign, of mind; so is posterity the sacrament of those who live after death. Each is the mechanism through which the other becomes effective.

"I grant that many live but a short time when the breath is out of them. Few seeds germinate as compared with those that rot or are eaten, and most of this world's denizens are little more than still-born as regards the larger life, while none are immortal to the end of time. But the end of time is not worth considering; not a few live as many centuries as either they or we need think about, and surely the world, so far as we can guess its object, was made rather to be enjoyed than

to last. 'Come and go' pervades all things of which we have knowledge, and if there was any provision made, it seems to have been for a short life and a merry one, with enough chance of extension beyond the grave to be worth trying for, rather than for the perpetuity even of the best and noblest.

"Granted, again, that few live after death as long or as fully as they had hoped to do, while many, when quick, can have had none but the faintest idea of the immortality that awaited them; it is nevertheless true that none are so still-born on death as not to enter into a life of some sort, however short and humble. A short life or a long one can no more be bargained for in the unseen world than in the seen; as, however, care on the part of parents can do much for the longer life and greater well-being of their offspring in this world, so the conduct of that offspring in this world does much both to secure for itself longer tenure of life in the next, and to determine whether that life shall be one of reward or punishment.

"'Reward or punishment,' some reader will perhaps exclaim; 'what mockery, when the essence of reward and punishment lies in their being felt by those who have earned them.' I can do nothing with those who either cry for the moon, or deny that it has two sides, on the ground that we can see but one. Here comes in faith, of which the Sunchild said, that though we can do little with it, we can do nothing without it. Faith does not consist, as some have falsely urged, in believing things on insufficient evidence; this is not faith, but faithlessness to all that we should hold most faithfully. Faith consists in holding that the instincts of the best men and women are in themselves an evidence which may not be set aside lightly; and the best men and women have ever held that death is better than dishonour, and desirable if honour is to be won thereby.

"It follows, then, that though our conscious flesh and blood life is the only one that we can fully apprehend, yet we do also indeed move, even here, in an unseen world, wherein, when our palpable life is ended, we shall continue to live for a shorter or longer time–reaping roughly, though not infallibly, much as we have sown. Of this unseen world the best men and women will be almost as heedless while in the flesh as they will be when their life in flesh is over; for, as the Sunchild often said, 'The Kingdom of Heaven cometh not by observation.' It will be all in all to them, and at the same time nothing, for the better people they are, the less they will think of anything but this present life.

"What an ineffable contradiction in terms have we not here. What a reversal, is it not, of all this world's canons, that we should hold even the best of all that we can know or feel in this life to be a poor thing as compared with hopes the fulfilment of which we can never either feel or know. Yet we all hold this, however little we may admit it to ourselves. For the world at heart despises its own canons."

I cannot quote further from Dr. Gurgoyle's pamphlet; suffice it that he presently dealt with those who say that it is not right of any man to aim at thrusting himself in among the living when he has had his day. "Let him die," say they, "and let die as his fathers before him." He argued that as we had a right to pester people till we got ourselves born, so also we have a right to pester them for extension of life beyond the grave. Life, whether before the grave or afterwards, is like love–all reason is against it, and all healthy instinct for it. Instinct on such matters is the older and safer guide; no one, therefore, should seek to efface himself as regards the next world more than as regards this. If he is to be effaced, let others efface him; do not let him commit suicide. Freely we have received; freely, therefore, let

us take as much more as we can get, and let it be a stand-up fight between ourselves and posterity to see whether it can get rid of us or no. If it can, let it; if it cannot, it must put up with us. It can better care for itself than we can for ourselves when the breath is out of us.

Not the least important duty, he continued, of posterity towards itself lies in passing righteous judgement on the forbears who stand up before it. They should be allowed the benefit of a doubt, and peccadilloes should be ignored; but when no doubt exists that a man was engrainedly mean and cowardly, his reputation must remain in the Purgatory of Time for a term varying from, say, a hundred to two thousand years. After a hundred years it may generally come down, though it will still be under a cloud. After two thousand years it may be mentioned in any society without holding up of hands in horror. Our sense of moral guilt varies inversely as the squares of its distance in time and space from ourselves.

Not so with heroism; this loses no lustre through time and distance. Good is gold; it is rare, but it will not tarnish. Evil is like dirty water–plentiful and foul, but it will run itself clear of taint.

The Doctor having thus expatiated on his own opinions concerning heaven and hell, concluded by tilting at those which all right-minded people hold among ourselves. I shall adhere to my determination not to reproduce his arguments; suffice it that though less flippant than those of the young student whom I have already referred to, they were more plausible; and though I could easily demolish them, the reader will probably prefer that I should not set them up for the mere pleasure of knocking them down. Here, then, I take my leave of good Dr. Gurgoyle and his pamphlet; neither can I interrupt my story further by saying anything about the other two pamphlets purchased by my father.

CHAPTER TWELVE: GEORGE FAILS TO FIND MY FATHER, WHEREON YRAM CAUTIONS THE PROFESSORS

ON THE MORNING AFTER THE INTERVIEW with her son described in a foregoing chapter, Yram told her husband what she had gathered from the Professors, and said that she was expecting Higgs every moment, inasmuch as she was confident that George would soon find him.

"Do what you like, my dear," said the Mayor. "I shall keep out of the way, for you will manage him better without me. You know what I think of you."

He then went unconcernedly to his breakfast, at which the Professors found him somewhat taciturn. Indeed they set him down as one of the dullest and most uninteresting people they had ever met.

When George returned and told his mother that though he had at last found the inn at which my father had slept, my father had left and could not be traced, she was disconcerted, but after a few minutes she said:

"He will come back here for the dedication, but there will be such crowds that we may not see him till he is inside the temple, and it will save trouble if we can lay hold on him sooner. Therefore, ride either to Clearwater or Fairmead, and see if you can find him. Try Fairmead first; it is more out of the way. If you cannot hear of him there, come back, get another horse, and try Clearwater. If you fail here too, we must give him up, and look out for him in the temple to-morrow morning."

"Are you going to say anything to the Professors?"

"Not if you can bring Higgs here before nightfall. If you cannot do this I must talk it over with my husband; I shall have some hours in which to make up my mind. Now go–the sooner the better."

It was nearly eleven, and in a few minutes George was on his way. By noon he was at Fairmead, where he tried all the inns in vain for news of a person answering the description of my father—for not knowing what name my father might choose to give, he could trust only to description. He concluded that since my father could not be heard of in Fairmead by one o'clock (as it nearly was by the time he had been round all the inns) he must have gone somewhere else; he therefore rode back to Sunch'ston, made a hasty lunch, got a fresh horse, and rode to Clearwater, where he met with no better success. At all the inns both at Fairmead and Clearwater he left word that if the person he had described came later in the day, he was to be told that the Mayoress particularly begged him to return at once to Sunch'ston, and come to the Mayor's house.

Now all the time that George was at Fairmead my father was inside the Musical Bank, which he had entered before going to any inn. Here he had been sitting for nearly a couple of hours, resting, dreaming, and reading Doctor Gurgoyle's pamphlet. If he had left the Bank five minutes earlier, he would probably have been seen by George in the main street of Fairmead—as he found out on reaching the inn which he selected and ordering dinner.

He had hardly got inside the house before the waiter told him that young Mr. Strong, the Ranger from Sunch'ston, had been enquiring for him and had left a message for him, which was duly delivered.

My father, though in reality somewhat disquieted, showed no uneasiness, and said how sorry he was to have missed seeing Mr. Strong. "But," he added, "it does not much matter; I need not go back this afternoon, for I shall be at Sunch'ston to-morrow morning and will go straight to the Mayor's."

He had no suspicion that he was discovered, but he was a good deal puzzled. Presently he inclined to the opinion that George, still believing him to be Professor Panky, had wanted to invite him to the banquet on the following day–for he had no idea that Hanky and Panky were staying with the Mayor and Mayoress. Or perhaps the Mayor and his wife did not like so distinguished a man's having been unable to find a lodging in Sunch'ston, and wanted him to stay with them. Ill satisfied as he was with any theory he could form, he nevertheless reflected that he could not do better than stay where he was for the night, inasmuch as no one would be likely to look for him a second time at Fairmead. He therefore ordered his room at once.

It was nearly seven before George got back to Sunch'ston. In the meantime Yram and the Mayor had considered the question whether anything was to be said to the Professors or no. They were confident that my father would not commit himself–why, indeed, should he have dyed his hair and otherwise disguised himself, if he had not intended to remain undiscovered? Oh no; the probability was that if nothing was said to the Professors now, nothing need ever be said, for my father might be escorted back to the statues by George on the Sunday evening and be told that he was not to return. Moreover, even though something untoward were to happen after all, the Professors would have no reason for thinking that their hostess had known of the Sunchild's being in Sunch'ston.

On the other hand, they were her guests, and it would not be handsome to keep Hanky, at any rate, in the dark, when the knowledge that the Sunchild was listening to every word he said might make him modify his sermon not a little. It might or it might not, but that was a matter for him, not her. The only question for her was whether or no it would be sharp practice to know what she knew and say nothing about it. Her husband hated *finesse* as much as she did, and they settled it that though the question was a nice one, the more proper thing to do would be to tell the Professors what it might so possibly concern one or both of them to know.

On George's return without news of my father, they found he thought just as they did; so it was arranged that they should let the Professors dine in peace, but tell them about the Sunchild's being again in Erewhon as soon as dinner was over.

"Happily," said George, "they will do no harm. They will wish Higgs's presence to remain unknown as much as we do, and they will be glad that he should be got out of the country immediately."

"Not so, my dear," said Yram. "'Out of the country' will not do for those people. Nothing short of 'out of the world' will satisfy them."

"That," said George promptly, "must not be."

"Certainly not, my dear, but that is what they will want. I do not like having to tell them, but I am afraid we must."

"Never mind," said the Mayor, laughing. "Tell them, and let us see what happens."

They then dressed for dinner, where Hanky and Panky were the only guests. When dinner was over Yram sent away her other children, George alone remaining. He sat opposite the Professors, while the Mayor and Yram were at the two ends of the table.

"I am afraid, dear Professor Hanky," said Yram, "that I was not quite open with you last night, but I wanted time to think things over, and I know you will forgive me when you remember what a number of guests I had to attend to." She then referred to what Hanky had told her about the supposed ranger, and showed him how obvious it was that this man was a foreigner, who had been for some time in Erewhon more than seventeen years ago, but had had no communication with it since then. Having pointed sufficiently, as she thought, to the Sunchild, she said, "You see who I believe this man to have been. Have I said enough, or shall I say more?"

"I understand you," said Hanky, "and I agree with you that the Sunchild will be in the temple to-morrow. It is a serious business, but I shall not alter my sermon. He must listen to what I may choose to say, and I wish I could tell him what a fool he was for coming here. If he behaves himself, well and good: your son will arrest him quietly after service, and by night he will be in the Blue Pool. Your son is bound to throw him there as a foreign devil, without the formality of a trial. It would be a most painful duty to me, but unless I am satisfied that that man has been thrown into the Blue Pool, I shall have no option but to report the matter at headquarters. If, on the other hand, the poor wretch makes a disturbance, I can set the crowd on to tear him in pieces."

George was furious, but he remained quite calm, and left everything to his mother.

"I have nothing to do with the Blue Pool," said Yram drily. "My son, I doubt not, will know how to do his duty; but if you let the people kill this man, his body will remain, and an inquest must be held, for the matter will have been too notorious to be hushed up. All Higgs's measurements and all marks on his body were recorded, and these alone would identify him. My father, too, who is still master of the gaol, and many another, could swear to him. Should the body prove, as no doubt it would, to be that of the Sunchild, what is to become of Sunchildism?"

Hanky smiled. "It would not be proved. The measurements of a man of twenty or thereabouts would not correspond with this man's. All we Professors should attend the inquest, and half Bridgeford is now in Sunch'ston. No matter though nine-tenths of the marks and measurements corresponded, so long as there is a tenth that does not do so, we should not be flesh and blood if we did not ignore the nine points and insist only on the tenth. After twenty years we shall find enough to serve our turn. Think of what all the learning of the country is committed to; think of the change in all our ideas and institutions; think of the King and of Court influence. I need not enlarge. We shall not permit the body to be the Sunchild's. No matter what evidence you may produce, we shall sneer it down, and say we must have more before you can expect us to take you seriously; if you bring more, we shall pay no attention; and the more you bring the more we shall laugh at you. No doubt those among us who are by way of being candid will admit that your arguments ought to be considered, but you must not expect that it will be any part of their duty to consider them.

"And even though we admitted that the body had been proved up to the hilt to be the Sunchild's, do you think that such a trifle as that could affect Sunchildism? Hardly. Sunch'ston is no match for Bridgeford and the King; our only difficulty would lie in settling which was the most plausible way of the many plausible ways in which the death could be explained. We should hatch up twenty theories in less than twenty hours, and the last state of Sunchildism would be stronger than the first. For the people want it, and so long as they want it they will have it. At the same time the supposed identification of the body, even by some few ignorant people here, might lead to a local heresy that is as well avoided, and it will be better that your son should arrest the man before the dedication, if he can be found, and throw him into the Blue Pool without any one but ourselves knowing that he has been here at all."

I need not dwell on the deep disgust with which this speech was listened to, but the Mayor, and Yram, and George said not a word.

"But, Mayoress," said Panky, who had not opened his lips so far, "are you sure that you are not too hasty in believing this stranger to be the Sunchild? People are continually thinking that such and such another is the Sunchild come down again from the sun's palace and going to and fro among us. How many such stories, sometimes very plausibly told, have we not had during the last twenty years? They never take root, and die out of themselves as suddenly as they spring up. That the man is a poacher can hardly be doubted; I thought so the moment I saw him; but I think I can also prove to you that he is not a foreigner, and, therefore, that he is not the Sunchild. He quoted the Sunchild's prayer with a corruption that can only have reached him from an Erewhonian source—"

Here Hanky interrupted him somewhat brusquely.

"The man, Panky," said he, "was the Sunchild; and he was not a poacher, for he had no idea that he was breaking the law; nevertheless, as you say, Sunchildism on the brain has been a common form of mania for several years. Several persons have even believed themselves to be the Sunchild. We must not forget this, if it should get about that Higgs has been here."

Then, turning to Yram, he said sternly, "But come what may, your son must take him to the Blue Pool at nightfall."

"Sir," said George, with perfect suavity, "you have spoken as though you doubted my readiness to do my duty. Let me assure you very solemnly that when the time comes for me to act, I shall act as duty may direct."

"I will answer for him," said Yram, with even more than her usual quick, frank smile, "that he will fulfil his instructions to the letter, unless," she added, "some black and white horses come down from heaven and snatch poor Higgs out of his grasp. Such things have happened before now."

"I should advise your son to shoot them if they do," said Hanky drily and sub-defiantly.

Here the conversation closed; but it was useless trying to talk of anything else, so the Professors asked Yram to excuse them if they retired early, in view of the fact that they had a fatiguing day before them. This excuse their hostess readily accepted.

"Do not let us talk any more now," said Yram as soon as they had left the room. "It will be quite time enough when the dedication is over. But I rather think the black and white horses will come."

"I think so too, my dear," said the Mayor laughing.

"They shall come," said George gravely; "but we have not yet got enough to make sure of bringing them. Higgs will perhaps be able to help me to-morrow."

*

"Now what," said Panky as they went upstairs, "does that woman mean–for she means something? Black and white horses indeed!"

"I do not know what she means to do," said the other, "but I know that she thinks she can best us."

"I wish we had not eaten those quails."

"Nonsense, Panky; no one saw us but Higgs, and the evidence of a foreign devil, in such straits as his, could not stand for a moment. We did not eat them. No, no; she has something that she thinks better than that. Besides, it is absolutely impossible that she should have heard what happened. What I do not understand is, why she should have told us about the Sunchild's being here at all. Why not have left us to find it out or to know nothing about it? I do not understand it."

So true is it, as Euclid long since observed, that the less cannot comprehend that which is the greater. True, however, as this is, it is also sometimes true that the greater cannot comprehend the less. Hanky went musing to his own room and threw himself into an easy chair to think the position over. After a few minutes he went to a table on which he saw pen, ink, and paper, and wrote a short letter; then he rang the bell.

When the servant came he said, " I want to send this note to the manager of the new temple, and it is important that he should have it to-night. Be pleased, therefore, to take it to him and deliver it into his own hands; but I had rather you said nothing about it to the Mayor or Mayoress, nor to any of your fellow-servants. Slip out unperceived if you can. When you have delivered the note, ask for an answer at once, and bring it to me."

So saying, he slipped a sum equal to about five shillings into the man's hand.

The servant returned in about twenty minutes, for the temple was quite near, and gave a note to Hanky, which ran, " Your wishes shall be attended to without fail."

" Good ! " said Hanky to the man. " No one in the house knows of your having run this errand for me ? "

" No one, sir."

" Thank you ! I wish you a very good night."

CHAPTER THIRTEEN: A VISIT TO THE PROVINCIAL DEFORMATORY AT FAIRMEAD

HAVING FINISHED HIS EARLY DINNER, and not fearing that he should be either recognized at Fairmead or again enquired after from Sunch'ston, my father went out for a stroll round the town, to see what else he could find that should be new and strange to him. He had not gone far before he saw a large building with an inscription saying that it was the Provincial Deformatory for Boys. Underneath the larger inscription there was a smaller one–one of those corrupt versions of my father's sayings, which, on dipping into the Sayings of the Sunchild, he had found to be so vexatiously common. The inscription ran:

"When the righteous man turneth away from the righteousness that he hath committed, and doeth that which is a little naughty and wrong, he will generally be found to have gained in amiability what he has lost in righteousness."–Sunchild Sayings, chap. xxii, v. 15.

The case of the little girl that he had watched earlier in the day had filled him with a great desire to see the working of one of these curious institutions; he therefore resolved to call on the head-master (whose name he found to be Turvey), and enquire about terms, alleging that he had a boy whose incorrigible rectitude was giving him much anxiety. The information he had gained in the forenoon would be enough to save him from appearing to know nothing of the system. On having rung the bell, he announced himself to the servant as a Mr. Senoj, and asked if he could see the Principal.

Almost immediately he was ushered into the presence of a beaming, dapper-looking, little old gentleman, quick of speech and movement, in spite of some little portliness.

"Ts, ts, ts," he said, when my father had enquired about terms and asked whether he might see the system at work. "How unfortunate that you should have called on a Saturday afternoon. We always have a half-holiday. But stay–yes–that will do very nicely; I will send for them into school as a means of stimulating their refractory system."

He called his servant and told him to ring the boys into school. Then, turning to my father he said, "Stand here, sir, by the window; you will see them all come trooping in. H'm, h'm, I am sorry to see them still come back as soon as they hear the bell. I suppose I shall ding some recalcitrancy into them some day, but it is uphill work. Do you see the head-boy–the third of those that are coming up the path? I shall have to get rid of him. Do you see him? he is going back to whip up the laggers–and now he has boxed a boy's ears: that boy is one of the most hopeful under my care. I feel sure he has been using improper language, and my head-boy has checked him instead of encouraging him." And so on till the boys were all in school.

"You see, my dear sir," he said to my father, "we are in an impossible position. We have to obey instructions from the Grand Council of Education at Bridgeford, and they have established these institutions in consequence of the Sunchild's having said that we should aim at promoting the greatest happiness of the greatest number. This, no doubt, is a sound principle, and the greatest number are by nature somewhat dull, conceited, and unscrupulous. They do not like those who are quick, unassuming, and sincere; how, then, consistently with the first principles either of morality or political economy as revealed to us by the Sunchild, can we encourage such people if we can bring sincerity and modesty fairly home to them? We cannot do so. And we must correct the young as far as possible from forming habits which, unless indulged in with the greatest moderation, are sure to ruin them.

"I cannot pretend to consider myself very successful.

I do my best, but I can only aim at making my school a reflection of the outside world. In the outside world we have to tolerate much that is prejudicial to the greatest happiness of the greatest number, partly because we cannot always discover in time who may be let alone as being genuinely insincere, and who are in reality masking sincerity under a garb of flippancy, and partly also because we wish to err on the side of letting the guilty escape, rather than of punishing the innocent. Thus many people who are perfectly well known to belong to the straightforward classes are allowed to remain at large, and may be even seen hobnobbing with the guardians of public immorality. Indeed it is not in the public interest that straightforwardness should be extirpated root and branch, for the presence of a small modicum of sincerity acts as a wholesome irritant to the academicism of the greatest number, stimulating it to consciousness of its own happy state, and giving it something to look down upon. Moreover, we hold it useful to have a certain number of melancholy examples, whose notorious failure shall serve as a warning to those who neglect cultivating that power of immoral self-control which shall prevent them from saying, or even thinking, anything that shall not immediately and palpably minister to the happiness, and hence meet the approval, of the greatest number."

By this time the boys were all in school. "There is not one prig in the whole lot," said the head-master sadly. "I wish there was, but only those boys come here who are notoriously too good to become current coin in the world unless they are hardened with an alloy of vice. I should have liked to show you our gambling, book-making, and speculation class, but the assistant-master who attends to this branch of our curriculum is gone to Sunch'ston this afternoon. He has friends who have asked him to see the dedication of the new temple, and he will not be back till Monday. I really do not know what I can do better for you than examine the boys in Counsels of Imperfection."

So saying, he went into the schoolroom, over the fireplace of which my father's eye caught an inscription, "Resist good, and it will fly from you.–Sunchild's Sayings, xvii. 2." Then, taking down a copy of the work just named from a shelf above his desk, he ran his eye over a few of its pages.

He called up a class of about twenty boys.

"Now, my boys," he said, "Why is it so necessary to avoid extremes of truthfulness?"

"It is not necessary, sir," said one youngster, "and the man who says that it is so is a scoundrel."

"Come here, my boy, and hold out your hand." When he had done so, Mr. Turvey gave him two sharp cuts with a cane. "There now, go down to the bottom of the class and try not to be so extremely truthful in future." Then, turning to my father, he said, "I hate caning them, but it is the only way to teach them. I really do believe that boy will know better than to say what he thinks another time."

He repeated his question to the class, and the head-boy answered, "Because, sir, extremes meet, and extreme truth will be mixed with extreme falsehood."

"Quite right, my boy. Truth is like religion; it has only two enemies–the too much and the too little. Your answer is more satisfactory than some of your recent conduct had led me to expect."

"But, sir, you punished me only three weeks ago for telling you a lie."

"Oh yes; why, so I did; I had forgotten. But then you overdid it. Still it was a step in the right direction."

"And now, my boy," he said to a very frank and ingenous youth about half way up the class, "and how is truth best reached?"

"Through the falling out of thieves, sir."

"Quite so. Then it will be necessary that the more earnest, careful, patient, self-sacrificing enquirers after truth should have a good deal of the thief about them, though they are very honest people at the same time. Now what does the man" (who on enquiry my father found to be none other than Mr. Turvey himself) "say about honesty?"

"He says, sir, that honesty does not consist in never stealing, but in knowing how and where it will be safe to do so."

"Remember," said Mr. Turvey to my father, "how necessary it is that we should have a plentiful supply of thieves, if honest men are ever to come by their own."

He spoke with the utmost gravity, evidently quite easy in his mind that his scheme was the only one by which truth could be successfully attained. "But pray let me have any criticism you may feel inclined to make."

"I have none," said my father. "Your system commends itself to common sense; it is the one adopted in the law courts, and it lies at the very foundation of party government. If your academic bodies can supply the country with a sufficient number of thieves–which I have no doubt they can–there seems no limit to the amount of truth that may be attained. If, however, I may suggest the only difficulty that occurs to me, it is that academic thieves shew no great alacrity in falling out, but incline rather to back each other up through thick and thin."

"Ah, yes," said Mr. Turvey, "there is that difficulty; nevertheless circumstances from time to time arise to get them by the ears in spite of themselves. But from whatever point of view you may look at the question, it is obviously better to aim at imperfection than perfection; for if we aim steadily at imperfection, we shall probably get it within a reasonable time, whereas to the end of our days we should never reach perfection. Moreover, from a worldly point of view, there is no mistake so great as that of being always right." He then turned to his class and said:

"And now tell me, what did the Sunchild tell us about God and Mammon?"

The head-boy answered: "He said that we must serve both, for no man can serve God well and truly who does not serve Mammon a little also; and no man can serve Mammon effectually unless he serve God largely at the same time."

"What were his words?"

"He said, 'Cursed be they that say, "Thou shalt not serve God and Mammon," for it is the whole duty of man to know how to adjust the conflicting claims of these two deities.'"

Here my father interposed. "I knew the Sunchild; and I more than once heard him speak of God and Mammon. He never varied the form of the words he used, which were to the effect that a man must serve either God or Mammon, but that he could not serve both."

"Ah!" said Mr. Turvey, "that no doubt was his exoteric teaching, but Professors Hanky and Panky have assured me most solemnly that his esoteric teaching was as I have given it. By the way, these gentlemen are both, I understand, at Sunch'ston, and I think it quite likely that I shall have a visit from them this afternoon. If you do not know them I should have great pleasure in introducing you to them; I was at Bridgeford with both of them."

"I have had the pleasure of meeting them already," said my father, "and as you are by no means certain that they will come, I will ask you to let me thank you for all that you have been good enough to show me, and bid you good-afternoon. I have a rather pressing engagement—"

"My dear sir, you must please give me five minutes more. I shall examine the boys in the Musical Bank Catechism." He pointed to one of them and said, "Repeat your duty towards your neighbour."

"My duty towards my neighbour," said the boy, "is to be quite sure that he is not likely to borrow money of me before I let him speak to me at all, and then to have as little to do with him as—"

At this point there was a loud ring at the door bell. "Hanky and Panky come to see me, no doubt," said Mr. Turvey. "I do hope it is so. You must stay and see them."

"My dear sir," said my father, putting his handkerchief up to his face, "I am taken suddenly unwell and must positively leave you." He said this in so peremptory a tone that Mr. Turvey had to yield. My father held his handkerchief to his face as he went through the passage and hall, but when the servant opened the door he took it down, for there was no Hanky or Panky–no one, in fact, but a poor, wizened old man who had come, as he did every other Saturday afternoon, to wind up the Deformatory clocks.

Nevertheless, he had been scared, and was in a very wicked-fleeth-when-no-man-pursueth frame of mind. He went to his inn, and shut himself up in his room for some time, taking notes of all that had happened to him in the last three days. But even at his inn he no longer felt safe. How did he know but that Hanky and Panky might have driven over from Sunch'ston to see Mr. Turvey, and might put up at this very house? or they might even be going to spend the night here. He did not venture out of his room till after seven by which time he had made rough notes of as much of the foregoing chapters as had come to his knowledge so far. Much of what I have told as nearly as I could in the order in which it happened, he did not learn till later.

After giving the merest outline of his interview with Mr. Turvey, he wrote a note as follows:

"I suppose I must have held forth about the greatest happiness of the greatest number, but I had quite forgotten it, though I remember repeatedly quoting my favourite proverb, 'Every man for himself, and the devil take the hindmost.' To this they have paid no attention."

By seven his panic about Hanky and Panky ended, for if they had not come by this time, they were not likely to do so. Not knowing that they were staying at the Mayor's, he had rather settled it that they would now stroll up to the place where they had left their hoard and bring it down as soon as night had fallen. And it is quite possible that they might have found some excuse for doing this, when dinner was over, if their hostess had not undesignedly hindered them by telling them about the Sunchild. When the conversation recorded in the preceding chapter was over, it was too late for them to make any plausible excuse for leaving the house; we may be sure, therefore, that much more had been said than Yram and George were able to remember and report to my father.

After another stroll about Fairmead, during which he saw nothing but what on a larger scale he had already seen at Sunch'ston, he returned to his inn at about half-past eight, and ordered supper in a public room that corresponded with the coffee-room of an English hotel.

CHAPTER FOURTEEN: MY FATHER MAKES THE ACQUAINTANCE OF MR. BALMY, AND WALKS WITH HIM NEXT DAY TO SUNCH'STON

UP TO THIS POINT, THOUGH HE HAD seen enough to show him the main drift of the great changes that had taken place in Erewhonian opinions, my father had not been able to glean much about the history of the transformation. He could see that it had all grown out of the supposed miracle of his balloon ascent, and he could understand that the ignorant masses had been so astounded by an event so contrary to all their experience, that their faith in experience was utterly routed and demoralised. If a man and a woman might rise from the earth and disappear into the sky, what else might not happen? If they had been wrong in thinking such a thing impossible, in how much else might they not be mistaken also? The ground was shaken under their very feet.

It was not as though the thing had been done in a corner. Hundreds of people had seen the ascent; and even if only a small number had been present, the disappearance of the balloon, of my mother, and of my father himself, would have confirmed their story. My father, then, could understand that a single incontrovertible miracle of the first magnitude should uproot the hedges of caution in the minds of the common people, but he could not understand how such men as Hanky and Panky, who evidently did not believe that there had been any miracle at all, had been led to throw themselves so energetically into a movement so subversive of all their traditions, when, as it seemed to him, if they had held out they might have pricked the balloon bubble easily enough, and maintained everything *in statu quo*.

How, again, had they converted the King—if they had converted him? The Queen had had full knowledge of all the preparations for the ascent. The King had had everything explained to him. The workmen and workwomen who had made the balloon and the gas could testify that none but natural means had been made use of–means which, if again employed any number of times, would effect a like result. How could it be that when the means of resistance were so ample and so easy, the movement should nevertheless have been irresistible? For had it not been irresistible, was it to be believed that astute men like Hanky and Panky would have let themselves be drawn into it?

What then had been its inner history? My father had so fully determined to make his way back on the following evening, that he saw no chance of getting to know the facts–unless, indeed, he should be able to learn something from Hanky's sermon; he was therefore not sorry to find an elderly gentleman of grave but kindly aspect seated opposite to him when he sat down to supper.

The expression on this man's face was much like that of the early Christians as shown in the S. Giovanni Laterano bas-reliefs at Rome, and again, though less aggressively self-confident, like that on the faces of those who have joined the Salvation Army. If he had been in England, my father would have set him down as a Swedenborgian; this being impossible, he could only note that the stranger bowed his head, evidently saying a short grace before he began to eat, as my father had always done when he was in Erewhon before. I will not say that my father had never omitted to say grace during the whole of the last twenty years, but he said it now, and unfortunately forgetting himself, he said it in the English language, not loud, but nevertheless audibly.

My father was alarmed at what he had done, but there was no need, for the stranger immediately said, "I hear, sir, that you have the gift of tongues. The Sunchild often mentioned it to us, as having been vouchsafed long since to certain of the people, to whom, for our learning, he saw fit to feign that he belonged. He thus foreshadowed prophetically its manifestation also among ourselves. All which, however, you must know as well as I do. Can you interpret?"

My father was much shocked, but he remembered having frequently spoken of the power of speaking in unknown tongues which was possessed by many of the early Christians, and he also remembered that in times of high religious enthusiasm this power had repeatedly been imparted, or supposed to be imparted, to devout believers in the middle ages. It grated upon him to deceive one who was so obviously sincere, but to avoid immediate discomfiture he fell in with what the stranger had said.

"Alas! sir," said he, "that rarer and more precious gift has been withheld from me; nor can I speak in an unknown tongue, unless as it is borne in upon me at the moment. I could not even repeat the words that have just fallen from me."

"That," replied the stranger, "is almost invariably the case. These illuminations of the spirit are beyond human control. You spoke in so low a tone that I cannot interpret what you have just said, but should you receive a second inspiration later, I shall doubtless be able to interpret it for you. I have been singularly gifted in this respect–more so, perhaps, than any other interpreter in Erewhon."

My father mentally vowed that no second inspiration should be vouchsafed to him, but presently remembering how anxious he was for information on the points touched upon at the beginning of this chapter, and seeing that fortune had sent him the kind of man who would be able to enlighten him, he changed his mind; nothing, he reflected, would be more likely to make the stranger talk freely with him, than the affording him an opportunity for showing off his skill as an interpreter.

Something, therefore, he would say, but what? No one could talk more freely when the train of his thoughts, or the conversation of others, gave him his cue, but when told to say an unattached "something," he could not even think of "How do you do this morning? it is a very fine day;" and the more he cudgelled his brains for "something," the more they gave no response. He could not even converse further with the stranger beyond plain "yes" and "no"; so he went on with his supper, and in thinking of what he was eating and drinking for the moment forgot to ransack his brain. No sooner had he left off ransacking it, than it suggested something–not, indeed, a very brilliant something, but still something. On having grasped it, he laid down his knife and fork, and with the air of one distraught he said:

"My name is Norval, on the Grampian Hills
My father feeds his flock–a frugal swain."

"I heard you," exclaimed the stranger, "and I can interpret every word of what you have said, but it would not become me to do so, for you have conveyed to me a message more comforting than I can bring myself to repeat even to him who has conveyed it."

Having said this he bowed his head, and remained for some time wrapped in meditation. My father kept a respectful silence, but after a little time he ventured to say in a low tone, how glad he was to have been the medium through whom a comforting assurance had been conveyed. Presently, on finding himself encouraged to renew the conversation, he threw out a deferential feeler as to the causes that might have induced Mr. Balmy to come to Fairmead. "Perhaps," he said, "you, like myself, have come to these parts in order to see the dedication of the new temple; I could not get a lodging in Sunch'ston, so I walked down here this morning."

This, it seemed, had been Mr. Balmy's own case, except that he had not yet been to Sunch'ston. Having heard that it was full to overflowing, he had determined to pass the night at Fairmead, and walk over in the morning–starting soon after seven, so as to arrive in good time for the dedication ceremony. When my father heard this, he proposed that they should walk together, to which Mr. Balmy gladly consented; it was therefore arranged that they should go to bed early, breakfast soon after six, and then walk to Sunch'ston. My father then went to his own room, where he again smoked a surreptitious pipe up the chimney.

Next morning the two men breakfasted together, and set out as the clock was striking seven. The day was lovely beyond the power of words, and still fresh–for Fairmead was some 2500 feet above the sea, and the sun did not get above the mountains that overhung it on the east side, till after eight o'clock. Many persons were also starting for Sunch'ston, and there was a procession got up by the Musical Bank Managers of the town, who walked in it, robed in rich dresses of scarlet and white embroidered with much gold thread. There was a banner displaying an open chariot in which the Sunchild and his bride were seated, beaming with smiles, and in attitudes suggesting that they were bowing to people who were below them. The chariot was, of course, drawn by the four black and white horses of which the reader has already heard, and the balloon had been ignored. Readers of my father's book will perhaps remember that my mother was not seen at all–she was smuggled into the car of the balloon along with sundry rugs, under which she lay concealed till the balloon had left the earth. All this went for nothing. It has been said that though God cannot alter the past, historians can; it is perhaps because they can be useful to Him in this respect that He tolerates their existence. Painters, my father now realized, can do all that historians can, with even greater effect.

Women headed the procession–the younger ones dressed in white, with veils and chaplets of roses, blue cornflower, and pheasant's eye narcissus, while the older women were more soberly attired. The Bank Managers and the banner headed the men, who were mostly peasants, but among them were a few who seemed to be of higher rank, and these, for the most part, though by no means all of them, wore their clothes reversed–as I have forgotten to say was done also by Mr. Balmy. Both men and women joined in singing a litany the words of which my father could not catch; the tune was one he had been used to play on his apology for a flute when he was in prison, being, in fact, none other than "Home, Sweet Home." There was no harmony; they never got beyond the first four bars, but these they must have repeated, my father thought, at least a hundred times between Fairmead and Sunch'ston. "Well," said he to himself, "however little else I may have taught them, I at any rate gave them the diatonic scale."

He now set himself to exploit his fellow-traveller, for they soon got past the procession.

"The greatest miracle," said he, "in connection with this whole matter, has been–so at least it seems to me–not the ascent of the Sunchild with his bride, but the readiness with which the people generally acknowledged its miraculous character. I was one of those that witnessed the ascent, but I saw no signs that the crowd appreciated its significance. They were astounded, but they did not fall down and worship."

"Ah," said the other, "but you forget the long drought and the rain that the Sunchild immediately prevailed on the air-god to send us. He had announced himself as about to procure it for us; it was on this ground that the King assented to the preparation of those material means that were necessary before the horses of the sun could attach themselves to the chariot into which the balloon was immediately transformed. Those horses might not be defiled by contact with this gross earth. I too witnessed the ascent; at the moment, I grant you, I saw neither chariot nor horses, and almost all those present shared my own temporary blindness; the whole action, from the moment when the balloon left the earth, moved so rapidly that we were flustered, and hardly knew what it was that we were really seeing. It was not till two or three years later that I found the scene presenting itself to my soul's imaginary sight in the full splendour which was no doubt witnessed, but not apprehended, by my bodily vision."

"There," said my father, "you confirm an opinion that I have long held. Nothing is so misleading as the testimony of eye-witnesses."

"A spiritual enlightenment from within," returned Mr. Balmy, "is more to be relied on than any merely physical affluence from external objects. Now, when I shut my eyes, I see the balloon ascend a little way, but almost immediately the heavens open, the horses descend, the balloon is transformed, and the glorious pageant careers onward till it vanishes into the heaven of heavens. Hundreds with whom I have conversed assure me that their experience has been the same as mine. Has yours been different?"

"Oh no, not at all; but I always see some storks circling round the balloon before I see any horses."

"How strange! I have heard others also say that they saw the storks you mention; but let me do my utmost I cannot force them into my mental image of the scene. This shows, as you were saying just now, how incomplete the testimony of an eye-witness often is. It is quite possible that the storks were there, but the horses and the chariot have impressed themselves more vividly on my mind than anything else has."

"Quite so; and I am not without hope that even at this late hour some further details may yet be revealed to us."

"It is possible, but we should be as cautious in accepting any fresh details as in rejecting them. Should some heresy obtain wide acceptance, visions will perhaps be granted to us that may be useful in refuting it, but otherwise I expect nothing more."

"Neither do I, but I have heard people say that inasmuch as the Sunchild said he was going to interview the air-god in order to send us rain, he was more probably son to the air-god than to the sun. Now here is a heresy which—"

"But, my dear sir," said Mr. Balmy, interrupting him with great warmth, "he spoke of his father in heaven as endowed with attributes far exceeding any that can be conceivably ascribed to the air-god. The power of the air-god does not extend beyond our own atmosphere."

"Pray believe me," said my father, who saw by the ecstatic gleam in his companion's eye that there was nothing to be done but to agree with him, "that I accept—"

"Hear me to the end," replied Mr. Balmy. "Who ever heard the Sunchild claim relationship with the air-god? He could command the air-god, and evidently did so, halting no doubt for this beneficent purpose on his journey towards his ultimate destination. Can we suppose that the air-god, who had evidently intended withholding the rain from us for an indefinite period, should have so immediately relinquished his designs against us at the intervention of any less exalted personage than the sun's own offspring? Impossible!"

"I quite agree with you," exclaimed my father, "it is out of the—"

"Let me finish what I have to say. When the rain came so copiously for days, even those who had not seen the miraculous ascent found its consequences come so directly home to them, that they had no difficulty in accepting the report of others. There was not a farmer or cottager in the land but heaved a sigh of relief at rescue from impending ruin, and they all knew it was the Sunchild who had promised the King that he would make the air-god send it. So abundantly, you will remember, did it come, that we had to pray to him to stop it, which in his own good time he was pleased to do."

"I remember," said my father, who was at last able to edge in a word, "that it nearly flooded me out of house and home. And yet, in spite of all this, I hear that there are many at Bridgeford who are still hardened unbelievers."

"Alas! you speak too truly. Bridgeford and the Musical Banks for the first three years fought tooth and nail to blind those whom it was their first duty to enlighten. I was a Professor of the hypothetical language, and you may perhaps remember how I was driven from my chair on account of the fearlessness with which I expounded the deeper mysteries of Sunchildism."

"Yes, I remember well how cruelly—" but my father was not allowed to get beyond "cruelly."

"It was I who explained why the Sunchild had represented himself as belonging to a people in many respects analogous to our own, when no such people can have existed. It was I who detected that the supposed nation spoken of by the Sunchild was an invention designed in order to give us instruction by the light of which we might more easily remodel our institutions. I have sometimes thought that my gift of interpretation was vouchsafed to me in recognition of the humble services that I was hereby allowed to render. By the way, you have received no illumination this morning, have you?"

"I never do, sir, when I am in the company of one

whose conversation I find supremely interesting. But you were telling me about Bridgeford: I live hundreds of miles from Bridgeford, and have never understood the suddenness, and completeness, with which men like Professors Hanky and Panky and Dr. Downie changed front. Do they believe as you and I do, or did they merely go with the times? I spent a couple of hours with Hanky and Panky only two evenings ago, and was not so much impressed as I could have wished with the depth of their religious fervour."

"They are sincere now–more especially Hanky–but I cannot think I am judging them harshly, if I say that they were not so at first. Even now, I fear, that they are more carnally than spiritually minded. See how they have fought for the aggrandisement of their own order. It is mainly their doing that the Musical Banks have usurped the spiritual authority formerly exercised by the straighteners."

"But the straighteners," said my father, "could not co-exist with Sunchildism, and it is hard to see how the claims of the Banks can be reasonably gainsaid."

"Perhaps; and after all the Banks are our main bulwark against the evils that I fear will follow from the repeal of the laws against machinery. This has already led to the development of a materialism which minimizes the miraculous element in the Sunchild's ascent, as our own people minimize the material means that were the necessary prologue to the miraculous."

Thus did they converse; but I will not pursue their conversation further. It will be enough to say that in further floods of talk Mr. Balmy confirmed what George had said about the Banks having lost their hold upon the masses. That hold was weak even in the time of my father's first visit; but when the people saw the hostility of the Banks to a movement which far the greater number of them accepted, it seemed as though both

Bridgeford and the Banks were doomed, for Bridgeford was heart and soul with the Banks. Hanky, it appeared, though under thirty, and not yet a Professor, grasped the situation, and saw that Bridgeford must either move with the times, or go. He consulted some of the most sagacious Heads of Houses and Professors, with the result that a committee of enquiry was appointed, which in due course reported that the evidence for the Sunchild's having been the only child of the sun was conclusive. It was about this time–that is to say some three years after his ascent–that " Higgsism," as it had been hitherto called, became " Sunchildism," and " Higgs " the " Sunchild."

My father also learned the King's fury at his escape (for he would call it nothing else) with my mother. This was so great that though he had hitherto been, and had ever since proved himself to be, a humane ruler, he ordered the instant execution of all who had been concerned in making either the gas or the balloon; and his cruel orders were carried out within a couple of hours. At the same time he ordered the destruction by fire of the Queen's workshops, and of all remnants of any materials used in making the balloon. It is said the Queen was so much grieved and outraged (for it was her doing that the material groundwork, so to speak, had been provided for the miracle) that she wept night and day without ceasing three whole months, and never again allowed her husband to embrace her, till he had also embraced Sunchildism.

When the rain came, public indignation at the King's action was raised almost to revolution pitch, and the King was frightened at once by the arrival of the promised downfall and the displeasure of his subjects. But he still held out, and it was only after concessions on the part of the Bridgeford committee, that he at last consented to the absorption of Sunchildism into the

Musical Bank system, and to its establishment as the religion of the country. The far-reaching changes in Erewhonian institutions with which the reader is already acquainted followed as a matter of course.

"I know the difficulty," said my father presently, "with which the King was persuaded to allow the way in which the Sunchild's dress should be worn to be a matter of opinion, not dogma. I see we have adopted different fashions. Have you any decided opinions upon the subject?"

"I have; but I will ask you not to press me for them. Let this matter remain as the King has left it."

My father thought that he might now venture on a shot. So he said, "I have always understood, too, that the King forced the repeal of the laws against machinery on the Bridgeford committee, as another condition of his assent?"

"Certainly. He insisted on this, partly to gratify the Queen, who had not yet forgiven him, and who had set her heart on having a watch, and partly because he expected that a development of the country's resources, in consequence of a freer use of machinery, would bring more money into his exchequer. Bridgeford fought hard and wisely here, but they had gained so much by the Musical Bank Managers being recognized as the authorized exponents of Sunchildism, that they thought it wise to yield–apparently with a good grace–and thus gild the pill which his Majesty was about to swallow. But even then they feared the consequences that are already beginning to appear, and which, if I mistake not, will assume far more serious proportions in the future."

"See," said my father suddenly, "we are coming to another procession, and they have got some banners; let us walk a little quicker and overtake it."

"Horrible!" replied Mr. Balmy fiercely. "You must be short-sighted, or you could never have called my attention to it. Let us get it behind us as fast as possible, and not so much as look at it."

"Oh yes, yes," said my father, "it is indeed horrible, I had not seen what it was."

He had not the faintest idea what the matter was, but he let Mr. Balmy walk a little ahead of him, so that he could see the banners, the most important of which he found to display a balloon pure and simple, with one figure in the car. True, at the top of the banner there was a smudge which might be taken for a little chariot, and some very little horses, but the balloon was the only thing insisted on. As for the procession, it consisted entirely of men, whom a smaller banner announced to be workmen from the Fairmead iron and steel works. There was a third banner, which said, "Science as well as Sunchildism."

CHAPTER FIFTEEN: THE TEMPLE IS DEDICATED TO MY FATHER, AND CERTAIN EXTRACTS ARE READ FROM HIS SUPPOSED SAYINGS

"IT IS ENOUGH TO BREAK ONE'S HEART," said Mr. Balmy when he had outstripped the procession, and my father was again beside him. "'As well as,' indeed! We know what that means. Wherever there is a factory there is a hot-bed of unbelief. 'As well as'! Why it is a defiance."

"What, I wonder," said my father innocently, "must the Sunchild's feelings be, as he looks down on this procession. For there can be little doubt that he is doing so."

"There can be no doubt at all," replied Mr. Balmy, "that he is taking note of it, and of all else that is happening this day in Erewhon. Heaven grant that he be not so angered as to chastise the innocent as well as the guilty."

"I doubt," said my father, "his being so angry even with this procession, as you think he is."

Here, fearing an outburst of indignation, he found an excuse for rapidly changing the conversation. Moreover he was angry with himself for playing upon this poor good creature. He had not done so of malice prepense; he had begun to deceive him, because he believed himself to be in danger if he spoke the truth; and though he knew the part to be an unworthy one, he could not escape from continuing to play it, if he was to discover things that he was not likely to discover otherwise.

Often, however, he had checked himself. It had been on the tip of his tongue to be illuminated with the words;

"Sukoh and Sukop were two pretty men,
They lay in bed till the clock struck ten,"

and to follow it up with,

> "Now with the drops of this most Yknarc time
> My love looks fresh,"

in order to see how Mr. Balmy would interpret the assertion here made about the Professors, and what statement he would connect with his own Erewhonian name; but he had restrained himself.

The more he saw, and the more he heard, the more shocked he was at the mischief he had done. See how he had unsettled the little mind this poor, dear, good gentleman had ever had, till he was now a mere slave to preconception. And how many more had he not in like manner brought to the verge of idiocy? How many again had he not made more corrupt than they were before, even though he had not deceived them–as for example, Hanky and Panky. And the young? how could such a lie as that a chariot and four horses came down out of the clouds enter seriously into the life of any one, without distorting his mental vision, if not ruining it?

And yet, the more he reflected, the more he also saw that he could do no good by saying who he was. Matters had gone so far that though he spoke with the tongues of men and angels he would not be listened to; and even if he were, it might easily prove that he had added harm to that which he had done already. No. As soon as he had heard Hanky's sermon, he would begin to work his way back, and if the Professors had not yet removed their purchase, he would recover it; but he would pin a bag containing about five pounds' worth of nuggets on to the tree in which they had hidden it, and, if possible, he would find some way of sending the rest to George.

He let Mr. Balmy continue talking, glad that this gentleman required little more than monosyllabic answers, and still more glad, in spite of some agitation, to see that they were now nearing Sunch'ston, towards which a great concourse of people was hurrying from Clearwater, and more distant towns on the main road. Many whole families were coming, the fathers and mothers carrying the smaller children, and also their own shoes and stockings, which they would put on when nearing the town. Most of the pilgrims brought provisions with them. All wore European costume, but only a few of them wore it reversed, and these were almost invariably of higher social status than the great body of the people, who were mainly peasants.

When they reached the town, my father was relieved at finding that Mr. Balmy had friends on whom he wished to call before going to the temple. He asked my father to come with him, but my father said that he too had friends, and would leave him for the present, while hoping to meet him again later in the day. The two, therefore, shook hands with great effusion, and went their several ways. My father's way took him first into a confectioner's shop, where he bought a couple of Sunchild buns, which he put into his pocket, and refreshed himself with a bottle of Sunchild cordial and water. All shops except those dealing in refreshments were closed, and the town was gaily decorated with flags and flowers, often festooned into words or emblems proper for the occasion.

My father, it being now a quarter to eleven, made his way towards the temple, and his heart was clouded with care as he walked along. Not only was his heart clouded, but his brain also was oppressed, and he reeled so much on leaving the confectioner's shop, that he had to catch hold of some railings till the faintness and giddiness left him. He knew the feeling to be the same as what he had felt on the Friday evening, but he had no idea of the cause, and as soon as the giddiness left him he thought there was nothing the matter with him.

Turning down a side street that led into the main square of the town, he found himself opposite the south end of the temple, with its two lofty towers that flanked the richly decorated main entrance. I will not attempt to describe the architecture, for my father could give me little information on this point. He only saw the south front for two or three minutes, and was not impressed by it, save in so far as it was richly ornamented—evidently at great expense—and very large. Even if he had had a longer look, I doubt whether I should have got more out of him, for he knew nothing of architecture, and I fear his test whether a building was good or bad, was whether it looked old and weather-beaten or no. No matter what a building was, if it was three or four hundred years old he liked it, whereas, if it was new, he would look to nothing but whether it kept the rain out. Indeed I have heard him say that the mediaeval sculpture on some of our great cathedrals often only pleases us because time and weather have set their seals upon it, and that if we could see it as it was when it left the mason's hands, we should find it no better than much that is now turned out in the Euston Road.

The ground plan here given will help the reader to understand the few following pages more easily.

The building was led up to by a flight of steps (M), and on entering it my father found it to consist of a spacious nave, with two aisles and an apse which was raised some three feet above the nave and aisles. There were no transepts. In the apse there was the table (*a*), with the two bowls of Musical Bank money mentioned on an earlier page, as also the alms-box in front of it.

At some little distance in front of the table stood the President's chair (*c*), or I might almost call it throne. It was so placed that his back would be turned towards the table, which fact again shows that the table was not

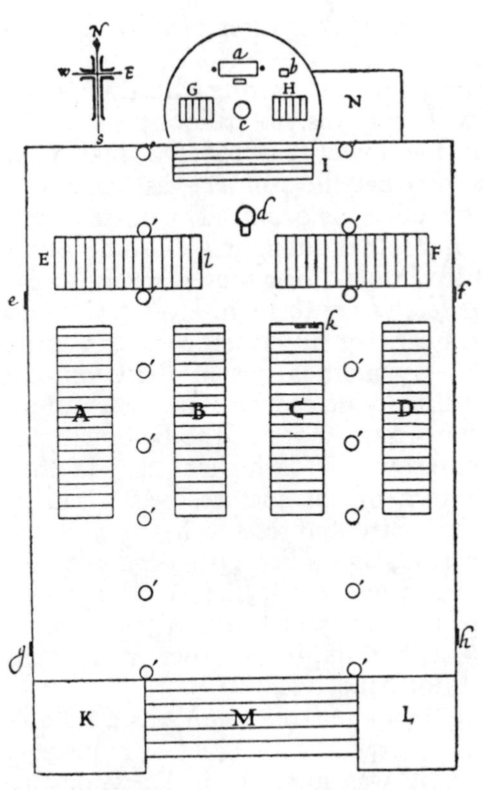

a. Table with cashier's seat on either side, and alms-box in front. The picture is exhibited on a scaffolding behind it.
b. The reliquary.
c. The President's chair.
d. Pulpit and lectern.
e.
f.
g.
h. } Side doors.

i. Yram's seat.
k. Seats of George and the Sun-child.
o′. Pillars.
A, B, C, D, E, F, G, H. Blocks of seats.
I. Steps leading from the apse to the nave.
K and L. Towers.
M. Steps and main entrance.
N. Robing-room.

regarded as having any greater sanctity than the rest of the temple.

Behind the table, the picture already spoken of was raised aloft. There was no balloon; some clouds that hung about the lower part of the chariot served to conceal the fact that the painter was uncertain whether it ought to have wheels or no. The horses were without driver, and my father thought that some one ought to have had them in hand, for they were in far too excited a state to be left safely to themselves. They had hardly any harness, but what little there was was enriched with gold bosses. My mother was in Erewhonian costume, my father in European, but he wore his clothes reversed. Both he and my mother seemed to be bowing graciously to an unseen crowd beneath them, and in the distance, near the bottom of the picture, was a fairly accurate representation of the Sunch'ston new temple. High up, on the right hand, was a disc, raised and gilt, to represent the sun; on it, in low relief, there was an indication of a gorgeous palace, in which, no doubt, the sun was supposed to live; though how they made it all out my father could not conceive.

On the right of the table there was a reliquary (*b*) of glass, much adorned with gold, or more probably gilding, for gold was so scarce in Erewhon that gilding would be as expensive as a thin plate of gold would be in Europe: but there is no knowing. The reliquary was attached to a portable stand some five feet high, and inside it was the relic already referred to. The crowd was so great that my father could not get near enough to see what it contained, but I may say here, that when, two days later, circumstances compelled him to have a close look at it, he saw that it consisted of about a dozen fine coprolites, deposited by some antediluvian creature or creatures, which, whatever else they may have been, were certainly not horses.

In the apse there were a few cross benches (G and H) on either side, with an open space between them, which was partly occupied by the President's seat already mentioned. Those on the right, as one looked towards the apse, were for the Managers and Cashiers of the Bank, while those on the left were for their wives and daughters.

In the centre of the nave, only a few feet in front of the steps leading to the apse, was a handsome pulpit and lectern (*d*). The pulpit was raised some feet above the ground, and was so roomy that the preacher could walk about in it. On either side of it there were cross benches with backs (E and F); those on the right were reserved for the Mayor, civic functionaries, and distinguished visitors, while those on the left were for their wives and daughters.

Benches with backs (A, B, C, D) were placed about half-way down both nave and aisles–those in the nave being divided so as to allow a free passage between them. The rest of the temple was open space, about which people might walk at their will. There were side doors (*e*, *g*, and *f*, *h*) at the upper and lower end of each aisle. Over the main entrance was a gallery in which singers were placed.

As my father was worming his way among the crowd, which was now very dense, he was startled at finding himself tapped lightly on the shoulder, and turning round in alarm was confronted by the beaming face of George.

" How do you do, Professor Panky ? " said the youth –who had decided thus to address him. " What are you doing here among the common people ? Why have you not taken your place in one of the seats reserved for our distinguished visitors ? I am afraid they must be all full by this time, but I will see what I can do for you. Come with me."

" Thank you," said my father. His heart beat so fast

that this was all he could say, and he followed meek as a lamb.

With some difficulty the two made their way to the right-hand corner seats of block C, for every seat in the reserved block was taken. The places which George wanted for my father and for himself were already occupied by two young men of about eighteen and nineteen, both of them well-grown, and of prepossessing appearance. My father saw by the truncheons they carried that they were special constables, but he took no notice of this, for there were many others scattered about the crowd. George whispered a few words to one of them, and to my father's surprise they both gave up their seats, which appear on the plan as *k*.

It afterwards transpired that these two young men were George's brothers, who by his desire had taken the seats some hours ago, for it was here that George had determined to place himself and my father if he could find him. He chose these places because they would be near enough to let his mother (who was at *i*, in the middle of the front row of block E, to the left of the pulpit) see my father without being so near as to embarrass him; he could also see and be seen by Hanky, and hear every word of his sermon; but perhaps his chief reason had been the fact that they were not far from the side-door at the upper end of the right-hand aisle, while there was no barrier to interrupt rapid egress should this prove necessary.

It was now high time that they should sit down, which they accordingly did. George sat at the end of the bench, and thus had my father on his left. My father was rather uncomfortable at seeing the young men whom they had turned out, standing against a column close by, but George said that this was how it was to be, and there was nothing to be done but to submit. The young men seemed quite happy, which puzzled my father, who of course had no idea that their action was preconcerted.

Panky was in the first row of block F, so that my father could not see his face except sometimes when he turned round. He was sitting on the Mayor's right hand, while Dr. Downie was on his left; he looked at my father once or twice in a puzzled way, as though he ought to have known him, but my father did not think he recognized him. Hanky was still with President Gurgoyle and others in the robing-room, N; Yram had already taken her seat: my father knew her in a moment, though he pretended not to do so when George pointed her out to him. Their eyes met for a second; Yram turned hers quickly away, and my father could not see a trace of recognition in her face. At no time during the whole ceremony did he catch her looking at him again.

"Why, you stupid man," she said to him later on in the day with a quick, kindly smile, "I was looking at you all the time. As soon as the President or Hanky began to talk about you I knew you would stare at him, and then I could look. As soon as they left off talking about you I knew you would be looking at me, unless you went to sleep–and as I did not know which you might be doing, I waited till they began to talk about you again."

My father had hardly taken note of his surroundings when the choir began singing, accompanied by a few treble flutes and lutes, or whatever the name of the instrument should be, but with no violins, for he knew nothing of the violin, and had not been able to teach the Erewhonians anything about it. The voices were all in unison, and the tune they sang was one which my father had taught Yram to sing; but he could not catch the words.

As soon as the singing began, a procession, headed

by the venerable Dr. Gurgoyle, President of the Musical Banks of the province, began to issue from the robing-room, and move towards the middle of the apse. The President was sumptuously dressed, but he wore no mitre, nor anything to suggest an English or European Bishop. The Vice-President, Head Manager, Vice-Manager, and some Cashiers of the Bank, now ranged themselves on either side of him, and formed an impressive group as they stood, gorgeously arrayed, at the top of the steps leading from the apse to the nave. Here they waited till the singers left off singing.

When the litany, or hymn, or whatever it should be called, was over, the Head Manager left the President's side and came down to the lectern in the nave, where he announced himself as about to read some passages from the Sunchild's Sayings. Perhaps because it was the first day of the year according to their new calendar, the reading began with the first chapter, the whole of which was read. My father told me that he quite well remembered having said the last verse, which he still held as true; hardly a word of the rest was ever spoken by him, though he recognized his own influence in almost all of it. The reader paused, with good effect, for about five seconds between each paragraph, and read slowly and very clearly. The chapter was as follows:

"These are the words of the Sunchild about God and man. He said:

"1. God is the baseless basis of all thoughts, things, and deeds.

"2. So that those who say that there is a God, lie, unless they also mean that there is no God; and those who say that there is no God, lie, unless they also mean that there is a God.

"3. It is very true to say that man is made after the likeness of God; and yet it is very untrue to say this.

"4. God lives and moves in every atom throughout the

universe. Therefore it is wrong to think of Him as 'Him' and 'He,' save as by the clutching of a drowning man at a straw.

"5. God is God to us only so long as we cannot see Him. When we are near to seeing Him He vanishes, and we behold Nature in His stead.

"6. We approach Him most nearly when we think of Him as our expression for Man's highest conception, of goodness, wisdom, and power. But we cannot rise to Him above the level of our own highest selves.

"7. We remove ourselves most far from Him when we invest Him with human form and attributes.

"8. My father the sun, the earth, the moon, and all planets that roll round my father, are to God but as a single cell in our bodies to ourselves.

"9. He is as much above my father, as my father is above men and women.

"10. The universe is instinct with the mind of God. The mind of God is in all that has mind throughout all worlds. There is no God but the Universe, and man, in this world is His prophet.

"11. God's conscious life, nascent, so far as this world is concerned, in the infusoria, adolescent in the higher mammals, approaches maturity on this earth in man. All these living beings are members one of another, and of God.

"12. Therefore, as man cannot live without God in the world, so neither can God live in this world without mankind.

"13. If we speak ill of God in our ignorance it may be forgiven us; but if we speak ill of His Holy Spirit indwelling in good men and women it may not be forgiven us."

The Head Manager now resumed his place by President Gurgoyle's side, and the President in the name of his Majesty the King declared the temple to be hereby dedicated to the contemplation of the Sunchild and the better exposition of his teaching. This was all that was said. The reliquary was then brought forward and placed at the top of the steps leading from the apse to the nave; but the original intention of carrying it round the temple was abandoned for fear of accidents through the pressure round it of the enormous multitudes who were assembled. More singing followed of a simple but impressive kind; during this I am afraid I must own that my father, tired with his walk, dropped off into a refreshing slumber, from which he did not wake till George nudged him and told him not to snore, just as the Vice-Manager was going towards the lectern to read another chapter of the Sunchild's Sayings–which was as follows:

"The Sunchild also spoke to us a parable about the unwisdom of the children yet unborn, who though they know so much, yet do not know as much as they think they do.

"He said:

"The unborn have knowledge of one another so long as they are unborn, and this without impediment from walls or material obstacles. The unborn children in any city form a population apart, who talk with one another and tell each other about their developmental progress.

"They have no knowledge, and cannot even conceive the existence of anything that is not such as they are themselves. Those who have been born are to them what the dead are to us. They can see no life in them, and know no more about them than they do of any stage in their own past development other than the one through which they are passing at the moment. They do not even know that their mothers are alive–much less that their mothers were once as they now are. To an embryo, its mother is simply the environment, and is looked upon much as our inorganic surroundings are by ourselves.

" The great terror of their lives is the fear of birth,— that they shall have to leave the only thing that they can think of as life, and enter upon a dark unknown which is to them tantamount to annihilation.

" Some, indeed, among them have maintained that birth is not the death which they commonly deem it, but that there is a life beyond the womb of which they as yet know nothing, and which is a million fold more truly life than anything they have yet been able even to imagine. But the greater number shake their yet unfashioned heads and say they have no evidence for this that will stand a moment's examination.

" 'Nay,' answer the others, 'so much work, so elaborate, so wondrous as that whereon we are now so busily engaged must have a purpose, though the purpose is beyond our grasp.'

" 'Never,' reply the first speakers; 'our pleasure in the work is sufficient justification for it. Who has ever partaken of this life you speak of, and re-entered into the womb to tell us of it? Granted that some few have pretended to have done this, but how completely have their stories broken down when subjected to the tests of sober criticism. No. When we are born we are born, and there is an end of us.'

" But in the hour of birth, when they can no longer re-enter the womb and tell the others, Behold! they find that it is not so."

Here the reader again closed his book and resumed his place in the apse.

CHAPTER SIXTEEN: PROFESSOR HANKY PREACHES A SERMON, IN THE COURSE OF WHICH MY FATHER DECLARES HIMSELF TO BE THE SUNCHILD

PROFESSOR HANKY THEN WENT UP INTO the pulpit, richly but soberly robed in vestments the exact nature of which I cannot determine. His carriage was dignified, and the harsh lines on his face gave it a strong individuality, which, though it did not attract, conveyed an impression of power that could not fail to interest. As soon as he had given attention time to fix itself upon him, he began his sermon without text or preliminary matter of any kind, and apparently without notes.

He spoke clearly and very quietly, especially at the beginning; he used action whenever it could point his meaning, or give it life and colour, but there was no approach to staginess or even oratorical display. In fact, he spoke as one who meant what he was saying, and desired that his hearers should accept his meaning, fully confident in his good faith. His use of pause was effective. After the word " mistake," at the end of the opening sentence, he held up his half-bent hand and paused for full three seconds, looking intently at his audience as he did so. Every one felt the idea to be here enounced that was to dominate the sermon.

The sermon–so much of it as I can find room for–was as follows:

" My friends, let there be no mistake. At such a time, as this, it is well we should look back upon the path by which we have travelled, and forward to the goal towards which we are tending. As it was necessary that the material foundations of this building should be so sure that there shall be no subsidence in the superstructure, so is it not less necessary to ensure that there shall be no subsidence in the immaterial structure that we have raised in consequence of the Sunchild's sojourn among us. Therefore, my friends, I again say, ' Let there be no mistake.' Each stone that goes towards the uprearing of this visible fane, each human soul that does its part in building the invisible temple of our national faith, is bearing witness to, and lending its support to, that which is either the truth of truths, or the baseless fabric of a dream.

"My friends, this is the only possible alternative. He in whose name we are here assembled, is either worthy of more reverential honour than we can ever pay him, or he is worthy of no more honour than any other honourable man among ourselves. There can be no halting between these two opinions. The question of questions is, Was he the child of the tutelary god of this world–the sun, and is it to the palace of the sun that he returned when he left us, or was he, as some amongst us still do not hesitate to maintain, a mere man, escaping by unusual but strictly natural means to some part of this earth with which we are unacquainted? My friends, either we are on a right path or on a very wrong one, and in a matter of such supreme importance–there must be no mistake.

"I need not remind those of you whose privilege it is to live in Sunch'ston, of the charm attendant on the Sunchild's personal presence and conversation, nor of his quick sympathy, his keen intellect, his readiness to adapt himself to the capacities of all those who came to see him while he was in prison. He adored children, and it was on them that some of his most conspicuous miracles were performed. Many a time when a child had fallen and hurt itself, was he known to make the place well by simply kissing it. Nor need I recall to your minds the spotless purity of his life–so spotless that not one breath of slander has ever dared to visit it. I was one of the not very many who had the privilege of being admitted to the inner circle of his friends during the later weeks that he was amongst us. I loved him dearly, and it will ever be the proudest recollection of my life that he deigned to return me no small measure of affection."

My father, furious as he was at finding himself dragged into complicity with this man's imposture, could not resist a smile at the effrontery with which he lowered his tone here, and appeared unwilling to dwell on an incident which he could not recall without being affected almost to tears, and mere allusion to which, had involved an apparent self-display that was above all things repugnant to him. What a difference between the Hanky of Thursday evening with its "Never set eyes on him and hope I never shall," and the Hanky of Sunday morning, who now looked as modest as Cleopatra might have done had she been standing godmother to a little blue-eyed girl–Bellerophon's first-born baby.

Having recovered from his natural, but promptly repressed, emotion, the Professor continued:

"I need not remind you of the purpose for which so many of us, from so many parts of our kingdom, are here assembled. We know what we have come hither to do: we are come each one of us to sign and seal by his presence the bond of his assent to those momentous changes, which have found their first great material expression in the temple that you see around you.

"You all know how, in accordance with the expressed will of the Sunchild, the Presidents and Vice-Presidents of the Musical Banks began as soon as he had left us to examine, patiently, carefully, earnestly, and without bias of any kind, firstly the evidences in support of the Sunchild's claim to be the son of the tutelar deity of this world, and secondly the precise nature of his instructions as regards the future position and authority of the Musical Banks.

"My friends, it is easy to understand why the Sunchild should have given us these instructions. With that foresight which is the special characteristic of divine, as compared with human wisdom, he desired that the evidences in support of his superhuman character should be collected, sifted, and placed on record, before anything was either lost through the death of those who could alone substantiate it, or unduly supplied through the enthusiasm of over-zealous visionaries. The greater any true miracle has been, the more certainly will false ones accrete round it; here, then, we find the explanation of the command the Sunchild gave to us to gather, verify, and record the facts of his sojourn here in Erewhon. For above all things he held it necessary to ensure that there should be neither mistake, nor even possibility of mistake.

" Consider for a moment what differences of opinion would infallibly have arisen, if the evidences for the miraculous character of the Sunchild's mission had been conflicting–if they had rested on versions each claiming to be equally authoritative, but each hopelessly irreconcilable on vital points with every single other. What would future generations have said in answer to those who bade them fling all human experience to the winds, on the strength of records written they knew not certainly by whom, nor how long after the marvels that they recorded, and of which all that could be certainly said was that no two of them told the same story?

" Who that believes either in God or man–who with any self-respect, or respect for the gift of reason with which God had endowed him, either would, or could, believe that a chariot and four horses had come down from heaven, and gone back again with human or quasi-human occupants, unless the evidences for the fact left no loophole for escape? If a single loophole were left him, he would be unpardonable, not for disbelieving the story, but for believing it. The sin against God would lie not in want of faith, but in faith.

"My friends, there are two sins in matters of belief. There is that of believing on too little evidence, and that of requiring too much before we are convinced. The guilt of the latter is incurred, alas! by not a few amongst us at the present day, but if the testimony to the truth of the wondrous event so faithfully depicted on the picture that confronts you had been less contemporaneous, less authoritative, less unanimous, future generations—and it is for them that we should now provide—would be guilty of the first-named, and not less heinous sin if they believed at all.

"Small wonder, then, that the Sunchild, having come amongst us for our advantage, not his own, would not permit his beneficent designs to be endangered by the discrepancies, mythical developments, idiosyncracies, and a hundred other defects inevitably attendant on amateur and irresponsible recording. Small wonder, then, that he should have chosen the officials of the Musical Banks, from the Presidents and Vice-Presidents downwards, to be the authoritative exponents of his teaching, the depositaries of his traditions, and his representatives here on earth till he shall again see fit to visit us. For he will come. Nay it is even possible that he may be here amongst us at this very moment, disguised so that none may know him, and intent only on watching our devotion towards him. If this be so, let me implore him, in the name of the sun his father, to reveal himself."

Now Hanky had already given my father more than one look that had made him uneasy. He had evidently recognized him as the supposed ranger of last Thursday evening. Twice he had run his eye like a searchlight over the front benches opposite to him, and when the beam had reached my father there had been no more searching. It was beginning to dawn upon my father that George might have discovered that he was not Professor Panky; was it for this reason that these two young special constables, though they gave up their places, still kept so close to him? Was George only waiting his opportunity to arrest him–not of course even suspecting who he was–but as a foreign devil who had tried to pass himself off as Professor Panky? Had this been the meaning of his having followed him to Fairmead? And should he have to be thrown into the Blue Pool by George after all? "It would serve me," said he to himself, "richly right."

These fears which had been taking shape for some few minutes were turned almost to certainties by the half-contemptuous glance Hanky threw towards him as he uttered what was obviously intended as a challenge. He saw that all was over, and was starting to his feet to declare himself, and thus fall into the trap that Hanky was laying for him, when George gripped him tightly by the knee and whispered, "Don't–you are in great danger." And he smiled kindly as he spoke.

My father sank back dumbfounded. "You know me?" he whispered in reply.

"Perfectly. So does Hanky, so does my mother; say no more," and he again smiled.

George, as my father afterwards learned, had hoped that he would reveal himself, and had determined in spite of his mother's instructions, to give him an opportunity of doing so. It was for this reason that he had not arrested him quietly, as he could very well have done, before the service began. He wished to discover what manner of man his father was, and was quite happy as soon as he saw that he would have spoken out if he had not been checked. He had not yet caught Hanky's motive in trying to goad my father, but on seeing that he was trying to do this, he knew that a trap was being laid, and that my father must not be allowed to speak.

Almost immediately, however, he perceived that while his eyes had been turned on Hanky, two burly vergers had wormed their way through the crowd and taken their stand close to his two brothers. Then he understood, and understood also how to frustrate.

As for my father, George's ascendancy over him—quite felt by George—was so absolute that he could think of nothing now but the exceeding great joy of finding his fears groundless, and of delivering himself up to his son's guidance in the assurance that the void in his heart was filled, and that his wager not only would be held as won, but was being already paid. How they had found out, why he was not to speak as he would assuredly have done—for he was in a white heat of fury—what did it all matter now that he had found that which he had feared he should fail to find? He gave George a puzzled smile, and composed himself as best he could to hear the continuation of Hanky's sermon, which was as follows:

"Who could the Sunchild have chosen, even though he had been gifted with no more than human sagacity, but the body of men whom he selected? It becomes me but ill to speak so warmly in favour of that body of whom I am the least worthy member, but what other is there in Erewhon so above all suspicion of slovenliness, self-seeking, preconceived bias, or bad faith? If there was one set of qualities more essential than another for the conduct of the investigations entrusted to us by the Sunchild, it was those that turn on meekness and freedom from all spiritual pride. I believe I can say quite truly that these are the qualities for which Bridgeford is more especially renowned. The readiness of her Professors to learn even from those who at first sight may seem least able to instruct them; the gentleness with which they correct an opponent if they feel it incumbent upon them to do so; the promptitude with which they acknowledge error when it is pointed out to them and quit a position, no matter how deeply they have been committed to it, at the first moment in which they see that they cannot hold it righteously; their delicate sense of honour; their utter immunity from what the Sunchild used to call log-rolling or intrigue; the scorn with which they regard anything like hitting below the belt–these I believe I may truly say are the virtues for which Bridgeford is pre-eminently renowned."

The Professor went on to say a great deal more about the fitness of Bridgeford and the Musical Bank managers for the task imposed on them by the Sunchild, but here my father's attention flagged–nor, on looking at the verbatim report of the sermon that appeared next morning in the leading Sunch'ston journal, do I see reason to reproduce Hanky's words on this head. It was all to show that there had been no possibility of mistake.

Meanwhile George was writing on a scrap of paper as though he were taking notes of the sermon. Presently he slipped this into my father's hand. It ran:

"You see those vergers standing near my brothers, who gave up their seats to us. Hanky tried to goad you into speaking that they might arrest you, and get you into the Bank prisons. If you fall into their hands you are lost. I must arrest you instantly on a charge of poaching on the King's preserves, and make you my prisoner. Let those vergers catch sight of the warrant which I shall now give you. Read it and return it to me. Come with me quietly after service. I think you had better not reveal yourself at all."

As soon as he had given my father time to read the foregoing, George took a warrant out of his pocket. My father pretended to read it and returned it. George then laid his hand on his shoulder, and in an undertone arrested him. He then wrote on another scrap of paper and passed it on to the elder of his two brothers. It was to the effect that he had now arrested my father, and that if the vergers attempted in any way to interfere between him and his prisoner, his brothers were to arrest both of them, which, as special constables, they had power to do.

Yram had noted Hanky's attempt to goad my father, and had not been prepared for his stealing a march upon her by trying to get my father arrested by Musical Bank officials, rather than by her son. On the preceding evening this last plan had been agreed upon; and she knew nothing of the note that Hanky had sent an hour or two later to the Manager of the temple–the substance of which the reader can sufficiently guess. When she had heard Hanky's words and saw the vergers, she was for a few minutes seriously alarmed, but she was reassured when she saw George give my father the warrant, and her two sons evidently explaining the position to the vergers.

Hanky had by this time changed his theme, and was warning his hearers of the dangers that would follow on the legalization of the medical profession, and the repeal of the edicts against machines. Space forbids me to give his picture of the horrible tortures that future generations would be put to by medical men, if these were not duly kept in check by the influence of the Musical Banks; the horrors of the inquisition in the middle ages are nothing to what he depicted as certain to ensue if medical men were ever to have much money at their command. The only people in whose hands money might be trusted safely were those who presided over the Musical Banks. This tirade was followed by one not less alarming about the growth of materialistic tendencies among the artisans employed in the production of mechanical inventions. My father, though his eyes had been somewhat opened by the second of the two processions he had seen on his way to Sunch'ston, was not prepared to find that in spite of the superficially almost universal acceptance of the new faith, there was a powerful, and it would seem growing, undercurrent of scepticism, with a desire to reduce his escape with my mother to a purely natural occurrence.

"It is not enough," said Hanky, "that the Sunchild should have ensured the preparation of authoritative evidence of his supernatural character. The evidences happily exist in overwhelming strength, but they must be brought home to minds that as yet have stubbornly refused to receive them. During the last five years there has been an enormous increase in the number of those whose occupation in the manufacture of machines inclines them to a materialistic explanation even of the most obviously miraculous events, and the growth of this class in our midst constituted, and still constitutes, a grave danger to the state.

"It was to meet this that the society was formed on behalf of which I appeal fearlessly to your generosity. It is called, as most of you doubtless know, the Sunchild Evidence Society; and his Majesty the King graciously consented to become its Patron. This society not only collects additional evidences–indeed it is entirely due to its labours that the precious relic now in this temple was discovered–but it is its beneficent purpose to lay those that have been authoritatively investigated before men who, if left to themselves, would either neglect them altogether, or worse still reject them.

"For the first year or two the efforts of the society met with but little success among those for whose benefit they were more particularly intended, but during the present year the working classes in some cities and towns (stimulated very much by the lectures of my illustrious friend Professor Panky) have shown a most remarkable and zealous interest in Sunchild evidences, and have formed themselves into local branches for the study and defence of Sunchild truth.

"Yet in spite of all this need–of all this patient labour and really very gratifying success–the subscriptions to the society no longer furnish it with its former very modest income–an income which is deplorably insufficient if the organization is to be kept effective, and the work adequately performed. In spite of the most rigid economy, the committee have been compelled to part with a considerable portion of their small reserve fund (provided by a legacy) to tide over difficulties. But this method of balancing expenditure and income is very unsatisfactory, and cannot be long continued.

"I am led to plead for the society with especial insistence at the present time, inasmuch as more than one of those whose unblemished life has made them fitting recipients of such a signal favour, have recently had visions informing them that the Sunchild will again shortly visit us. We know not when he will come, but when he comes, my friends, let him not find us unmindful of, nor ungrateful for, the inestimable services he has rendered us. For come he surely will. Either in winter, what time icicles hang by the wall and milk comes frozen home in pail–or in summer when days are at their longest and the mowing grass is about–there will be an hour, either at morn, or eve, or in the middle day, when he will again surely come. May it be mine to be among those who are then present to receive him."

Here he again glared at my father, whose blood was boiling. George had not positively forbidden him to speak out; he therefore sprang to his feet, "You lying hound," he cried, "I am the Sunchild, and you know it."

George, who knew that he had my father in his own hands, made no attempt to stop him, and was delighted that he should have declared himself though he had felt it his duty to tell him not to do so. Yram turned pale. Hanky roared out, "Tear him in pieces–leave not a single limb on his body. Take him out and burn him alive." The vergers made a dash for him–but George's brothers seized them. The crowd seemed for a moment inclined to do as Hanky bade them, but Yram rose from her place, and held up her hand as one who claimed attention. She advanced towards George and my father as unconcernedly as though she were merely walking out of church, but she still held her hand uplifted. All eyes were turned on her, as well as on George and my father, and the icy calm of her self-possession chilled those who were inclined for the moment to take Hanky's words literally. There was not a trace of fluster in her gait, action, or words, as she said:

"My friends, this temple, and this day, must not be profaned with blood. My son will take this poor madman to the prison. Let him be judged and punished according to law. Make room, that he and my son may pass."

Then, turning to my father, she said, "Go quietly with the Ranger."

Having so spoken, she returned to her seat as unconcernedly as she had left it.

Hanky for a time continued to foam at the mouth and roar out, "Tear him to pieces! burn him alive!" but when he saw that there was no further hope of getting the people to obey him, he collapsed on to a seat in his pulpit, mopped his bald head, and consoled himself with a great pinch of a powder which corresponds very closely to our own snuff.

George led my father out by the side door at the north end of the western aisle; the people eyed him intently, but made way for him without demonstration. One voice alone was heard to cry out, "Yes, he is the Sunchild!" My father glanced at the speaker, and saw that he was the interpreter who had taught him the Erewhonian language when he was in prison.

George, seeing a special constable close by, told him to bid his brothers release the vergers, and let them arrest the interpreter—this the vergers, foiled as they had been in the matter of my father's arrest, were very glad to do. So the poor interpreter, to his dismay, was lodged at once in one of the Bank prison-cells, where he could do no further harm.

CHAPTER SEVENTEEN: GEORGE TAKES HIS FATHER TO PRISON, AND THERE OBTAINS SOME USEFUL INFORMATION

BY THIS TIME GEORGE HAD GOT MY father into the open square, where he was surprised to find that a large bonfire had been made and lighted. There had been nothing of the kind an hour before; the wood, therefore, must have been piled and lighted while people had been in church. He had no time at the moment to enquire why this had been done, but later on he discovered that on the Sunday morning the Manager of the new temple had obtained leave from the Mayor to have the wood piled in the square, representing that this was Professor Hanky's contribution to the festivities of the day. There had, it seemed, been no intention of lighting it until nightfall; but it had accidentally caught fire through the carelessness of a workman, much about the time when Hanky began to preach. No one for a moment believed that there had been any sinister intention, or that Professor Hanky when he urged the crowd to burn my father alive, even knew that there was a pile of wood in the square at all–much less that it had been lighted–for he could hardly have supposed that the wood had been got together so soon. Nevertheless both George and my father, when they knew all that had passed, congratulated themselves on the fact that my father had not fallen into the hands of the vergers, who would probably have tried to utilise the accidental fire, though in no case is it likely they would have succeeded.

As soon as they were inside the gaol, the old Master recognized my father. "Bless my heart–what? You here again, Mr. Higgs? Why, I thought you were in the palace of the sun your father."

"I wish I was," answered my father, shaking hands with him, but he could say no more.

"You are as safe here as if you were," said George laughing, "and safer." Then turning to his grandfather, he said, " You have the record of Mr. Higgs's marks and measurements? I know you have: take him to his old cell; it is the best in the prison; and then please bring me the record."

The old man took George and my father to the cell which he had occupied twenty years earlier–but I cannot stay to describe his feelings on finding himself again within it. The moment his grandfather's back was turned, George said to my father, " And now shake hands also with your son."

As he spoke he took my father's hand and pressed it warmly between both his own.

" Then you know you are my son," said my father as steadily as the strong emotion that mastered him would permit.

" Certainly."

" But you did not know this when I was walking with you on Friday? "

" Of course not. I thought you were Professor Panky; if I had not taken you for one of the two persons named in your permit, I should have questioned you closely, and probably ended by throwing you into the Blue Pool." He shuddered as he said this.

" But you knew who I was when you called me Panky in the temple? "

" Quite so. My mother told me everything on Friday evening."

" And that is why you tried to find me at Fairmead? "

" Yes, but where in the world were you? "

" I was inside the Musical Bank of the town, resting and reading."

George laughed, and said, " On purpose to hide? "

" Oh no; pure chance. But on Friday evening? How could your mother have found out by that time that I was in Erewhon? Am I on my head or my heels? "

" On your heels, my father, which shall take you back

to your own country as soon as we can get you out of this."

"What have I done to deserve so much goodwill? I have done you nothing but harm?" Again he was quite overcome.

George patted him gently on the hand, and said, "You made a bet and you won it. During the very short time that we can be together, you shall be paid in full, and may heaven protect us both."

As soon as my father could speak he said, "But how did your mother find out that I was in Erewhon?"

"Hanky and Panky were dining with her, and they told her some things that she thought strange. She cross-questioned them, put two and two together, learned that you had got their permit out of them, saw that you intended to return on Friday, and concluded that you would be sleeping in Sunch'ston. She sent for me, told me all, bade me scour Sunch'ston to find you, intending that you should be at once escorted safely over the preserves by me. I found your inn, but you had given us the slip. I tried first Fairmead and then Clearwater, but did not find you till this morning. For reasons too long to repeat, my mother warned Hanky and Panky that you would be in the temple; whereon Hanky tried to get you into his clutches. Happily he failed, but if I had known what he was doing I should have arrested you before the service. I ought to have done this, but I wanted you to win your wager, and I shall get you safely away in spite of them. My mother will not like my having let you hear Hanky's sermon and declare yourself."

"You half told me not to say who I was."

"Yes, but I was delighted when you disobeyed me."

"I did it very badly. I never rise to great occasions, I always fall to them; but these things must come as they come."

"You did it as well as it could be done, and good will come of it."

"And now," he continued, "describe exactly all that passed between you and the Professors. On which side of Panky did Hanky sit, and did they sit north and south or east and west? How did you get—oh yes, I know that–you told them it would be of no further use to them. Tell me all else you can."

My father said that the Professors were sitting pretty well east and west, so that Hanky, who was on the east side, nearest the mountains, had Panky, who was on the Sunch'ston side, on his right hand. George made a note of this. My father then told what the reader already knows, but when he came to the measurement of the boots, George said, "Take your boots off," and began taking off his own. "Foot for foot," said he, "we are not father and son, but brothers. Yours will fit me; they are less worn than mine, but I daresay you will not mind that."

On this George *ex abundanti cautela* knocked a nail out of the right boot that he had been wearing and changed boots with my father; but he thought it more plausible not to knock out exactly the same nail that was missing on my father's boot. When the change was made, each found–or said he found–the other's boots quite comfortable.

My father all the time felt as though he were a basket given to a dog. The dog had got him, was proud of him, and no one must try to take him away. The promptitude with which George took to him, the obvious pleasure he had in "running" him, his quick judgement, verging as it should towards rashness, his confidence that my father trusted him without reserve, the conviction of perfect openness that was conveyed by the way in which his eyes never budged from my father's when he spoke to him, his genial, kindly, manner, perfect physical health, and the air he had of being on the best possible terms with himself and every one else–the combination of all this so overmastered my poor father (who indeed had been sufficiently mastered before he had been five minutes in George's company) that he resigned himself as gratefully to being a basket, as George had cheerfully undertaken the task of carrying him.

In passing I may say that George could never get his own boots back again, though he tried more than once to do so. My father always made some excuse. They were the only memento of George that he brought home with him; I wonder that he did not ask for a lock of his hair, but he did not. He had the boots put against a wall in his bedroom, where he could see them from his bed, and during his illness, while consciousness yet remained with him, I saw his eyes continually turn towards them. George, in fact, dominated him as long as anything in this world could do so. Nor do I wonder; on the contrary, I love his memory the better; for I too, as will appear later, have seen George, and whatever little jealousy I may have felt, vanished on my finding him almost instantaneously gain the same ascendancy over me his brother, that he had gained over his and my father. But of this no more at present. Let me return to the gaol in Sunch'ston.

"Tell me more," said George, "about the Professors."

My father told him about the nuggets, the sale of his kit, the receipt he had given for the money, and how he had got the nuggets back from a tree, the position of which he described.

"I know the tree; have you got the nuggets here?"

"Here they are, with the receipt, and the pocket handkerchief marked with Hanky's name. The pocket handkerchief was found wrapped round some dried leaves that we call tea, but I have not got these with me."

As he spoke he gave everything to George, who showed the utmost delight in getting possession of them.

"I suppose the blanket and the rest of the kit are still in the tree?"

"Unless Hanky and Panky have got them away, or some one has found them."

"This is not likely. I will now go to my office, but I will come back very shortly. My grandfather shall bring you something to eat at once. I will tell him to send enough for two"–which he accordingly did.

On reaching the office, he told his next brother (whom he had made an under-ranger) to go to the tree he described, and bring back the bundle he should find concealed therein. "You can go there and back," he said, "in an hour and a half, and I shall want the bundle by that time."

The brother, whose name I never rightly caught, set out at once. As soon as he was gone, George took from a drawer the feathers and bones of quails, that he had shown my father on the morning when he met him. He divided them in half, and made them into two bundles, one of which he docketed, "Bones of quails eaten, XIX. xii. 29, by Professor Hanky, P.O.W.W., etc." And he labelled Panky's quail bones in like fashion.

Having done this, he returned to the gaol, but on his way he looked in at the Mayor's, and left a note saying that he should be at the gaol, where any message would reach him, but that he did not wish to meet Professors Hanky and Panky for another couple of hours. It was now about half-past twelve, and he caught sight of a crowd coming quietly out of the temple, whereby he knew that Hanky would soon be at the Mayor's house.

Dinner was brought in almost at the moment when George returned to the gaol. As soon as it was over George said:

"Are you quite sure you have made no mistake about

the way in which you got the permit out of the Professors ? "

" Quite sure. I told them they would not want it, and said I could save them trouble if they gave it me. They never suspected why I wanted it. Where do you think I may be mistaken ? "

" You sold your nuggets for rather less than a twentieth part of their value, and you threw in some curiosities, that would have fetched about half as much as you got for the nuggets. You say you did this because you wanted money to keep you going till you could sell some of your nuggets. This sounds well at first, but the sacrifice is too great to be plausible when considered. It looks more like a case of good honest manly straightforward corruption."

" But surely you believe me ? "

" Of course I do. I believe every syllable that comes from your mouth, but I shall not be able to make out that the story was as it was not, unless I am quite certain what it really was."

" It was exactly as I have told you."

" That is enough. And now, may I tell my mother that you will put yourself in her, and the Mayor's, and my hands, and will do whatever we tell you ? "

" I will be obedience itself–but you will not ask me to do anything that will make your mother or you think less well of me ? "

" If we tell you what you are to do, we shall not think any the worse of you for doing it. Then I may say to my mother that you will be good and give no trouble–not even though we bid you shake hands with Hanky and Panky ? "

" I will embrace them and kiss them on both cheeks, if you and she tell me to do so. But what about the Mayor ? "

" He has known everything, and condoned everything, these last twenty years. He will leave everything to my mother and me."

"Shall I have to see him?"

"Certainly. You must be brought up before him to-morrow morning."

"How can I look him in the face?"

"As you would me, or any one else. It is understood among us that nothing happened. Things may have looked as though they had happened, but they did not happen."

"And you are not yet quite twenty?"

"No, but I am son to my mother–and," he added, "to one who can stretch a point or two in the way of honesty as well as other people."

Having said this with a laugh, he again took my father's hand between both his, and went back to his office–where he set himself to think out the course he intended to take when dealing with the Professors.

CHAPTER EIGHTEEN: YRAM INVITES DR. DOWNIE AND MRS. HUMDRUM TO LUNCHEON, A PASSAGE AT ARMS BETWEEN HER AND HANKY IS AMICABLY ARRANGED

THE DISTURBANCE CAUSED BY MY father's outbreak was quickly suppressed, for George got him out of the temple almost immediately; it was bruited about, however, that the Sunchild had come down from the palace of the sun, but had disappeared as soon as any one had tried to touch him. In vain did Hanky try to put fresh life into his sermon; its back had been broken, and large numbers left the church to see what they could hear outside, or failing information, to discourse more freely with one another.

Hanky did his best to quiet his hearers when he found that he could not infuriate them.

" This poor man," he said, " is already known to me, as one of those who have deluded themselves into believing that they are the Sunchild. I have known of his so declaring himself, more than once, in the neighbourhood of Bridgeford, and others have not infrequently done the same; I did not at first recognize him, and regret that the shock of horror his words occasioned me should have prompted me to suggest violence against him. Let this unfortunate affair pass from your minds, and let me again urge upon you the claims of the Sunchild Evidence Society."

The audience on hearing that they were to be told more about the Sunchild Evidence Society melted away even more rapidly than before, and the sermon fizzled out to an ignominious end quite unworthy of its occasion.

About half-past twelve, the service ended, and Hanky went to the robing-room to take off his vestments. Yram, the Mayor, and Panky waited for him at the door opposite to that through which my father had been taken; while waiting, Yram scribbled off two notes in pencil, one to Dr. Downie, and another to Mrs. Humdrum, begging them to come to lunch at once–for it would be one o'clock before they could reach the Mayor's. She gave these notes to the Mayor, and bade him bring both the invited guests along with him.

The Mayor left just as Hanky was coming towards her. " This, Mayoress," he said with some asperity, " is a very serious business. It has ruined my collection. Half the people left the temple without giving anything at all. You seem," he added in a tone the significance of which could not be mistaken, " to be very fond, Mayoress, of this Mr. Higgs."

" Yes," said Yram, " I am; I always liked him, and I am sorry for him, but he is not the person I am most sorry for at this moment–he, poor man, is not going to be horsewhipped within the next twenty minutes." And she spoke the " he " in italics.

" I do not understand you, Mayoress."

" My husband will explain, as soon as I have seen him."

" Hanky," said Panky, " you must withdraw, and apologize at once."

Hanky was not slow to do this, and when he had disavowed everything, withdrawn everything, apologized for everything, and eaten humble pie to Yram's satisfaction, she smiled graciously, and held out her hand, which Hanky was obliged to take.

" And now, Professor," she said, " let me return to your remark that this is a very serious business, and let me also claim a woman's privilege of being listened to whenever she chooses to speak. I propose, then, that we say nothing further about this matter till after luncheon. I have asked Dr. Downie and Mrs. Humdrum to join us—"

" Why Mrs. Humdrum ? " interrupted Hanky none too pleasantly, for he was still furious about the duel that had just taken place between himself and his hostess.

" My dear Professor," said Yram good-humouredly, " pray say all you have to say and I will continue."

Hanky was silent.

" I have asked," resumed Yram, " Dr. Downie and Mrs. Humdrum to join us, and after luncheon we can discuss the situation or no as you may think proper. Till then let us say no more. Luncheon will be over by two o'clock or soon after, and the banquet will not begin till seven, so we shall have plenty of time."

Hanky looked black and said nothing. As for Panky he was morally in a state of collapse, and did not count.

Hardly had they reached the Mayor's house when the Mayor also arrived with Dr. Downie and Mrs. Humdrum, both of whom had seen and recognized my father in spite of his having dyed his hair. Dr. Downie had met him at supper in Mr. Thims's rooms when he had visited Bridgeford, and naturally enough had observed him closely. Mrs. Humdrum, as I have already said, had seen him more than once when he was in prison. She and Dr. Downie were talking earnestly over the strange reappearance of one whom they had believed long since dead, but Yram imposed on them the same silence that she had already imposed on the Professors.

" Professor Hanky," said she to Mrs. Humdrum, in Hanky's hearing, " is a little alarmed at my having asked you to join our secret conclave. He is not married, and does not know how well a woman can hold her tongue when she chooses. I should have told you all that passed, for I mean to follow your advice, so I thought you had better hear everything yourself."

Hanky still looked black, but he said nothing. Luncheon was promptly served, and done justice to in spite of much preoccupation; for if there is one thing that gives a better appetite than another, it is a Sunday morning's service with a charity sermon to follow. As the guests might not talk on the subject they wanted to talk about, and were in no humour to speak of anything else, they gave their whole attention to the good things that were before them, without so much as a thought about reserving themselves for the evening's banquet. Nevertheless, when luncheon was over, the Professors were in no more genial, manageable state of mind than they had been when it began.

When the servants had left the room, Yram said to Hanky, " You saw the prisoner, and he was the man you met on Thursday night ? "

" Certainly; he was wearing the forbidden dress and he had many quails in his possession. There is no doubt also that he was a foreign devil."

At this point, it being now nearly half-past two, George came in, and took a seat next to Mrs. Humdrum—between her and his mother—who of course sat at the head of the table with the Mayor opposite to her. On one side of the table sat the Professors, and on the other Dr. Downie, Mrs. Humdrum, and George, who had heard the last few words that Hanky had spoken.

CHAPTER NINETEEN: A COUNCIL IS HELD AT THE MAYOR'S, IN THE COURSE OF WHICH GEORGE TURNS THE TABLES ON THE PROFESSORS

"NOW WHO," SAID YRAM, "IS THIS UNfortunate creature to be, when he is brought up to-morrow morning, on the charge of poaching?"

"It is not necessary," said Hanky severely, "that he should be brought up for poaching. He is a foreign devil, and as such your son is bound to fling him without trial into the Blue Pool. Why bring a smaller charge when you must inflict the death penalty on a more serious one? I have already told you that I shall feel it my duty to report the matter at headquarters, unless I am satisfied that the death penalty has been inflicted."

"Of course," said George, "we must all of us do our duty, and I shall not shrink from mine–but I have arrested this man on a charge of poaching, and must give my reasons; the case cannot be dropped, and it must be heard in public. Am I, or am I not, to have the sworn depositions of both you gentlemen to the fact that the prisoner is the man you saw with quails in his possession? If you can depose to this he will be convicted, for there can be no doubt he killed the birds himself. The least penalty my father can inflict is twelve months' imprisonment with hard labour; and he must undergo this sentence before I can Blue-Pool him.

"Then comes the question whether or no he is a foreign devil. I may decide this in private, but I must have depositions on oath before I do so, and at present I have nothing but hearsay. Perhaps you gentlemen can give me the evidence I shall require, but the case is one of such importance that were the prisoner proved never so clearly to be a foreign devil, I should not Blue-Pool him till I had taken the King's pleasure concerning him. I shall rejoice, therefore, if you gentlemen can help me to sustain the charge of poaching, and thus give me legal standing-ground for deferring action which the King might regret, and which once taken cannot be recalled."

Here Yram interposed. "These points," she said, "are details. Should we not first settle, not what, but who, we shall allow the prisoner to be, when he is brought up to-morrow morning? Settle this, and the rest will settle itself. He has declared himself to be the Sunchild, and will probably do so again. I am prepared to identify him, so is Dr. Downie, so is Mrs. Humdrum, the interpreter, and doubtless my father. Others of known respectability will also do so, and his marks and measurements are sure to correspond quite sufficiently. The question is, whether all this is to be allowed to appear in evidence, or whether it is to be established, as it easily may, if we give our minds to it, that he is not the Sunchild."

"Whatever else he is," said Hanky, "he must not be the Sunchild. He must, if the charge of poaching cannot be dropped, be a poacher and a foreign devil. I was doubtless too hasty when I said that I believed I recognized the man as one who had more than once declared himself to be the Sunchild—"

"But, Hanky," interrupted Panky, "are you sure that you can swear to this man's being the man we met on Thursday night? We only saw him by firelight, and I doubt whether I should feel justified in swearing to him."

"Well, well: on second thoughts I am not sure, Panky, but what you may be right after all; it is possible that he may be what I said he was in my sermon."

"I rejoice to hear you say so," said George, "for in this case the charge of poaching will fall through. There will be no evidence against the prisoner. And I rejoice also to think that I shall have nothing to warrant me in believing him to be a foreign devil. For if he is not to be the Sunchild, and not to be your poacher, he becomes a mere monomaniac. If he apologizes for having made a disturbance in the temple, and promises not to offend again, a fine, and a few days' imprisonment, will meet the case, and he may be discharged."

"I see, I see," said Hanky very angrily. "You are determined to get this man off if you can."

"I shall act," said George, "in accordance with sworn evidence, and not otherwise. Choose whether you will have the prisoner to be your poacher or no: give me your sworn depositions one way or the other, and I shall know how to act. If you depose on oath to the identity of the prisoner and your poacher, he will be convicted and imprisoned. As to his being a foreign devil, if he is the Sunchild, of course he is one; but otherwise I cannot Blue-Pool him even when his sentence is expired, without testimony deposed to me on oath in private, though no open trial is required. A case for suspicion was made out in my hearing last night, but I must have depositions on oath to all the leading facts before I can decide what my duty is. What will you swear to?"

"All this," said Hanky, in a voice husky with passion, "shall be reported to the King."

"I intend to report every word of it; but that is not the point: the question is what you gentlemen will swear to?"

"Very well. I will settle it thus. We will swear that the prisoner is the poacher we met on Thursday night, and that he is also a foreign devil: his wearing the forbidden dress; his foreign accent; the foot-tracks we found in the snow, as of one coming over from the other side; his obvious ignorance of the Afforesting Act, as shown by his having lit a fire and making no effort to conceal his quails till our permit showed him his blunder; the cock-and-bull story he told us about your orders, and that other story about his having killed a foreign devil–if these facts do not satisfy you, they will satisfy the King that the prisoner is a foreign devil as well as a poacher."

"Some of these facts," answered George, "are new to me. How do you know that the foot-tracks were made by the prisoner?"

Panky brought out his note-book and read the details he had noted.

"Did you examine the man's boots?"

"One of them, the right foot; this, with the measurements, was quite enough."

"Hardly. Please to look at both soles of my own boots; you will find that those tracks were mine. I will have the prisoner's boots examined; in the meantime let me tell you that I was up at the statues on Thursday morning, walked three or four hundred yards beyond them, over ground where there was less snow, returned over the snow, and went two or three times round them, as it is the Ranger's duty to do once a year in order to see that none of them are beginning to lean."

He showed the soles of his boots, and the Professors were obliged to admit that the tracks were his. He cautioned them as to the rest of the points on which they relied. Might they not be as mistaken as they had just proved to be about the tracks? He could not, however, stir them from sticking to it that there was enough evidence to prove my father to be a foreign devil, and declaring their readiness to depose to the facts on oath. In the end Hanky again fiercely accused him of trying to shield the prisoner.

"You are quite right," said George, "and you will see my reasons shortly."

"I have no doubt," said Hanky significantly, "that they are such as would weigh with any man of ordinary feeling."

"I understand, then," said George, appearing to take

no notice of Hanky's innuendo, " that you will swear to the facts as you have above stated them ? "

" Certainly."

" Then kindly wait while I write them on the form that I have brought with me; the Mayor can administer the oath and sign your depositions. I shall then be able to leave you, and proceed with getting up the case against the prisoner."

So saying, he went to a writing-table in another part of the room, and made out the depositions.

Meanwhile the Mayor, Mrs. Humdrum, and Dr. Downie (who had each of them more than once vainly tried to take part in the above discussion) conversed eagerly in an undertone among themselves. Hanky was blind with rage, for he had a sense that he was going to be outwitted; the Mayor, Yram, and Mrs. Humdrum had already seen that George thought he had all the trumps in his own hand, but they did not know more. Dr. Downie was frightened, and Panky so muddled as to be *hors de combat*.

George now rejoined the Professors, and read the depositions: the Mayor administered the oath according to Erewhonian custom; the Professors signed without a word, and George then handed the document to his father to countersign.

The Mayor examined it, and almost immediately said, " My dear George, you have made a mistake; these depositions are on a form reserved for deponents who are on the point of death."

" Alas ! " answered George, " there is no help for it. I did my utmost to prevent their signing. I knew that those depositions were their own death warrant, and that is why, though I was satisfied that the prisoner is a foreign devil, I had hoped to be able to shut my eyes. I can now no longer do so, and as the inevitable consequence, I must Blue-Pool both the Professors before midnight. What man of ordinary feeling would not under these circumstances have tried to dissuade them from deposing as they have done?"

By this time the Professors had started to their feet, and there was a look of horrified astonishment on the faces of all present, save that of George, who seemed quite happy.

"What monstrous absurdity is this?" shouted Hanky; "do you mean to murder us?"

"Certainly not. But you have insisted that I should do my duty, and I mean to do it. You gentlemen have now been proved to my satisfaction to have had traffic with a foreign devil; and under section 37 of the Afforesting Act, I must at once Blue-Pool any such persons without public trial."

"Nonsense, nonsense, there was nothing of the kind on our permit, and as for trafficking with this foreign devil, we spoke to him, but we neither bought nor sold. Where is the Act?"

"Here. On your permit you were referred to certain other clauses not set out therein, which might be seen at the Mayor's office. Clause 37 is as follows:

"It is furthermore enacted that should any of his Majesty's subjects be found, after examination by the Head Ranger, to have had traffic of any kind by way of sale or barter with any foreign devil, the said Ranger, on being satisfied that such traffic has taken place, shall forthwith, with or without the assistance of his under-rangers, convey such subjects of his Majesty to the Blue Pool, bind them, weight them, and fling them into it, without the formality of a trial, and shall report the circumstances of the case to his Majesty."

"But we never bought anything from the prisoner. What evidence can you have of this but the word of a foreign devil in such straits that he would swear to anything?"

" The prisoner has nothing to do with it. I am convinced by this receipt in Professor Panky's handwriting which states that he and you jointly purchased his kit from the prisoner, and also this bag of gold nuggets worth about £100 in silver, for the absurdly small sum of £4, 10*s*. in silver. I am further convinced by this handkerchief marked with Professor Hanky's name, in which was found a broken packet of dried leaves that are now at my office with the rest of the prisoner's kit."

" Then we were watched and dogged," said Hanky, " on Thursday evening."

" That, sir," replied George, " is my business, not yours."

Here Panky laid his arms on the table, buried his head in them, and burst into tears. Every one seemed aghast, but the Mayor, Yram, and Mrs. Humdrum saw that George was enjoying it all far too keenly to be serious. Dr. Downie was still frightened (for George's surface manner was Rhadamanthine) and did his utmost to console Panky. George pounded away ruthlessly at his case.

" I say nothing about your having bought quails from the prisoner and eaten them. As you justly remarked just now, there is no object in preferring a smaller charge when one must inflict the death penalty on a more serious one. Still, Professor Hanky, these are bones of the quails you ate as you sate opposite the prisoner on the side of the fire nearest Sunch'ston; these are Professor Panky's bones, with which I need not disturb him. This is your permit, which was found upon the prisoner, and which there can be no doubt you sold him, having been bribed by the offer of the nuggets for—"

" Monstrous, monstrous ! Infamous falsehood ! Who will believe such a childish trumped-up story ! "

" Who, sir, will believe anything else ? You will hardly contend that you did not know the nuggets were gold, and no one will believe you mean enough to have tried to get this poor man's property out of him for a song–you knowing its value, and he not knowing the same. No one will believe that you did not know the man to be a foreign devil, or that he could hoodwink two such learned Professors so cleverly as to get their permit out of them. Obviously he seduced you into selling him your permit, and–I presume because he wanted a little of our money–he made you pay him for his kit. I am satisfied that you have not only had traffic with a foreign devil, but traffic of a singularly atrocious kind, and this being so, I shall Blue-Pool both of you as soon as I can get you up to the Pool itself. The sooner we start the better. I shall gag you, and drive you up in a closed carriage as far as the road goes; from that point you can walk up, or be dragged up as you may prefer, but you will probably find walking more comfortable."

"But," said Hanky, "come what may, I must be at the banquet. I am set down to speak."

"The Mayor will explain that you have been taken somewhat suddenly unwell."

Here Yram, who had been talking quietly with her husband, Dr. Downie, and Mrs. Humdrum, motioned her son to silence.

"I feared," she said, "that difficulties might arise, though I did not foresee how seriously they would affect my guests. Let Mrs. Humdrum on our side, and Dr. Downie on that of the Professors, go into the next room and talk the matter quietly over; let us then see whether we cannot agree to be bound by their decision. I do not doubt but they will find some means of averting any catastrophe more serious–No, Professor Hanky, the doors are locked–than a little perjury in which we shall all share and share alike."

"Do what you like," said Hanky, looking for all the

world like a rat caught in a trap. As he spoke he seized a knife from the table, whereon George pulled a pair of handcuffs from his pocket and slipped them on to his wrists before he well knew what was being done to him.

"George," said the Mayor, "this is going too far. Do you mean to Blue-Pool the Professors or no?"

"Not if they will compromise. If they will be reasonable, they will not be Blue-Pooled; if they think they can have everything their own way, the eels will be at them before morning."

A voice was heard from the head of Panky which he had buried in his arms upon the table. "Co–co–co–co–compromise," it said; and the effect was so comic that every one except Hanky smiled. Meanwhile Yram had conducted Dr. Downie and Mrs. Humdrum into an adjoining room.

CHAPTER TWENTY: MRS. HUMDRUM AND DR. DOWNIE PROPOSE A COMPROMISE, WHICH, AFTER AN AMENDMENT BY GEORGE, IS CARRIED *nem. con.*

THEY RETURNED IN ABOUT TEN MINUTES, and Dr. Downie asked Mrs. Humdrum to say what they had agreed to recommend.

"We think," said she very demurely, "that the strict course would be to drop the charge of poaching, and Blue-Pool both the Professors and the prisoner without delay.

"We also think that the proper thing would be to place on record that the prisoner is the Sunchild–about which neither Dr. Downie nor I have a shadow of doubt.

"These measures we hold to be the only legal ones, but at the same time we do not recommend them. We think it would offend the public conscience if it came to be known, as it certainly would, that the Sunchild was violently killed, on the very day that had seen us dedicate a temple in his honour, and perhaps at the very hour when laudatory speeches were being made about him at the Mayor's banquet; we think also that we should strain a good many points rather than Blue-Pool the Professors.

"Nothing is perfect, and Truth makes her mistakes like other people; when she goes wrong and reduces herself to such an absurdity as she has here done, those who love her must save her from herself, correct her, and rehabilitate her.

"Our conclusion, therefore, is this:

"The prisoner must recant on oath his statement that he is the Sunchild. The interpreter must be squared, or convinced of his mistake. The Mayoress, Dr. Downie, I, and the gaoler (with the interpreter if we can manage him), must depose on oath that the prisoner is not Higgs. This must be our contribution to the rehabilitation of Truth.

"The Professors must contribute as follows: They

must swear that the prisoner is not the man they met with quails in his possession on Thursday night. They must further swear that they have one or both of them known him, off and on, for many years past, as a monomaniac with Sunchildism on the brain but otherwise harmless. If they will do this, no proceedings are to be taken against them.

" The Mayor's contribution shall be to reprimand the prisoner, and order him to repeat his recantation in the new temple before the Manager and Head Cashier, and to confirm his statement on oath by kissing the reliquary containing the newly found relic.

" The Ranger and the Master of the Gaol must contribute that the prisoner's measurements, and the marks found on his body, negative all possibility of his identity with the Sunchild, and that all the hair on the covered as well as the uncovered parts of his body was found to be jet black.

" We advise further that the prisoner should have his nuggets and his kit returned to him, and that the receipt given by the Professors together with Professor Hanky's handkerchief be given back to the Professors.

" Furthermore, seeing that we should all of us like to have a quiet evening with the prisoner, we should petition the Mayor and Mayoress to ask him to meet all here present at dinner to-morrow evening, after his discharge, on the plea that Professors Hanky and Panky and Dr. Downie may give him counsel, convince him of his folly, and if possible free him henceforth from the monomania under which he now suffers.

" The prisoner shall give his word of honour never to return to Erewhon, nor to encourage any of his countrymen to do so. After the dinner to which we hope the Mayoress will invite us, the Ranger, if the night is fair, shall escort the prisoner as far as the statues, whence he will find his own way home.

"Those who are in favour of this compromise hold up their hands."

The Mayor and Yram held up theirs. "Will you hold up yours, Professor Hanky," said George, "if I release you?"

"Yes," said Hanky with a gruff laugh, whereon George released him and he held up both his hands.

Panky did not hold up his, whereon Hanky said, "Hold up your hands, Panky, can't you? We are really very well out of it."

Panky, hardly lifting his head, sobbed out, "I think we ought to have our f-f-fo-fo-four pounds ten returned to us."

"I am afraid, sir," said George, "that the prisoner must have spent the greater part of this money."

Every one smiled, indeed it was all George could do to prevent himself from laughing outright. The Mayor brought out his purse, counted the money, and handed it good-humouredly to Panky, who gratefully received it, and said he would divide it with Hanky. He then held up his hands, "But," he added, turning to his brother Professor, "so long as I live, Hanky, I will never go out anywhere again with you."

George then turned to Hanky and said, "I am afraid I must now trouble you and Professor Panky to depose on oath to the facts which Mrs. Humdrum and Dr. Downie propose you should swear to in open court to-morrow. I knew you would do so, and have brought an ordinary form, duly filled up, which declares that the prisoner is not the poacher you met on Thursday; and also, that he has been long known to both of you as a harmless monomaniac."

As he spoke he brought out depositions to the above effect which he had just written in his office; he showed the Professors that the form was this time an innocent one, whereon they made no demur to signing and swearing in the presence of the Mayor, who attested.

"The former depositions," said Hanky, "had better be destroyed at once."

"That," said George, "may hardly be, but so long as you stick to what you have just sworn to, they will not be used against you."

Hanky scowled, but knew that he was powerless and said no more.

*

The knowledge of what ensued did not reach me from my father. George and his mother, seeing how ill he looked, and what a shock the events of the last few days had given him, resolved that he should not know of the risk that George was about to run; they therefore said nothing to him about it. What I shall now tell, I learned on the occasion already referred to when I had the happiness to meet George. I am in some doubt whether it is more fitly told here, or when I come to the interview between him and me; on the whole, however, I suppose chronological order is least outraged by dealing with it here.

As soon as the Professors had signed the second depositions, George said, "I have not yet held up my hands, but I will hold them up if Mrs. Humdrum and Dr. Downie will approve of what I propose. Their compromise does not go far enough, for swear as we may, it is sure to get noised abroad, with the usual exaggerations, that the Sunchild has been here, and that he has been spirited away either by us, or by the sun his father. For one person whom we know of as having identified him, there will be five, of whom we know nothing, and whom we cannot square. Reports will reach the King sooner or later, and I shall be sent for. Meanwhile the Professors will be living in fear of intrigue on my part, and I, however unreasonably, shall fear the like on theirs. This should not be. I mean, therefore, on the day following my return from escorting the prisoner, to set out for the capital, see the King, and make a clean breast of the whole matter. To this end I must have the nuggets, the prisoner's kit, his receipt, Professor Hanky's handkerchief, and, of course, the two depositions just sworn to by the Professors. I hope and think that the King will pardon us all round; but whatever he may do I shall tell him everything."

Hanky was up in arms at once. "Sheer madness," he exclaimed. Yram and the Mayor looked anxious; Dr. Downie eyed George as though he were some curious creature, which he had heard of but had never seen, and was rather disposed to like. Mrs. Humdrum nodded her head approvingly.

"Quite right, George," said she, "tell his Majesty everything."

Dr. Downie then said, "Your son, Mayoress, is a very sensible fellow. I will go with him, and with the Professors–for they had better come too: each will hear what the other says, and we will tell the truth, the whole truth, and nothing but the truth. I am, as you know, a *persona grata* at Court; I will say that I advised your son's action. The King has liked him ever since he was a boy, and I am not much afraid about what he will do. In public, no doubt, we had better hush things up, but in private the King must be told."

Hanky fought hard for some time, but George told him that it did not matter whether he agreed or no. "You can come," he said, "or stop away, just as you please. If you come, you can hear and speak; if you do not, you will not hear, but these two depositions will speak for you. Please yourself."

"Very well," he said at last. "I suppose we had better go."

Every one having now understood what his or her part was to be, Yram said they had better shake hands all round and take a couple of hours' rest before getting ready for the banquet. George said that the Professors did not shake hands with him very cordially, but the farce was gone through. When the hand-shaking was over, Dr. Downie and Mrs. Humdrum left the house, and the Professors retired grumpily to their own room.

I will say here that no harm happened either to George or the Professors in consequence of his having told the King, but will reserve particulars for my concluding chapter.

CHAPTER TWENTY-ONE: YRAM, ON GETTING RID OF HER GUESTS, GOES TO THE PRISON TO SEE MY FATHER

YRAM DID NOT TAKE THE ADVICE SHE had given her guests, but set about preparing a basket of the best cold dainties she could find, including a bottle of choice wine that she knew my father would like; thus loaded she went to the gaol, which she entered by her father's private entrance.

It was now about half-past four, so that much more must have been said and done after luncheon at the Mayor's than ever reached my father. The wonder is that he was able to collect so much. He, poor man, as soon as George left him, flung himself on to the bed that was in his cell and lay there wakeful, but not unquiet, till near the time when Yram reached the gaol.

The old gaoler came to tell him that she had come and would be glad to see him; much as he dreaded the meeting there was no avoiding it, and in a few minutes Yram stood before him.

Both were agitated, but Yram betrayed less of what she felt than my father. He could only bow his head and cover his face with his hands. Yram said, " We are old friends; take your hands from your face and let me see you. There! That is well."

She took his right hand between both hers, looked at him with eyes full of kindness, and said softly:

" You are not much changed, but you look haggard, worn, and ill; I am uneasy about you. Remember, you are among friends, who will see that no harm befalls you. There is a look in your eyes that frightens me."

As she spoke she took the wine out of her basket, and poured him out a glass, but rather to give him some little thing to distract his attention, than because she expected him to drink it–which he could not do.

She never asked him whether he found her altered, or turned the conversation ever such a little on to herself; all was for him; to soothe and comfort him, not in words alone, but in look, manner, and voice. My father knew that he could thank her best by controlling himself, and letting himself be soothed and comforted—at any rate so far as he could seem to be.

Up to this time they had been standing, but now Yram, seeing my father calmer, said, " Enough, let us sit down."

So saying she seated herself at one end of the small table that was in the cell, and motioned my father to sit opposite to her. " The light hurts you ? " she said, for the sun was coming into the room. " Change places with me, I am a sun worshipper. No, we can move the table, and we can then see each other better."

This done, she said, still very softly, " And now tell me what it is all about. Why have you come here ? "

" Tell me first," said my father, " what befell you after I had been taken away. Why did you not send me word when you found what had happened ? or come after me ? You know I should have married you at once, unless they bound me in fetters."

" I know you would; but you remember Mrs. Humdrum ? Yes, I see you do. I told her everything; it was she who saved me. We thought of you, but she saw that it would not do. As I was to marry Mr. Strong, the more you were lost sight of the better, but with George ever with me I have not been able to forget you. I might have been very happy with you, but I could not have been happier than I have been ever since that short dreadful time was over. George must tell you the rest. I cannot do so. All is well. I love my husband with my whole heart and soul, and he loves me with his. As between him and me, he knows everything; George is his son, not yours; we have settled it so, though we both know otherwise; as between you and me, for this one hour, here, there is no use in pretending that you are not George's father. I have said

all I need say. Now, tell me what I asked you–Why are you here?"

"I fear," said my father, set at rest by the sweetness of Yram's voice and manner–he told me he had never seen any one to compare with her except my mother–"I fear, to do as much harm now as I did before, and with as little wish to do any harm at all."

He then told her all that the reader knows, and explained how he had thought he could have gone about the country as a peasant, and seen how she herself had fared, without her, or any one, even suspecting that he was in the country.

"You say your wife is dead, and that she left you with a son–is he like George?"

"In mind and disposition, wonderfully; in appearance, no; he is dark and takes after his mother, and though he is handsome, he is not so good-looking as George."

"No one," said George's mother, "ever was, or ever will be, and he is as good as he looks."

"I should not have believed you if you had said he was not."

"That is right. I am glad you are proud of him. He irradiates the lives of every one of us."

"And the mere knowledge that he exists will irradiate the rest of mine."

"Long may it do so. Let us now talk about this morning–did you mean to declare yourself?"

"I do not know what I meant; what I most cared about was the doing what I thought George would wish to see his father do."

"You did that; but he says he told you not to say who you were."

"So he did, but I knew what he would think right. He was uppermost in my thoughts all the time."

Yram smiled, and said, "George is a dangerous

person; you were both of you very foolish; one as bad as the other."

"I do not know. I do not know anything. It is beyond me; but I am at peace about it, and hope I shall do the like again to-morrow before the Mayor."

"I heartily hope you will do nothing of the kind. George tells me you have promised him to be good and to do as we bid you."

"So I will; but he will not tell me to say that I am not what I am."

"Yes, he will, and I will tell you why. If we permit you to be Higgs the Sunchild, he must either throw his own father into the Blue Pool–which he will not do–or run great risk of being thrown into it himself, for not having Blue-Pooled a foreigner. I am afraid we shall have to make you do a good deal that neither you nor we shall like."

She then told him briefly of what had passed after luncheon at her house, and what it had been settled to do, leaving George to tell the details while escorting him towards the statues on the following evening. She said that every one would be so completely in every one else's power that there was no fear of any one's turning traitor. But she said nothing about George's intention of setting out for the capital on Wednesday morning to tell the whole story to the King.

"Now," she said, when she had told him as much as was necessary, "be good, and do as you said you would."

"I will. I will deny myself, not once, nor twice, but as often as is necessary. I will kiss the reliquary, and when I meet Hanky and Panky at your table, I will be sworn brother to them–so long, that is, as George is out of hearing; for I cannot lie well to them when he is listening."

"Oh yes, you can. He will understand all about it;

he enjoys falsehood as well as we all do, and has the nicest sense of when to lie and when not to do so."

"What gift can be more invaluable?"

My father, knowing that he might not have another chance of seeing Yram alone, now changed the conversation.

"I have something," he said, "for George, but he must know nothing about it till after I am gone."

As he spoke, he took from his pockets the nine small bags of nuggets that remained to him.

"But this," said Yram, "being gold, is a large sum: can you indeed spare it, and do you really wish George to have it all?"

"I shall be very unhappy if he does not, but he must know nothing about it till I am out of Erewhon."

My father then explained to her that he was now very rich, and would have brought ten times as much, if he had known of George's existence.

"Then," said Yram, musing, "if you are rich, I accept and thank you heartily on his behalf. I can see a reason for his not knowing what you are giving him at present, but it is too long to tell."

The reason was, that if George knew of this gold before he saw the King, he would be sure to tell him of it, and the King might claim it, for George would never explain that it was a gift from father to son; whereas if the King had once pardoned him, he would not be so squeamish as to open up the whole thing again with a postscript to his confession. But of this she said not a word.

My father then told her of the box of sovereigns that he had left in his saddle-bags. "They are coined," he said, "and George will have to melt them down, but he will find some way of doing this. They will be worth rather more than these nine bags of nuggets."

"The difficulty will be to get him to go down and

fetch them, for it is against his oath to go far beyond the statues. If you could be taken faint and say you wanted help, he would see you to your camping ground without a word, but he would be angry if he found he had been tricked into breaking his oath in order that money might be given him. It would never do. Besides, there would not be time, for he must be back here on Tuesday night. No; if he breaks his oath he must do it with his eyes open–and he will do it later on–or I will go and fetch the money for him myself. He is in love with a grand-daughter of Mrs. Humdrum's, and this sum, together with what you are now leaving with me, will make him a well-to-do man. I have always been unhappy about his having any of the Mayor's money and his salary was not quite enough for him to marry on. What can I say to thank you ? "

" Tell me, please, about Mrs. Humdrum's grand-daughter. You like her as a wife for George ? "

" Absolutely. She is just such another as her grand-mother must have been. She and George have been sworn lovers ever since he was ten, and she eight. The only drawback is that her mother, Mrs. Humdrum's second daughter, married for love, and there are many children, so that there will be no money with her ; but what you are leaving will make everything quite easy, for he will sell the gold at once. I am so glad about it."

" Can you ask Mrs. Humdrum to bring her grand-daughter with her to-morrow evening ? "

" I am afraid not, for we shall want to talk freely at dinner, and she must not know that you are the Sun-child; she shall come to my house in the afternoon and you can see her then. You will be quite happy about her, but of course she must not know that you are her father-in-law that is to be."

" One thing more. As George must know nothing about the sovereigns, I must tell you how I will hide them. They are in a silver box, which I will bind to the bough of some tree close to my camp; or if I can find a tree with a hole in it I will drop the box into the hole. He cannot miss my camp; he has only to follow the stream that runs down from the pass till it gets near a large river, and on a small triangular patch of flat ground he will see the ashes of my camp fire, a few yards away from the stream on his right hand as he descends. In whatever tree I may hide the box, I will strew wood ashes for some yards in a straight line towards it. I will then light another fire underneath, and blaze the tree with a knife that I have left at my camping ground. He is sure to find it."

Yram again thanked him, and then my father, to change the conversation, asked whether she thought that George really would have Blue-Pooled the Professors.

"There is no knowing," said Yram. "He is the gentlest creature living till some great provocation rouses him, and I never saw him hate and despise any one as he does the Professors. Much of what he said was merely put on, for he knew the Professors must yield. I do not like his ever having to throw any one into that horrid place, no more does he, but the Rangership is exactly the sort of thing to suit him, and the opening was too good to lose. I must now leave you, and get ready for the Mayor's banquet. We shall meet again to-morrow evening. Try and eat what I have brought you in this basket. I hope you will like the wine." She put out her hand, which my father took, and in another moment she was gone, for she saw a look in his face as though he would fain have asked her to let him once more press his lips to hers. Had he done this, without thinking about it, it is likely enough she would not have been ill pleased. But who can say?

For the rest of the evening my father was left very much to his own not too comfortable reflections. He spent part of it in posting up the notes from which, as well as from his own mouth, my story is in great part taken. The good things that Yram had left with him, and his pipe, which she had told him he might smoke quite freely, occupied another part, and by ten o'clock he went to bed.

CHAPTER TWENTY-TWO: MAINLY OCCUPIED WITH A VERACIOUS EXTRACT FROM A SUNCH'STONIAN JOURNAL

WHILE MY FATHER WAS THUS WILING away the hours in his cell, the whole town was being illuminated in his honour, and not more than a couple of hundred yards off, at the Mayor's banquet, he was being extolled as a superhuman being.

The banquet, which was at the town hall, was indeed a very brilliant affair, but the little space that is left me forbids my saying more than that Hanky made what was considered the speech of the evening, and betrayed no sign of ill effects from the bad quarter of an hour which he had spent so recently. Not a trace was to be seen of any desire on his part to change his tone as regards Sunchildism–as, for example, to minimize the importance of the relic, or to remind his hearers that though the chariot and horses had undoubtedly come down from the sky and carried away my father and mother, yet that the earlier stage of the ascent had been made in a balloon. It almost seemed, so George told my father, as though he had resolved that he would speak lies, all lies, and nothing but lies.

Panky, who was also to have spoken, was excused by the Mayor on the ground that the great heat and the excitement of the day's proceedings had quite robbed him of his voice.

Dr. Downie had a jumping cat before his mental vision. He spoke quietly and sensibly, dwelling chiefly on the benefits that had already accrued to the kingdom through the abolition of the edicts against machinery, and the great developments which he foresaw as probable in the near future. He held up the Sunchild's example, and his ethical teaching, to the imitation and admiration of his hearers, but he said nothing about the miraculous element in my father's career, on which he declared that his friend Professor Hanky had already so eloquently enlarged as to make further allusion to it superfluous.

The reader knows what was to happen on the following morning. The programme concerted at the Mayor's was strictly adhered to. The following account, however, which appeared in the Sunch'ston bi-weekly newspaper two days after my father had left, was given me by George a year later, on the occasion of that interview to which I have already more than once referred. There were other accounts in other papers, but the one I am giving departs the least widely from the facts. It ran:

"*The close of a disagreeable incident.*—Our readers will remember that on Sunday last during the solemn inauguration of the temple now dedicated to the Sunchild, an individual on the front bench of those set apart for the public suddenly interrupted Professor Hanky's eloquent sermon by declaring himself to be the Sunchild, and saying that he had come down from the sun to sanctify by his presence the glorious fane which the piety of our fellow-citizens and others has erected in his honour.

"Wild rumours obtained credence throughout the congregation to the effect that this person was none other than the Sunchild himself, and in spite of the fact that his complexion and the colour of his hair showed this to be impossible, more than one person was carried away by the excitement of the moment, and by some few points of resemblance between the stranger and the Sunchild. Under the influence of this belief, they were preparing to give him the honour which they supposed justly due to him, when to the surprise of every one he was taken into custody by the deservedly popular Ranger of the King's preserves, and in the course of the afternoon it became generally known that he had been arrested on the charge of being one of a gang of poachers who have been known for some time past to be making much havoc among the quails on the preserves.

"This offence, at all times deplored by those who desire that his Majesty should enjoy good sport when he honours us with a visit, is doubly deplorable during the season when, on the higher parts of the preserves, the young birds are not yet able to shift for themselves; the Ranger, therefore, is indefatigable in his efforts to break up the gang, and with this end in view, for the last fortnight has been out night and day on the remoter sections of the forest–little suspecting that the marauders would venture so near Sunch'ston as it now seems they have done. It is to his extreme anxiety to detect and punish these miscreants that we must ascribe the arrest of a man, who, however foolish, and indeed guilty, he is in other respects, is innocent of the particular crime imputed to him. The circumstances that led to his arrest have reached us from an exceptionally well-informed source, and are as follows:

"Our distinguished guests, Professors Hanky and Panky, both of them justly celebrated archaeologists, had availed themselves of the opportunity afforded them by their visit to Sunch'ston, to inspect the mysterious statues at the head of the stream that comes down near this city, and which have hitherto baffled all those who have tried to ascertain their date and purpose.

"On their descent after a fatiguing day the Professors were benighted, and lost their way. Seeing the light of a small fire among some trees near them, they made towards it, hoping to be directed rightly, and found a man, respectably dressed, sitting by the fire with several brace of quails beside him, some of them plucked. Believing that in spite of his appearance, which would not have led them to suppose that he was a poacher, he must unquestionably be one, they hurriedly enquired their way, intending to leave him as soon as they had got their answer; he, however, attacked them, or made as though he would do so, and said he would show them a way which they should be in no fear of losing, whereon Professor Hanky, with a well-directed blow, felled him to the ground. The two Professors, fearing that other poachers might come to his assistance, made off as nearly as they could guess in the direction of Sunch'ston. When they had gone a mile or two onward at haphazard, they sat down under a large tree, and waited till day began to break; they then resumed their journey, and before long struck a path which led them to a spot from which they could see the towers of the new temple.

"Fatigued though they were, they waited before taking the rest of which they stood much in need, till they had reported their adventure at the Ranger's office. The Ranger was still out on the preserves, but immediately on his return on Saturday morning he read the description of the poacher's appearance and dress, about which last, however, the only remarkable feature was that it was better than a poacher might be expected to possess, and gave an air of respectability to the wearer that might easily disarm suspicion.

"The Ranger made enquiries at all the inns in Sunch'ston, and at length succeeded in hearing of a stranger who appeared to correspond with the poacher whom the Professors had seen; but the man had already left, and though the Ranger did his best to trace him he did not succeed. On Sunday morning, however, he observed the prisoner, and found that he answered the description given by the Professors; he therefore arrested him quietly in the temple, but told him that he should not take him to prison till the service was over. The man said he would come quietly inasmuch as he should easily be able to prove his innocence. In the meantime, however, he professed the utmost anxiety to hear Professor Hanky's sermon, which he said he believed would concern him nearly. The Ranger paid no attention to this, and was as much astounded as the rest of the congregation were, when immediately after one of Professor Hanky's most eloquent passages, the man started up and declared himself to be the Sunchild. On this the Ranger took him away at once, and for the man's own protection hurried him off to prison.

" Professor Hanky was so much shocked at such outrageous conduct, that for the moment he failed to recognize the offender; after a few seconds, however, he grasped the situation, and knew him to be one who on previous occasions, near Bridgeford, had done what he was now doing. It seems that he is notorious in the neighbourhood of Bridgeford, as a monomaniac who is so deeply impressed with the beauty of the Sunchild's character–and we presume also of his own–as to believe that he is himself the Sunchild.

" Recovering almost instantly from the shock the interruption had given him, the learned Professor calmed his hearers by acquainting them with the facts of the case, and continued his sermon to the delight of all who heard it. We should say, however, that the gentleman who twenty years ago instructed the Sunchild in the Erewhonian language, was so struck with some few points of resemblance between the stranger and his former pupil, that he acclaimed him, and was removed forcibly by the vergers.

" On Monday morning the prisoner was brought up before the Mayor. We cannot say whether it was the sobering effect of prison walls, or whether he had been drinking before he entered the temple, and had now had time enough to recover himself–at any rate for some reason or other he was abjectly penitent when his case came on for hearing. The charge of poaching was first gone into, but was immediately disposed of by the evidence of the two Professors, who stated that the prisoner bore no resemblance to the poacher they had seen, save that he was about the same height and age, and was respectably dressed.

" The charge of disturbing the congregation by declaring himself the Sunchild was then proceeded with, and unnecessary as it may appear to be, it was thought advisable to prevent all possibility of the man's assertion being accepted by the ignorant as true, at some later date, when those who could prove its falsehood were no longer living. The prisoner, therefore, was removed to his cell, and there measured by the Master of the Gaol, and the Ranger in the presence of the Mayor, who attested the accuracy of the measurements. Not one single one of them corresponded with those recorded of the Sunchild himself, and a few marks such as moles, and permanent scars on the Sunchild's body were not found on the prisoner's. Furthermore the prisoner was shaggy-breasted, with much coarse jet black hair on the fore-arms and from the knees downwards, whereas the Sunchild had little hair save on his head, and what little there was, was fine, and very light in colour.

" Confronted with these discrepancies, the gentleman who had taught the Sunchild our language was convinced of his mistake, though he still maintained that there was some superficial likeness between his former pupil and the prisoner. Here he was confirmed by the Master of the Gaol, the Mayoress, Mrs. Humdrum, and Professors Hanky and Panky, who all of them could see what the interpreter meant, but denied that the prisoner could be mistaken for the Sunchild for more than a few seconds. No doubt the prisoner's unhappy delusion has been fostered, if not entirely caused, by his having been repeatedly told that he was like the Sunchild. The celebrated Dr. Downie, who well remembers the Sunchild, was also examined, and gave his evidence with so much convincing detail as to make it unnecessary to call further witnesses.

" It having been thus once for all officially and authoritatively placed on record that the prisoner was not the Sunchild, Professors Hanky and Panky then identified him as a well-known monomaniac on the subject of Sunchildism, who in other respects was harmless. We withhold his name and place of abode, out of consideration for the well-known and highly respectable family to which he belongs. The prisoner admitted with much contrition that he had made a disturbance in the temple, but pleaded that he had been carried away by the eloquence of Professor Hanky; he promised to avoid all like offence in future, and threw himself on the mercy of the court.

"The Mayor, unwilling that Sunday's memorable ceremony should be the occasion of a serious punishment to any of those who took part in it, reprimanded the prisoner in a few severe but not unkindly words, inflicted a fine of forty shillings, and ordered that the prisoner should be taken directly to the temple, where he should confess his folly to the Manager and Head Cashier, and confirm his words by kissing the reliquary in which the newly found relic has been placed. The prisoner being unable to pay the fine, some of the ladies and gentlemen in court kindly raised the amount amongst them, in pity for the poor creature's obvious contrition, rather than see him sent to prison for a month in default of payment.

"The prisoner was then conducted to the temple, followed by a considerable number of people. Strange to say, in spite of the overwhelming evidence that they had just heard, some few among the followers, whose love of the marvellous overpowered their reason, still maintained that the prisoner was the Sunchild. Nothing could be more decorous than the prisoner's behaviour when, after hearing the recantation that was read out to him by the Manager, he signed the document with his name and address, which we again withhold, and kissed the reliquary in confirmation of his words.

"The Mayor then declared the prisoner to be at

liberty. When he had done so he said, 'I strongly urge you to place yourself under my protection for the present, that you may be freed from the impertinent folly and curiosity of some whose infatuation might lead you from that better mind to which I believe you are now happily restored. I wish you to remain for some few hours secluded in the privacy of my own study, where Dr. Downie and the two excellent Professors will administer that ghostly counsel to you, which will be likely to protect you from any return of your unhappy delusion.'

"The man humbly bowed assent, and was taken by the Mayor's younger sons to the Mayor's own house, where he was duly cared for. About midnight, when all was quiet, he was conducted to the outskirts of the town towards Clearwater, and furnished with enough money to provide for his more pressing necessities till he could reach some relatives who reside three or four days' walk down on the road towards the capital. He desired the man who accompanied him to repeat to the Mayor his heartfelt thanks for the forbearance and generosity with which he had been treated. The remembrance of this, he said, should be ever present with him, and he was confident would protect him if his unhappy monomania showed any signs of returning.

"Let us now, however, remind our readers that the poacher who threatened Professors Hanky and Panky on Thursday evening last is still at large. He is evidently a man of desperate character, and it is to be hoped that our fellow-citizens will give immediate information at the Ranger's office if they see any stranger in the neighbourhood of the preserves whom they may have reasonable grounds for suspecting.

"*P.S.*–As we are on the point of going to press we learn that a dangerous lunatic, who has been for some years confined in the Clearwater asylum, succeeded in escaping on the night of Wednesday last, and it is surmised with much probability, that this was the man who threatened the two Professors on Thursday evening. His being alone, his having dared to light a fire, probably to cook quails which he had been driven to kill from stress of hunger, the respectability of his dress, and the fury with which he would have attacked the two Professors single-handed, but for Professor Hanky's presence of mind in giving him a knock-down blow, all point in the direction of thinking that he was no true poacher, but, what is even more dangerous–a madman at large. We have not received any particulars as to the man's appearance, nor the clothes he was wearing, but we have little doubt that these will confirm the surmise to which we now give publicity. If it is correct it becomes doubly incumbent on all our fellow-citizens to be both on the watch and on their guard.

" We may add that the man was fully believed to have taken the direction towards the capital; hence no attempts were made to look for him in the neighbourhood of Sunch'ston, until news of the threatened attack on the Professors led the keeper of the asylum to feel confident that he had hitherto been on a wrong scent."

CHAPTER TWENTY-THREE: MY FATHER IS ESCORTED TO THE MAYOR'S HOUSE, AND IS INTRODUCED TO A FUTURE DAUGHTER-IN-LAW

MY FATHER SAID HE WAS FOLLOWED to the Mayor's house by a good many people, whom the Mayor's sons in vain tried to get rid of. One or two of these still persisted in saying he was the Sunchild–whereon another said, "But his hair is black."

"Yes," was the answer, "but a man can dye his hair, can he not? look at his blue eyes and his eyelashes?"

My father was doubting whether he ought not to again deny his identity out of loyalty to the Mayor and Yram, when George's next brother said, "Pay no attention to them, but step out as fast as you can." This settled the matter, and in a few minutes they were at the Mayor's, where the young men took him into the study; the elder said with a smile, "We should like to stay and talk to you, but my mother said we were not to do so." Whereon they left him much to his regret, but he gathered rightly that they had not been officially told who he was, and were to be left to think what they liked, at any rate for the present.

In a few minutes the Mayor entered, and going straight up to my father shook him cordially by the hand.

"I have brought you this morning's paper," said he. "You will find a full report of Professor Hanky's sermon, and of the speeches at last night's banquet. You see they pass over your little interruption with hardly a word, but I dare say they will have made up their minds about it all by Thursday's issue."

He laughed as he produced the paper–which my father brought home with him, and without which I should not have been able to report Hanky's sermon as fully as I have done. But my father could not let things pass over thus lightly.

"I thank you," he said, "but I have much more to thank you for, and know not how to do it."

"Can you not trust me to take everything as said?"

"Yes, but I cannot trust myself not to be haunted if I do not say–or at any rate try to say–some part of what I ought to say."

"Very well; then I will say something myself. I have a small joke, the only one I ever made, which I inflict periodically upon my wife. You, and I suppose George, are the only two other people in the world to whom it can ever be told; let me see, then, if I cannot break the ice with it. It is this. Some men have twin sons; George in this topsy-turvy world of ours has twin fathers–you by luck, and me by cunning. I see you smile; give me your hand."

My father took the Mayor's hand between both his own. "Had I been in your place," he said, "I should be glad to hope that I might have done as you did."

"And I," said the Mayor, more readily than might have been expected of him, "fear that if I had been in yours–I should have made it the proper thing for you to do. There! The ice is well broken, and now for business. You will lunch with us, and dine in the evening. I have given it out that you are of good family, so there is nothing odd in this. At lunch you will not be the Sunchild, for my younger children will be there; at dinner all present will know who you are, so we shall be free as soon as the servants are out of the room.

"I am sorry, but I must send you away with George as soon as the streets are empty–say at midnight–for the excitement is too great to allow of your staying longer. We must keep your rug and the things you cook with, but my wife will find you what will serve your turn. There is no moon, so you and George will camp out as soon as you get well on to the preserves; the weather is hot, and you will neither of you take any harm. To-morrow by mid-day you will be at the statues, where George must bid you good-bye, for he must be at Sunch'ston to-morrow night. You will doubtless get safely home; I wish with all my heart that I could hear of your having done so, but this, I fear, may not be."

"So be it," replied my father, "but there is something I should yet say. The Mayoress has no doubt told you of some gold, coined and uncoined, that I am leaving for George. She will also have told you that I am rich; this being so, I should have brought him much more, if I had known that there was any such person. You have other children; if you leave him anything, you will be taking it away from your own flesh and blood; if you leave him nothing, it will be a slur upon him. I must therefore send you enough gold to provide for George as your other children will be provided for; you can settle it upon him at once, and make it clear that the settlement is instead of provision for him by will. The difficulty is in the getting the gold into Erewhon, and until it is actually here, he must know nothing about it."

I have no space for the discussion that followed. In the end it was settled that George was to have £2000 in gold, which the Mayor declared to be too much, and my father too little. Both, however, were agreed that Erewhon would before long be compelled to enter into relations with foreign countries, in which case the value of gold would decline so much as to make £2000 worth little more than it would be in England. The Mayor proposed to buy land with it, which he would hand over to George as a gift from himself, and this my father at once acceded to. All sorts of questions such as will occur to the reader were raised and settled, but I must beg him to be content with knowing that everything was arranged with the good sense that two such men were sure to bring to bear upon it.

The getting the gold into Erewhon was to be managed thus. George was to know nothing, but a promise was to be got from him that at noon on the following New Year's day, or whatever day might be agreed upon, he would be at the statues, where either my father or myself would meet him, spend a couple of hours with him, and then return. Whoever met George was to bring the gold as though it were for the Mayor, and George could be trusted to be human enough to bring it down, when he saw that it would be left where it was if he did not do so.

" He will kick a good deal," said the Mayor, " at first, but he will come round in the end."

Luncheon was now announced. My father was feeling faint and ill; more than once during the forenoon he had had a return of the strange giddiness and momentary loss of memory which had already twice attacked him, but he had recovered in each case so quickly that no one had seen he was unwell. He, poor man, did not yet know what serious brain exhaustion these attacks betokened, and finding himself in his usual health as soon as they passed away, set them down as simply effects of fatigue and undue excitement.

George did not lunch with the others. Yram explained that he had to draw up a report which would occupy him till dinner time. Her three other sons, and her three lovely daughters, were there. My father was delighted with all of them, for they made friends with him at once. He had feared that he would have been disgraced in their eyes by his having just come from prison, but whatever they may have thought, no trace of anything but a little engaging timidity on the girls' part was to be seen. The two elder boys–or rather young men, for they seemed fully grown, though, like George, not yet bearded–treated him as already an old acquaintance, while the youngest, a lad of fourteen, walked straight up to him, put out his hand, and said, "How do you do, sir?" with a pretty blush that went straight to my father's heart.

"These boys," he said to Yram aside, "who have nothing to blush for–see how the blood mantles into their young cheeks, while I, who should blush at being spoken to by them, cannot do so."

"Do not talk nonsense," said Yram, with mock severity.

But it was no nonsense to my poor father. He was awed at the goodness and beauty with which he found himself surrounded. His thoughts were too full of what had been, what was, and what was yet to be, to let him devote himself to these young people as he would dearly have liked to do. He could only look at them, wonder at them, fall in love with them, and thank heaven that George had been brought up in such a household.

When luncheon was over, Yram said, "I will now send you to a room where you can lie down and go to sleep for a few hours. You will be out late to-night, and had better rest while you can. Do you remember the drink you taught us to make of corn parched and ground? You used to say you liked it. A cup shall be brought to your room at about five, for you must try and sleep till then. If you notice a little box on the dressing-table of your room, you will open it or no as you like. About half-past five there will be a visitor, whose name you can guess, but I shall not let her stay long with you. Here comes the servant to take you to your room." On this she smiled, and turned somewhat hurriedly away.

My father on reaching his room went to the dressing-table, where he saw a small unpretending box, which he immediately opened. On the top was a paper with the words, "Look–say nothing–forget." Beneath this was some cotton wool, and then–the two buttons and the lock of his own hair that he had given Yram when he said good-bye to her.

The ghost of the lock that Yram had then given him rose from the dead, and smote him as with a whip across the face. On what dust-heap had it not been thrown how many long years ago? Then she had never forgotten him? To have been remembered all these years by such a woman as that, and never to have heeded it—never to have found out what she was though he had seen her day after day for months. Ah! but she was then still budding. That was no excuse. If a loveable woman—aye, or any woman—has loved a man, even though he cannot marry her, or wish to do so, at any rate let him not forget her—and he had forgotten Yram as completely, until the last few days, as though he had never seen her. He took her little missive, and under "Look," he wrote, "I have;" under "say nothing," "I will;" under "forget," "never." "And I never shall," he said to himself, as he replaced the box upon the table. He then lay down to rest upon the bed, but he could get no sleep.

When the servant brought him his imitation coffee—an imitation so successful that Yram made him a packet of it to replace the tea that he must leave behind him—he rose and presently came downstairs into the drawing-room, where he found Yram and Mrs. Humdrum's grand-daughter, of whom I will say nothing, for I have never seen her, and know nothing about her, except that my father found her a sweet-looking girl, of graceful figure and very attractive expression. He was quite happy about her, but she was too young and shy to make it possible for him to do more than admire her appearance, and take Yram's word for it that she was as good as she looked.

CHAPTER TWENTY-FOUR: AFTER DINNER, DR. DOWNIE AND THE PROFESSORS WOULD BE GLAD TO KNOW WHAT IS TO BE DONE ABOUT SUNCHILDISM

IT WAS ABOUT SIX WHEN GEORGE'S *fiancée* left the house, and as soon as she had done so, Yram began to see about the rug and the best substitutes she could find for the billy and pannikin. She had a basket packed with all that my father and George would want to eat and drink while on the preserves, and enough of everything, except meat, to keep my father going till he could reach the shepherd's hut of which I have already spoken. Meat would not keep, and my father could get plenty of flappers—*i.e.* ducks that cannot yet fly—when he was on the river-bed down below.

The above preparations had not been made very long, before Mrs. Humdrum arrived, followed presently by Dr. Downie and in due course by the Professors, who were still staying in the house. My father remembered Mrs. Humdrum's good honest face, but could not bring Dr. Downie to his recollection till the Doctor told him when and where they had met, and then he could only very uncertainly recall him, though he vowed that he could now do so perfectly well.

"At any rate," said Hanky, advancing towards him with his best Bridgeford manner, "you will not have forgotten meeting my brother Professor and myself."

"It has been rather a forgetting sort of a morning," said my father demurely, "but I can remember that much, and am delighted to renew my acquaintance with both of you."

As he spoke he shook hands with both Professors.

George was a little late, but when he came, dinner was announced. My father sat on Yram's right hand, Dr. Downie on her left. George was next my father, with Mrs. Humdrum opposite to him. The Professors sat one on either side of the Mayor. During dinner the conversation turned almost entirely on my father's flight, his narrow escape from drowning, and his adventures on his return to England; about these last my father was very reticent, for he said nothing about his book, and antedated his accession of wealth by some fifteen years, but as he walked up towards the statues with George he told him everything.

My father repeatedly tried to turn the conversation from himself, but Mrs. Humdrum and Yram wanted to know about Nna Haras, as they persisted in calling my mother–how she endured her terrible experiences in the balloon, when she and my father were married, all about my unworthy self, and England generally. No matter how often he began to ask questions about the Nosnibors and other old acquaintances, both the ladies soon went back to his own adventures. He succeeded, however, in learning that Mr. Nosnibor was dead, and Zulora, an old maid of the most unattractive kind, who had persistently refused to accept Sunchildism, while Mrs. Nosnibor was the recipient of honours hardly inferior to those conferred by the people at large on my father and mother, with whom, indeed, she believed herself to have frequent interviews by way of visionary revelations. So intolerable were these revelations to Zulora, that a separate establishment had been provided for her. George said to my father quietly–" Do you know I begin to think that Zulora must be rather a nice person."

" Perhaps," said my father grimly, " but my wife and I did not find it out."

When the ladies left the room, Dr. Downie took Yram's seat, and Hanky Dr. Downie's; the Mayor took Mrs. Humdrum's, leaving my father, George, and Panky in their old places. Almost immediately, Dr. Downie said, " And now, Mr. Higgs, tell us, as a man of the world, what we are to do about Sunchildism ? "

My father smiled at this. " You know, my dear sir,

as well as I do, that the proper thing would be to put me back in prison, and keep me there till you can send me down to the capital. You should eat your oaths of this morning, as I would eat mine; tell every one here who I am; let them see that my hair has been dyed; get all who knew me when I was here before to come and see me; appoint an unimpeachable committee to examine the record of my marks and measurements, and compare it with those of my own body. You should let me be seen in every town at which I lodged on my way down, and tell people that you had made a mistake. When you get to the capital, hand me over to the King's tender mercies and say that our oaths were only taken this morning to prevent a ferment in the town. I will play my part very willingly. The King can only kill me, and I should die like a gentleman."

"They will not do it," said George quietly to my father, "and I am glad of it."

He was right. "This," said Dr. Downie, "is a counsel of perfection. Things have gone too far, and we are flesh and blood. What would those who in your country come nearest to us Musical Bank Managers do, if they found they had made such a mistake as we have, and dared not own it?"

"Do not ask me," said my father; "the story is too long, and too terrible."

"At any rate, then, tell us what you would have us do that is within our reach."

"I have done you harm enough, and if I preach, as likely as not I shall do more."

Seeing, however, that Dr. Downie was anxious to hear what he thought, my father said:

"Then I must tell you. Our religion sets before us an ideal which we all cordially accept, but it also tells us of marvels like your chariot and horses, which we most of us reject. Our best teachers insist on the ideal, and keep the marvels in the background. If they could say outright that our age has outgrown them, they would say so, but this they may not do; nevertheless they contrive to let their opinions be sufficiently well known, and their hearers are content with this.

"We have others who take a very different course, but of these I will not speak. Roughly, then, if you cannot abolish me altogether, make me a peg on which to hang all your own best ethical and spiritual conceptions. If you will do this, and wriggle out of that wretched relic, with that not less wretched picture–if you will make me out to be much better and abler than I was, or ever shall be, Sunchildism may serve your turn for many a long year to come. Otherwise it will tumble about your heads before you think it will.

"Am I to go on or stop?"

"Go on," said George softly. That was enough for my father, so on he went.

"You are already doing part of what I wish. I was delighted with the two passages I heard on Sunday, from what you call the Sunchild's Sayings. I never said a word of either passage; I wish I had; I wish I could say anything half so good. And I have read a pamphlet by President Gurgoyle, which I liked extremely; but I never said what he says I did. Again, I wish I had. Keep to this sort of thing, and I will be as good a Sunchildist as any of you. But you must bribe some thief to steal that relic, and break it up to mend the roads with; and–for I believe that here as elsewhere fires sometimes get lighted through the carelessness of a workman–set the most careless workman you can find to do a plumbing job near that picture."

Hanky looked black at this, and George trod lightly on my father's toe, but he told me that my father's face was innocence itself.

"These are hard sayings," said Dr. Downie.

"I know they are," replied my father, "and I do not like saying them, but there is no royal road to unlearning, and you have much to unlearn. Still, you Musical Bank people bear witness to the fact that beyond the kingdoms of this world there is another, within which the writs of this world's kingdoms do not run. This is the great service which our church does for us in England, and hence many of us uphold it, though we have no sympathy with the party now dominant within it. 'Better,' we think, 'a corrupt church than none at all.' Moreover, those who in my country would step into the church's shoes are as corrupt as the church, and more exacting. They are also more dangerous, for the masses distrust the church, and are on their guard against aggression, whereas they do not suspect the doctrinaires and faddists, who, if they could, would interfere in every concern of our lives.

"Let me return to yourselves. You Musical Bank Managers are very much such a body of men as your country needs–but when I was here before you had no figurehead; I have unwittingly supplied you with one, and it is perhaps because you saw this, that you good people of Bridgeford took up with me. Sunchildism is still young and plastic; if you will let the cock-and-bull stories about me tacitly drop, and invent no new ones, beyond saying what a delightful person I was, I really cannot see why I should not do for you as well as any one else.

"There. What I have said is nine-tenths of it rotten and wrong, but it is the most practicable rotten and wrong that I can suggest, seeing into what a rotten and wrong state of things you have drifted. And now, Mr. Mayor, do you not think we may join the Mayoress and Mrs. Humdrum?"

"As you please, Mr. Higgs," answered the Mayor.

"Then let us go, for I have said too much already,

and your son George tells me that we must be starting shortly."

As they were leaving the room Panky sidled up to my father and said, " There is a point, Mr. Higgs, which you can settle for me, though I feel pretty certain how you will settle it. I think that a corruption has crept into the text of the very beautiful—"

At this moment, as my father, who saw what was coming, was wondering what in the world he could say, George came up to him and said, " Mr. Higgs, my mother wishes me to take you down into the store-room, to make sure that she has put everything for you as you would like it." On this my father said he would return directly and answer what he knew would be Panky's question.

When Yram had shown what she had prepared–all of it, of course, faultless–she said, " And now, Mr. Higgs, about our leave-taking. Of course we shall both of us feel much. I shall; I know you will; George will have a few more hours with you than the rest of us, but his time to say good-bye will come, and it will be painful to both of you. I am glad you came–I am glad you have seen George, and George you, and that you took to one another. I am glad my husband has seen you; he has spoken to me about you very warmly, for he has taken to you much as George did. I am very, very glad to have seen you myself, and to have learned what became of you–and of your wife. I know you wish well to all of us; be sure that we all of us wish most heartily well to you and yours. I sent for you and George, because I could not say all this unless we were alone; it is all I can do," she said, with a smile, " to say it now."

Indeed it was, for the tears were in her eyes all the time, as they were also in my father's.

" Let this," continued Yram, " be our leave-taking–

for we must have nothing like a scene upstairs. Just shake hands with us all, say the usual conventional things, and make it as short as you can; but I could not bear to send you away without a few warmer words than I could have said when others were in the room."

"May heaven bless you and yours," said my father, "for ever and ever."

"That will do," said George gently. "Now, both of you shake hands, and come upstairs with me."

*

When all three of them had got calm, for George had been moved almost as much as his father and mother, they went upstairs, and Panky came for his answer. "You are very possibly right," said my father—"the version you hold to be corrupt is the one in common use amongst ourselves, but it is only a translation, and very possibly only a translation of a translation, so that it may perhaps have been corrupted before it reached us."

"That," said Panky, "will explain everything," and he went contentedly away.

My father talked a little aside with Mrs. Humdrum about her grand-daughter and George, for Yram had told him that she knew all about the attachment, and then George, who saw that my father found the greatest difficulty in maintaining an outward calm, said, "Mr. Higgs, the streets are empty; we had better go."

My father did as Yram had told him; shook hands with every one, said all that was usual and proper as briefly as he could, and followed George out of the room. The Mayor saw them to the door, and saved my father from embarrassment by saying, "Mr. Higgs, you and I understand one another too well to make it necessary for us to say so. Good-bye to you, and may no ill befall you ere you get home."

My father grasped his hand in both his own. " Again," he said, " I can say no more than that I thank you from the bottom of my heart."

As he spoke he bowed his head, and went out with George into the night.

CHAPTER TWENTY-FIVE: GEORGE ESCORTS MY FATHER TO THE STATUES, THE TWO THEN PART

THE STREETS WERE QUITE DESERTED AS George had said they would be, and very dark, save for an occasional oil lamp.

"As soon as we can get within the preserves," said George, "we had better wait till morning. I have a rug for myself as well as for you."

"I saw you had two," answered my father; "you must let me carry them both; the provisions are much the heavier load."

George fought as hard as a dog would do, till my father said that they must not quarrel during the very short time they had to be together. On this George gave up one rug meekly enough, and my father yielded about the basket and the other rug.

It was about half-past eleven when they started, and it was after one before they reached the preserves. For the first mile from the town they were not much hindered by the darkness, and my father told George about his book and many another matter; he also promised George to say nothing about this second visit. Then the road became more rough, and when it dwindled away to be a mere lane–becoming presently only a foot track–they had to mind their footsteps, and got on but slowly. The night was starlit, and warm, considering that they were more than three thousand feet above the sea, but it was very dark, so that my father was well enough pleased when George showed him the white stones that marked the boundary, and said they had better soon make themselves as comfortable as they could till morning.

"We can stay here," he said, "till half-past three, there will be a little daylight then; we will rest half an hour for breakfast at about five, and by noon we shall be at the statues, where we will dine."

This being settled, George rolled himself up in his rug, and in a few minutes went comfortably off to sleep.

Not so my poor father. He wound up his watch, wrapped his rug round him, and lay down; but he could get no sleep. After such a day, and such an evening, how could any one have slept?

About three the first signs of dawn began to show, and half an hour later my father could see the sleeping face of his son–whom it went to his heart to wake. Nevertheless he woke him, and in a few minutes the two were on their way–George as fresh as a lark–my poor father intent on nothing so much as on hiding from George how ill and unsound in body and mind he was feeling.

They walked on, saying but little, till at five by my father's watch George proposed a halt for breakfast. The spot he chose was a grassy oasis among the trees, carpeted with subalpine flowers, now in their fullest beauty, and close to a small stream that here came down from a side valley. The freshness of the morning air, the extreme beauty of the place, the lovely birds that flitted from tree to tree, the exquisite shapes and colours of the flowers, still dew-bespangled, and above all, the tenderness with which George treated him, soothed my father, and when he and George had lit a fire and made some hot corn-coffee–with a view to which Yram had put up a bottle of milk–he felt so much restored as to look forward to the rest of his journey without alarm. Moreover he had nothing to carry, for George had left his own rug at the place where they had slept, knowing that he should find it on his return; he had therefore insisted on carrying my father's. My father fought as long as he could, but he had to give in.

"Now tell me," said George, glad to change the subject, "what will those three men do about what you said to them last night? Will they pay any attention to it?"

My father laughed. "My dear George, what a question–I do not know them well enough."

"Oh yes, you do. At any rate say what you think most likely."

"Very well. I think Dr. Downie will do much as I said. He will not throw the whole thing over, through fear of schism, loyalty to a party from which he cannot well detach himself, and because he does not think that the public is quite tired enough of its toy. He will neither preach nor write against it, but he will live lukewarmly against it, and this is what the Hankys hate. They can stand either hot or cold, but they are afraid of lukewarm. In England Dr. Downie would be a Broad Churchman."

"Do you think we shall ever get rid of Sunchildism altogether?"

"If they stick to the cock-and-bull stories they are telling now, and rub them in, as Hanky did on Sunday, it may go, and go soon. It has taken root too quickly and easily; and its top is too heavy for its roots; still there are so many chances in its favour that it may last a long time."

"And how about Hanky?"

"He will brazen it out, relic, chariot, and all: and he will welcome more relics and more cock-and-bull stories; his single eye will be upon his own aggrandisement and that of his order. Plausible, unscrupulous, heartless scoundrel that he is, he will play for the queen and the women of the court, as Dr. Downie will play for the king and the men. He and his party will sleep neither night nor day, but they will have one redeeming feature – whoever they may deceive, they will not deceive themselves. They believe every one else to be as bad as they are, and see no reason why they should not push their own wares in the way of business. Hanky is everything that we in England rightly or wrongly believe a typical Jesuit to be."

"And Panky – what about him?"

"Panky must persuade himself of his own lies, before he is quite comfortable about telling them to other people. Hanky keeps Hanky well out of it; Panky must have a base of operations in Panky. Hanky will lead him by the nose, bit by bit, for his is the master spirit. In England Panky would be what we call an extreme ritualist."

"Then the real battle will be between Hanky and Dr. Downie. Which will carry the day?"

"For the present, probably Hanky. He is the more vigilant and energetic; in this case Sunchildism will have to go, and I am afraid your whole Musical Bank system will be swept away along with it."

"And why not?"

"Because, my dear boy, though false in the letter, if good counsels prevail, it may be made true enough in spirit. If it were to go, its place would be soon filled by men who would be as false in letter as the others were, and much more false in spirit. You want a heart to check your head, and a head to check your heart. As in our English body politic there are two parties opposed to one another, neither of which can thrive if the other is unduly weakened, so in our spiritual and intellectual world two parties more or less antagonistic are equally necessary. Those who are at the head of science provide us with the one party; those whom we call our churchmen are the other. Both are corrupt, but we can spare neither, for each checks as far as it can the corruptions of the other."

"Then you would have us uphold Sunchildism, knowing it to be untrue?"

"Do what you will, you will not get perfect truth. And if you can follow the lead which I believe Dr. Downie will give you, that is to say, get rid of cock-and-bull stories, idealize my unworthy self, and, as I said last night, make me a peg on which to hang your own best thoughts – Sunchildism will be as near truth as anything you are likely to get. But if Hankyism triumphs, come what may you must get rid of it, for he and his school will tamper with the one sure and everlasting word of God revealed to us by human experience. He who plays fast and loose with this is as one who would forge God's signature to a cheque drawn on God's own bank."

"Are we to foster the belief that it was indeed the Sunchild who interrupted Hanky's sermon?"

"Yes, where you safely can, but not otherwise; and commit the facts to writing as soon as you can find time. Do nothing to jeopardize your own safety; you can do more by perfunctory acquiescence than by open dissent. And tell those friends whom you can trust what these my parting words to you have been. But above all I charge you solemnly, do nothing to jeopardize your own safety; you cannot play into Hanky's hands more certainly than by risking this. Think how he and Panky would rejoice, and how Dr. Downie would grieve. Be wise and wary; bide your time; do what you prudently can, and you will find you can do much; try to do more, and you will do nothing. Be guided by the Mayor, by your mother – and by that dear old lady whose grandson you will—"

"Then they have told you," interrupted the youth blushing scarlet.

"My dearest boy, of course they have, and I have seen her, and am head over ears in love with her myself."

He was all smiles and blushes, and vowed for a few minutes that it was a shame of them to tell my father, but presently he said:

"Then you like her."

"Rather!" said my father vehemently, and shaking George by the hand. But he said nothing about the nuggets and the sovereigns, knowing that Yram did not wish him to do so. Neither did George say anything about his determination to start for the capital in the morning, and make a clean breast of everything to the King. So soon does it become necessary even for those who are most cordially attached to hide things from one another. My father, however, was made comfortable by receiving a promise from the youth that he would take no step of which the persons he had named would disapprove.

When once Mrs. Humdrum's grand-daughter had been introduced there was no more talking about Hanky and Panky; for George began to bubble over with the subject that was nearest his heart, and how much he feared that it would be some time yet before he could be married. Many a story did he tell of his early attachment and of its course for the last ten years, but my space will not allow me to inflict one of them on the reader. My father saw that the more he listened and sympathized and encouraged, the fonder George became of him, and this was all he cared about.

Thus did they converse hour after hour. They passed the Blue Pool, without seeing it or even talking about it for more than a minute. George kept an eye on the quails and declared them fairly plentiful and strong on the wing, but nothing now could keep him from pouring out his whole heart about Mrs. Humdrum's grand-daughter, until towards noon they caught sight of the statues, and a halt was made which gave my father the first pang he had felt that morning, for he knew that the statues would be the beginning of the end.

There was no need to light a fire, for Yram had packed for them two bottles of a delicious white wine, something like White Capri, which went admirably with the many more solid good things that she had provided for them. As soon as they had finished a hearty meal my father said to George, " You must have my watch for a keepsake; I see you are not wearing my boots. I fear you did not find them comfortable, but I am glad you have not got them on, for I have set my heart on keeping yours."

"Let us settle about the boots first. I rather fancied that that was why you put me off when I wanted to get my own back again; and then I thought I should like yours for a keepsake, so I put on another pair last night, and they are nothing like so comfortable as yours were."

"Now I wonder," said my father to me, "whether this was true, or whether it was only that dear fellow's pretty invention; but true or false I was as delighted as he meant me to be."

I asked George about this when I saw him, and he confessed with an ingenuous blush that my father's boots had hurt him, and that he had never thought of making a keepsake of them, till my father's words stimulated his invention.

As for the watch, which was only a silver one, but of the best make, George protested for a time, but when he had yielded, my father could see that he was overjoyed at getting it; for watches, though now permitted, were expensive and not in common use.

Having thus bribed him, my father broached the possibility of his meeting him at the statues on that day twelvemonth, but of course saying nothing about why he was so anxious that he should come.

"I will come," said my father, "not a yard farther than the statues, and if I cannot come I will send your brother. And I will come at noon; but it is possible that the river down below may be in fresh, and I may not be able to hit off the day, though I will move heaven and earth to do so. Therefore if I do not meet you on the day appointed, do your best to come also at noon on the following day. I know how inconvenient this will be for you, and will come true to the day if it is possible."

To my father's surprise, George did not raise so many difficulties as he had expected. He said it might be done, if neither he nor my father were to go beyond the statues. "And difficult as it will be for you," said George, "you had better come a second day if necessary, as I will, for who can tell what might happen to make the first day impossible?"

"Then," said my father, "we shall be spared that horrible feeling that we are parting without hope of seeing each other again. I find it hard enough to say good-bye even now, but I do not know how I could have faced it if you had not agreed to our meeting again."

"The day fixed upon will be our XXI. i. 3, and the hour noon as near as may be?"

"So. Let me write it down: 'XXI. i. 3, *i.e.* our 9th December 1891, I am to meet George at the statues, at twelve o'clock, and if he does not come, I am to be there again on the following day.'"

In like manner, George wrote down what he was to do: "XXI. i. 3, or failing this XXI. i. 4. Statues. Noon."

"This," he said, "is a solemn covenant, is it not?"

"Yes," said my father, "and may all good omens attend it!"

The words were not out of his mouth before a mountain bird, something like our jackdaw, but smaller and of a bluer black, flew out of the hollow mouth of one of the statues, and with a hearty chuckle perched on the ground at his feet, attracted doubtless by the scraps of food that were lying about. With the fearlessness of birds in that country, it looked up at him and George, gave another hearty chuckle, and flew back to its statue with the largest fragment it could find.

They settled that this was an omen so propitious that they could part in good hope. "Let us finish the wine," said my father, "and then, do what must be done."

They finished the wine to each other's good health;

George drank also to mine, and said he hoped my father would bring me with him, while my father drank to Yram, the Mayor, their children, Mrs. Humdrum, and above all to Mrs. Humdrum's grand-daughter. They then re-packed all that could be taken away; my father rolled his rug to his liking, slung it over his shoulder, gripped George's hand, and said, " My dearest boy, when we have each turned our backs upon one another, let us walk our several ways as fast as we can, and try not to look behind us."

So saying he loosed his grip of George's hand, bared his head, lowered it, and turned away.

George burst into tears, and followed him after he had gone two paces; he threw his arms round him, hugged him, kissed him on his lips, cheeks, and forehead, and then turning round, strode full speed towards Sunch'ston. My father never took his eyes off him till he was out of sight, but the boy did not look round. When he could see him no more, my father with faltering gait, and feeling as though a prop had suddenly been taken from under him, began to follow the stream down towards his old camp.

CHAPTER TWENTY-SIX: MY FATHER REACHES HOME, AND DIES NOT LONG AFTERWARDS

MY FATHER COULD WALK BUT SLOWLY, for George's boots had blistered his feet, and it seemed to him that the river-bed, of which he caught glimpses now and again, never got any nearer; but all things come to an end, and by seven o'clock on the night of Tuesday, he was on the spot which he had left on the preceding Friday morning. Three entire days had intervened, but he felt that something, he knew not what, had seized him, and that whereas before these three days life had been one thing, what little might follow them, would be another—and a very different one.

He soon caught sight of his horse which had strayed a mile lower down the river-bed, and in spite of his hobbles had crossed one ugly stream that my father dared not ford on foot. Tired though he was, he went after him, bridle in hand, and when the friendly creature saw him, it recrossed the stream, and came to him of its own accord—either tired of his own company, or tempted by some bread my father held out towards him. My father took off the hobbles, and rode him bare-backed to the camping ground, where he rewarded him with more bread and biscuit, and then hobbled him again for the night.

"It was here," he said to me on one of the first days after his return, "that I first knew myself to be a broken man. As for meeting George again, I felt sure that it would be all I could do to meet his brother; and though George was always in my thoughts, it was for you and not him that I was now yearning. When I gave George my watch, how glad I was that I had left my gold one at home, for that is yours, and I could not have brought myself to give it him."

"Never mind that, my dear father," said I, "but tell me how you got down the river, and thence home again."

"My very dear boy," he said, "I can hardly remember, and I had no energy to make any more notes. I remember putting a scrap of paper into the box of sovereigns, merely sending George my love along with the money; I remember also dropping the box into a hole in a tree, which I blazed, and towards which I drew a line of wood-ashes. I seem to see a poor unhinged creature gazing moodily for hours into a fire which he heaps up now and again with wood. There is not a breath of air. Nature sleeps so calmly that she dares not even breathe for fear of waking; the very river has hushed his flow. Without, the starlit calm of a summer's night in a great wilderness; within, a hurricane of wild and incoherent thoughts battling with one another in their fury to fall upon him and rend him–and on the other side of the great wall of mountain, thousands of children praying at their mother's knee to this poor dazed thing. I suppose this half delirious wretch must have been myself. But I must have been more ill when I left England than I thought I was, or Erewhon would not have broken me down as it did."

No doubt he was right. Indeed it was because Mr. Cathie and his doctor saw that he was out of health and in urgent need of change, that they left off opposing his wish to travel. There is no use, however, in talking about this now.

I never got from him how he managed to reach the shepherd's hut, but I learned some little from the shepherd, when I stayed with him both on going towards Erewhon, and on returning.

"He did not seem to have drink in him," said the shepherd, "when he first came here; but he must have been pretty full of it, or he must have had some bottles in his saddle-bags; for he was awful when he came back. He had got them worse than any man I ever saw, only that he was not awkward. He said there was a bird flying out of a giant's mouth and laughing at him, and he kept muttering about a blue pool, and hanky-panky of all sorts, and he said he knew it was all hanky-panky, at least I thought he said so, but it was no use trying to follow him, for it was all nothing but horrors. He said I was to stop the people from trying to worship him. Then he said the sky opened and he could see the angels going about and singing 'Hallelujah.'"

"How long did he stay with you?" I asked.

"About ten days, but the last three he was himself again, only too weak to move. He thought he was cured except for weakness."

"Do you know how he had been spending the last two days or so before he got down to your hut?"

I said two days, because this was the time I supposed he would take to descend the river.

"I should say drinking all the time. He said he had fallen off his horse two or three times, till he took to leading him. If he had had any other horse than old Doctor he would have been a dead man. Bless you, I have known that horse ever since he was foaled, and I never saw one like him for sense. He would pick fords better than that gentleman could, I know, and if the gentleman fell off him he would just stay stock still. He was badly bruised, poor man, when he got here. I saw him through the gorge when he left me, and he gave me a sovereign; he said he had only one other left to take him down to the port, or he would have made it more."

"He was my father," said I, "and he is dead, but before he died he told me to give you five pounds which I have brought you. I think you are wrong in saying that he had been drinking."

"That is what they all say; but I take it very kind of him to have thought of me."

The Homeward Journey

My father's illness for the first three weeks after his return played with him as a cat plays with a mouse; now and again it would let him have a day or two's run, during which he was so cheerful and unclouded that his doctor was quite hopeful about him. At various times on these occasions I got from him that when he left the shepherd's hut, he thought his illness had run itself out, and that he should now reach the port from which he was to sail for San Francisco without misadventure. This he did, and he was able to do all he had to do at the port, though frequently attacked with passing fits of giddiness. I need not dwell upon his voyage to San Francisco, and thence home; it is enough to say that he was able to travel by himself in spite of gradually, but continually, increasing failure.

"When," he said, "I reached the port, I telegraphed as you know, for more money. How puzzled you must have been. I sold my horse to the man from whom I bought it, at a loss of only about £10, and I left with him my saddle, saddle-bags, small hatchet, my hobbles, and in fact everything that I had taken with me, except what they had impounded in Erewhon. Yram's rug I dropped into the river when I knew that I should no longer need it—as also her substitutes for my billy and pannikin; and I burned her basket. The shepherd would have asked me questions. You will find an order to deliver everything up to bearer. You need therefore take nothing from England."

At another time he said, "When you go, for it is plain I cannot, and go one or other of us must, try and get the horse I had: he will be nine years old, and he knows all about the rivers: if you leave everything to him, you may shut your eyes, but do not interfere with him. Give the shepherd what I said and he will attend to you, but go a day or two too soon, for the margin of one day was not enough to allow in case of a fresh in the river; if the water is discoloured you must not cross it–not even with Doctor. I could not ask George to come up three days running from Sunch'ston to the statues and back."

Here he became exhausted. Almost the last coherent string of sentences I got from him was as follows:

"About George's money if I send him £2000 you will still have nearly £150,000 left, and Mr. Cathie will not let you try to make it more. I know you would give him four or five thousand, but the Mayor and I talked it over, and settled that £2000 in gold would make him a rich man. Consult our good friend Alfred" (meaning, of course, Mr. Cathie) "about the best way of taking the money. I am afraid there is nothing for it but gold, and this will be a great weight for you to carry–about, I believe, 36 lbs. Can you do this? I really think that if you lead your horse you . . . no– there will be the getting him down again—"

"Don't worry about it, my dear father," said I, "I can do it easily if I stow the load rightly, and I will see to this. I shall have nothing else to carry, for I shall camp down below both morning and evening. But would you not like to send some present to the Mayor, Yram, their other children, and Mrs. Humdrum's granddaughter?"

"Do what you can," said my father. And these were the last instructions he gave me about those adventures with which alone this work is concerned.

The day before he died, he had a little flicker of intelligence, but all of a sudden his face became clouded as with great anxiety; he seemed to see some horrible chasm in front of him which he had to cross, or which he feared that I must cross, for he gasped out words, which, as near as I could catch them, were, "Look out! John! Leap! Leap! Le . . ." but he could not say all that he was trying to say and closed his eyes, having, as

I then deemed, seen that he was on the brink of that gulf which lies between life and death; I took it that in reality he died at that moment; for there was neither struggle, nor hardly movement of any kind afterwards—nothing but a pulse which for the next several hours grew fainter and fainter so gradually, that it was not till some time after it had ceased to beat that we were certain of its having done so.

CHAPTER TWENTY-SEVEN: I MEET MY BROTHER GEORGE AT THE STATUES ON THE TOP OF THE PASS INTO EREWHON

THIS BOOK HAS ALREADY BECOME longer than I intended, but I will ask the reader to have patience while I tell him briefly of my own visit to the threshold of that strange country of which I fear that he may be already beginning to tire.

The winding-up of my father's estate was a very simple matter, and by the beginning of September 1891 I should have been free to start; but about that time I became engaged, and naturally enough I did not want to be longer away than was necessary. I should not have gone at all if I could have helped it. I left, however, a fortnight later than my father had done.

Before starting I bought a handsome gold repeater for the Mayor, and a brooch for Yram, of pearls and diamonds set in gold, for which I paid £200. For Yram's three daughters and for Mrs. Humdrum's granddaughter I took four brooches each of which cost about £15 15*s*., and for the boys I got three ten-guinea silver watches. For George I only took a strong English knife of the best make, and the two thousand pounds' worth of uncoined gold, which for convenience' sake I had had made into small bars. I also had a knapsack made that would hold these and nothing else–each bar being strongly sewn into its place, so that none of them could shift. Whenever I went on board ship, or went on shore, I put this on my back, so that no one handled it except myself–and I can assure the reader that I did not find it a light weight to handle. I ought to have taken something for old Mrs. Humdrum, but I am ashamed to say that I forgot her.

I went as directly as I could to the port of which my father had told me, and reached it on 27th November, one day later than he had done in the preceding year.

On the following day, which was a Saturday, I went to the livery stables from which my father had bought his horse, and found to my great delight that Doctor could be at my disposal, for, as it seemed to me, the very reasonable price of fifteen shillings a day. I showed the owner of the stables my father's order, and all the articles he had left were immediately delivered to me. I was still wearing crape round one arm, and the horse-dealer, whose name was Baker, said he was afraid the other gentleman might be dead.

" Indeed, he is so," said I, " and a great grief it is to me; he was my father."

" Dear, dear," answered Mr. Baker, " that is a very serious thing for the poor gentleman. He seemed quite unfit to travel alone, and I feared he was not long for this world, but he was bent on going."

I had nothing now to do but to buy a blanket, pannikin, and billy, with some tea, tobacco, two bottles of brandy, some ship's biscuits, and whatever other few items were down on the list of requisites which my father had dictated to me. Mr. Baker, seeing that I was what he called a new chum, showed me how to pack my horse, but I kept my knapsack full of gold on my back, and though I could see that it puzzled him, he asked no questions. There was no reason why I should not set out at once for the principal town of the colony, which was some ten miles inland; I, therefore, arranged at my hotel that the greater part of my luggage should await my return, and set out to climb the high hills that back the port. From the top of these I had a magnificent view of the plains that I should have to cross, and of the long range of distant mountains which bounded them north and south as far as the eye could reach. On some of the mountains I could still see streaks of snow, but my father had explained to me that the ranges I should see here were not those dividing the English colony from Erewhon. I also saw, some nine miles or so out upon the plains, the more prominent buildings of a large town which seemed to be embosomed in trees, and this I reached in about an hour and a half; for I had to descend at a foot pace, and Doctor's many virtues did not comprise a willingness to go beyond an amble.

At the town above referred to I spent the night, and began to strike across the plains on the following morning. I might have crossed these in three days at twenty-five miles a day, but I had too much time on my hands, and my load of gold was so uncomfortable that I was glad to stay at one accommodation house after another, averaging about eighteen miles a day. I have no doubt that if I had taken advice, I could have stowed my load more conveniently, but I could not unpack it, and made the best of it as it was.

On the evening of Wednesday, 2nd December, I reached the river which I should have to follow up; it was here nearing the gorge through which it had to pass before the country opened out again at the back of the front range. I came upon it quite suddenly on reaching the brink of a great terrace, the bank of which sloped almost precipitously down towards it, but was covered with grass. The terrace was some three hundred feet above the river, and faced another similar one, which was from a mile and a half to two miles distant. At the bottom of this huge yawning chasm, rolled the mighty river, and I shuddered at the thought of having to cross and recross it. For it was angry, muddy, evidently in heavy fresh, and filled bank and bank for nearly a mile with a flood of seething waters.

I followed along the northern edge of the terrace, till I reached the last accommodation house that could be said to be on the plains–which, by the way, were here some eight or nine hundred feet above sea level. When I reached this house, I was glad to learn that the river was not likely to remain high for more than a day or two, and that if what was called a Southerly Burster came up, as it might be expected to do at any moment, it would be quite low again before three days were over.

At this house I stayed the night, and in the course of the evening a stray dog–a retriever, hardly full grown, and evidently very much down on his luck–took up with me; when I inquired about him, and asked if I might take him with me, the landlord said he wished I would, for he knew nothing about him and was trying to drive him from the house. Knowing what a boon the companionship of this poor beast would be to me when I was camping out alone, I encouraged him, and next morning he followed me as a matter of course.

In the night the Southerly Burster which my host anticipated had come up, cold and blustering, but invigorating after the hot, dry wind that had been blowing hard during the daytime as I had crossed the plains. A mile or two higher up I passed a large sheep-station, but did not stay there. One or two men looked at me with surprise, and asked me where I was going, whereon I said I was in search of rare plants and birds for the Museum of the town at which I had slept the night after my arrival. This satisfied their curiosity, and I ambled on accompanied by the dog. In passing I may say that I found Doctor not to excel at any pace except an amble, but for a long journey, especially for one who is carrying a heavy, awkward load, there is no pace so comfortable; and he ambled fairly fast.

I followed the horse track which had been cut through the gorge, and in many places I disliked it extremely, for the river, still in fresh, was raging furiously; twice, for some few yards, where the gorge was wider and the stream less rapid, it covered the track, and I had no confidence that it might not have washed it away; on these occasions Doctor pricked his ears towards the water, and was evidently thinking exactly what his rider was. He decided, however, that all would be sound, and took to the water without any urging on my part. Seeing his opinion, I remembered my father's advice, and let him do what he liked, but in one place for three or four yards the water came nearly up to his belly, and I was in great fear for the watches that were in my saddle-bags. As for the dog, I feared I had lost him, but after a time he rejoined me, though how he contrived to do so I cannot say.

Nothing could be grander than the sight of this great river pent into a narrow compass, and occasionally becoming more like an immense waterfall than a river, but I was in continual fear of coming to more places where the water would be over the track, and perhaps of finding myself unable to get any farther. I therefore failed to enjoy what was really far the most impressive sight in its way that I had ever seen. "Give me," I said to myself, "the Thames at Richmond," and right thankful was I, when at about two o'clock I found that I was through the gorge and in a wide valley, the greater part of which, however, was still covered by the river. It was here that I heard for the first time the curious sound of boulders knocking against each other underneath the great body of water that kept rolling them round and round.

I now halted, and lit a fire, for there was much dead scrub standing that had remained after the ground had been burned for the first time some years previously. I made myself some tea, and turned Doctor out for a couple of hours to feed. I did not hobble him, for my father had told me that he would always come for bread. When I had dined, and smoked, and slept for a couple of hours or so, I reloaded Doctor and resumed my journey towards the shepherd's hut, which I caught sight of about a mile before I reached it. When nearly half a mile off it, I dismounted, and made a written note of the exact spot at which I did so. I then turned for a couple of hundred yards to my right, at right angles to the track, where some huge rocks were lying–fallen ages since from the mountain that flanked this side of the valley. Here I deposited my knapsack in a hollow underneath some of the rocks, and put a good-sized stone in front of it, for I meant spending a couple of days with the shepherd to let the river go down. Moreover, as it was now only 3rd December, I had too much time on my hands, but I had not dared to cut things finer.

I reached the hut at about six o'clock, and introduced myself to the shepherd, who was a nice, kind old man, commonly called Harris, but his real name he told me was Horace–Horace Taylor. I had the conversation with him of which I have already told the reader, adding that my father had been unable to give a coherent account of what he had seen, and that I had been sent to get the information he had failed to furnish.

The old man said that I must certainly wait a couple of days before I went higher up the river. He had made himself a nice garden, in which he took the greatest pride, and which supplied him with plenty of vegetables. He was very glad to have company, and to receive the newspapers which I had taken care to bring him. He had a real genius for simple cookery, and fed me excellently. My father's £5, and the ration of brandy which I nightly gave him, made me a welcome guest, and though I was longing to be at any rate as far as the foot of the pass into Erewhon, I amused myself very well in an abundance of ways with which I need not trouble the reader.

One of the first things that Harris said to me was, "I wish I knew what your father did with the nice red blanket he had with him when he went up the river. He had none when he came down again; I have no horse here, but I borrowed one from a man who came up one day from down below, and rode to a place where I found what I am sure were the ashes of the last fire he made, but I could find neither the blanket nor the billy and pannikin he took away with him. He said he supposed he must have left the things there, but he could remember nothing about it."

"I am afraid," said I, "that I cannot help you."

"At any rate," continued the shepherd, "I did not have my ride for nothing, for as I was coming back I found this rug half covered with sand on the river-bed."

As he spoke he pointed to an excellent warm rug, on the spare bunk in his hut. "It is none of our make," said he; "I suppose some foreign digger has come over from the next river down south and got drowned, for it had not been very long where I found it, at least I think not, for it was not much fly-blown, and no one had passed here to go up the river since your father."

I knew what it was, but I held my tongue beyond saying that the rug was a very good one.

The next day, 4th December, was lovely, after a night that had been clear and cold, with frost towards early morning. When the shepherd had gone for some three hours in the forenoon to see his sheep (that were now lambing), I walked down to the place where I had left my knapsack, and carried it a good mile above the hut, where I again hid it. I could see the great range from one place, and the thick new-fallen snow assured me that the river would be quite normal shortly. Indeed, by evening it was hardly at all discoloured, but I waited another day, and set out on the morning of Sunday, 6th December. The river was now almost as low as in winter, and Harris assured me that if I used my eyes I could not miss finding a ford over one stream or another every half mile or so. I had the greatest difficulty in preventing him from accompanying me on foot for some little distance, but I got rid of him in the end; he came with me beyond the place where I had hidden my knapsack, but when he had left me long enough, I rode back and got it.

I see I am dwelling too long upon my own small adventures. Suffice it that, accompanied by my dog, I followed the north bank of the river till I found I must cross one stream before I could get any farther. This place would not do, and I had to ride half a mile back before I found one that seemed as if it might be safe. I fancy my father must have done just the same thing, for Doctor seemed to know the ground, and took to the water the moment I brought him to it. It never reached his belly, but I confess I did not like it. By and by I had to recross, and so on, off and on, till at noon I camped for dinner. Here the dog found me a nest of young ducks, nearly fledged, from which the parent birds tried with great success to decoy me. I fully thought I was going to catch them, but the dog knew better and made straight for the nest, from which he returned immediately with a fine young duck in his mouth, which he laid at my feet, wagging his tail and barking. I took another from the nest and left two for the old birds.

The afternoon was much as the morning and towards seven I reached a place which suggested itself as a good camping ground. I had hardly fixed on it and halted, before I saw a few pieces of charred wood, and felt sure that my father must have camped at this very place before me. I hobbled Doctor, unloaded, plucked and singed a duck, and gave the dog some of the meat with which Harris had furnished me; I made tea, laid my duck on the embers till it was cooked, smoked, gave myself a nightcap of brandy and water, and by and by rolled myself round in my blanket, with the dog curled up beside me. I will not dwell upon the strangeness of my feelings–nor the extreme beauty of the night. But for the dog, and Doctor, I should have been frightened, but I knew that there were no savage creatures or venomous snakes in the country, and both the dog and Doctor were such good companionable creatures, that I did not feel so much oppressed by the solitude as I had feared I should be. But the night was cold, and my blanket was not enough to keep me comfortably warm.

The following day was delightfully warm as soon as the sun got to the bottom of the valley, and the fresh fallen snow disappeared so fast from the snowy range that I was afraid it would raise the river—which, indeed, rose in the afternoon and became slightly discoloured, but it cannot have been more than three or four inches deeper, for it never reached the bottom of my saddle-bags. I believe Doctor knew exactly where I was going, for he wanted no guidance. I halted again at mid-day, got two more ducks, crossed and recrossed the river, or some of its streams, several times, and at about six, caught sight, after a bend in the valley, of the glacier descending on to the river-bed. This I knew to be close to the point at which I was to camp for the night, and from which I was to ascend the mountain. After another hour's slow progress over the increasing roughness of the river-bed, I saw the triangular delta of which my father had told me, and the stream that had formed it, bounding down the mountain side. Doctor went right up to the place where my father's fire had been, and I again found many pieces of charred wood and ashes.

As soon as I had unloaded Doctor and hobbled him, I went to a tree hard by, on which I could see the mark of a blaze, and towards which I thought I could see a line of wood ashes running. There I found a hole in which some bird had evidently been wont to build, and surmised correctly that it must be the one in which my father had hidden his box of sovereigns. There was no box in the hole now, and I began to feel that I was at last within measurable distance of Erewhon and the Erewhonians.

I camped for the night here, and again found my single blanket insufficient. The next day, *i.e.* Tuesday, 8th December, I had to pass as I best could, and it occurred to me that as I should find the gold a great weight, I had better take it some three hours up the mountain side and leave it there, so as to make the following day less fatiguing, and this I did, returning to my camp for dinner; but I was panic-stricken all the rest of the day lest I should not have hidden it safely, or lest I should be unable to find it next day–conjuring up a hundred absurd fancies as to what might befall it. And after all, heavy though it was, I could have carried it all the way. In the afternoon I saddled Doctor and rode him up to the glaciers, which were indeed magnificent, and then I made the few notes of my journey from which this chapter has been taken. I made excuses for turning in early, and at daybreak rekindled my fire and got my breakfast. All the time the companionship of the dog was an unspeakable comfort to me.

It was now the day my father had fixed for my meeting with George, and my excitement (with which I have not yet troubled the reader, though it had been consuming me ever since I had left Harris's hut) was beyond all bounds, so much so that I almost feared I was in a fever which would prevent my completing the little that remained of my task; in fact, I was in as great a panic as I had been about the gold that I had left. My hands trembled as I took the watches, and the brooches for Yram and her daughters from my saddle-bags, which I then hung, probably on the very bough on which my father had hung them. Needless to say, I also hung my saddle and bridle along with the saddle-bags.

It was nearly seven before I started, and about ten

before I reached the hiding-place of my knapsack. I found it, of course, quite easily, shouldered it, and toiled on towards the statues. At a quarter before twelve I reached them, and almost beside myself as I was, could not refrain from some disappointment at finding them a good deal smaller than I expected. My father, correcting the measurement he had given in his book, said he thought that they were about four or five times the size of life; but really I do not think they were more than twenty feet high, any one of them. In other respects my father's description of them is quite accurate. There was no wind, and as a matter of course, therefore, they were not chanting. I whiled away the quarter of an hour before the time when George became due, with wondering at them, and in a way admiring them, hideous though they were; but all the time I kept looking towards the part from which George should come.

At last my watch pointed to noon, but there was no George. A quarter past twelve, but no George. Half-past, still no George. One o'clock, and all the quarters till three o'clock, but still no George. I tried to eat some of the ship's biscuits I had brought with me, but I could not. My disappointment was now as great as my excitement had been all the forenoon; at three o'clock I fairly cried, and for half an hour could only fling myself on the ground and give way to all the unreasonable spleen that extreme vexation could suggest. True, I kept telling myself that for aught I knew George might be dead, or down with a fever; but this would not do; for in this last case he should have sent one of his brothers to meet me, and it was not likely that he was dead. I am afraid I thought it most probable that he had been casual–of which unworthy suspicion I have long since been heartily ashamed.

I put the brooches inside my knapsack, and hid it in a place where I was sure no one would find it; then, with a heavy heart, I trudged down again to my camp—broken in spirit, and hopeless for the morrow.

I camped again, but it was some hours before I got a wink of sleep; and when sleep came it was accompanied by a strange dream. I dreamed that I was by my father's bedside, watching his last flicker of intelligence, and vainly trying to catch the words that he was not less vainly trying to utter. All of a sudden the bed seemed to be at my camping ground, and the largest of the statues appeared, quite small, high up the mountain side, but striding down like a giant in seven league boots till it stood over me and my father, and shouted out " Leap, John, leap." In the horror of this vision I woke with a loud cry that woke my dog also, and made him show such evident signs of fear, that it seemed to me as though he too must have shared my dream.

Shivering with cold I started up in a frenzy, but there was nothing, save a night of such singular beauty that I did not even try to go to sleep again. Naturally enough, on trying to keep awake I dropped asleep before many minutes were over.

In the morning I again climbed up to the statues, without, to my surprise, being depressed with the idea that George would again fail to meet me. On the contrary, without rhyme or reason, I had a strong presentiment that he would come. And sure enough, as soon as I caught sight of the statues, which I did about a quarter to twelve, I saw a youth coming towards me, with a quick step, and a beaming face that had only to be seen to be fallen in love with.

" You are my brother," said he to me. " Is my father with you ? "

I pointed to the crape on my arm, and to the ground, but said nothing.

He understood me, and bared his head. Then he flung his arms about me and kissed my forehead according to Erewhonian custom. I was a little surprised at his saying nothing to me about the way in which he had disappointed me on the preceding day; I resolved, however, to wait for the explanation that I felt sure he would give me presently.

CHAPTER TWENTY-EIGHT: GEORGE AND I SPEND A FEW HOURS TOGETHER AT THE STATUES, AND THEN PART, I REACH HOME, POSTSCRIPT

I HAVE SAID ON AN EARLIER PAGE THAT George gained an immediate ascendancy over me, but ascendancy is not the word–he took me by storm; how, or why, I neither know nor want to know, but before I had been with him more than a few minutes I felt as though I had known and loved him all my life. And the dog fawned upon him as though he felt just as I did.

"Come to the statues," said he, as soon as he had somewhat recovered from the shock of the news I had given him. "We can sit down there on the very stone on which our father and I sat a year ago. I have brought a basket, which my mother packed for–for–him and me. Did he talk to you about me?"

"He talked of nothing so much, and he thought of nothing so much. He had your boots put where he could see them from his bed until he died."

Then followed the explanation about these boots, of which the reader has already been told. This made us both laugh, and from that moment we were cheerful.

I say nothing about our enjoyment of the luncheon with which Yram had provided us, and if I were to detail all that I told George about my father, and all the additional information that I got from him–(many a point did he clear up for me that I had not fully understood)–I should fill several chapters, whereas I have left myself only one. Luncheon being over I said:

"And are you married?"

"Yes" (with a blush), "and are you?"

I could not blush. Why should I? And yet young people–especially the most ingenuous among them–are apt to flush up on being asked if they are, or are going to be married. If I could have blushed, I would. As it was I could only say that I was engaged and should marry as soon as I got back.

"Then you have come all this way for me, when you were wanting to get married?"

"Of course I have. My father on his death-bed told me to do so, and to bring you something that I have brought you."

"What trouble I have given! How can I thank you?"

"Shake hands with me."

Whereon he gave my hand a stronger grip than I had quite bargained for.

"And now," said I, "before I tell you what I have brought, you must promise me to accept it. Your father said I was not to leave you till you had done so, and I was to say that he sent it with his dying blessing."

After due demur George gave his promise, and I took him to the place where I had hidden my knapsack.

"I brought it up yesterday," said I.

"Yesterday? but why?"

"Because yesterday–was it not?–was the first of the two days agreed upon between you and our father?"

"No–surely to-day is the first day–I was to come XXI. i. 3, which would be your 9th December."

"But yesterday was 9th December with us–to-day is 10th December."

"Strange! What day of the week do you make it?"

"To-day is Thursday, 10th December."

"This is still stranger–we make it Wednesday; yesterday was Tuesday."

Then I saw it. The year XX. had been a leap year with the Erewhonians, and 1891 in England had not. This, then, was what had crossed my father's brain in his dying hours, and what he had vainly tried to tell me. It was also what my unconscious self had been struggling to tell my conscious one, during the past night, but which my conscious self had been too stupid to understand. And yet my conscious self had caught it in an imperfect sort of a way after all, for from the moment that my dream had left me I had been composed, and easy in my mind that all would be well. I wish some one would write a book about dreams and parthenogenesis–for that the two are part and parcel of the same story–a brood of folly without father bred–I cannot doubt.

I did not trouble George with any of this rubbish, but only showed him how the mistake had arisen. When we had laughed sufficiently over my mistake–for it was I who had come up on the wrong day, not he–I fished my knapsack out of its hiding-place.

"Do not unpack it," said I, "beyond taking out the brooches, or you will not be able to pack it so well; but you can see the ends of the bars of gold, and you can feel the weight; my father sent them for you. The pearl brooch is for your mother, the smaller brooches are for your sisters, and your wife."

I then told him how much gold there was, and from my pockets brought out the watches and the English knife.

"This last," I said, "is the only thing that I am giving you; the rest is all from our father. I have many many times as much gold myself, and this is legally your property as much as mine is mine."

George was aghast, but he was powerless alike to express his feelings, or to refuse the gold.

"Do you mean to say that my father left me this by his will?"

"Certainly he did," said I, inventing a pious fraud.

"It is all against my oath," said he, looking grave.

"Your oath be hanged," said I. "You must give the gold to the Mayor, who knows that it is coming, and it will appear to the world, as though he were giving it you now instead of leaving you anything."

" But it is ever so much too much ! "

" It is not half enough. You and the Mayor must settle all that between you. He and our father talked it all over, and this was what they settled."

" And our father planned all this, without saying a word to me about it while we were on our way up here ? "

" Yes. There might have been some hitch in the gold's coming. Besides the Mayor told him not to tell you."

" And he never said anything about the other money he left for me–which enabled me to marry at once ? Why was this ? "

" Your mother said he was not to do so."

" Bless my heart, how they have duped me all round. But why would not my mother let your father tell me ? Oh yes–she was afraid I should tell the King about it, as I certainly should, when I told him all the rest."

" Tell the King ? " said I, " what have you been telling the King ? "

" Everything; except about the nuggets and the sovereigns, of which I knew nothing; and I have felt myself a blackguard ever since for not telling him about these when he came up here last autumn–but I let the Mayor and my mother talk me over, as I am afraid they will do again."

" When did you tell the King ? "

Then followed all the details that I have told in the latter part of chapter 21. When I asked how the King took the confession, George said:

" He was so much flattered at being treated like a reasonable being, and Dr. Downie, who was chief spokesman, played his part so discreetly, without attempting to obscure even the most compromising issues, that though his Majesty made some show of displeasure at first, it was plain that he was heartily enjoying the whole story.

" Dr. Downie showed very well. He took on himself the onus of having advised our action, and he gave me all the credit of having proposed that we should make a clean breast of everything.

" The King, too, behaved with truly royal politeness; he was on the point of asking why I had not taken our father to the Blue Pool at once, and flung him into it on the Sunday afternoon, when something seemed to strike him: he gave me a searching look, on which he said in an undertone, ' Oh yes,' and did not go on with his question. He never blamed me for anything, and when I begged him to accept my resignation of the Rangership, he said:

" ' No. Stay where you are till I lose confidence in you, which will not, I think, be very soon. I will come and have a few days' shooting about the middle of March, and if I have good sport I shall order your salary to be increased. If any more foreign devils come over, do not Blue-Pool them; send them down to me, and I will see what I think of them; I am much disposed to encourage a few of them to settle here.'

" I am sure," continued George, " that he said this because he knew I was half a foreign devil myself. Indeed he won my heart not only by the delicacy of his consideration, but by the obvious good will be bore me. I do not know what he did with the nuggets, but he gave orders that the blanket and the rest of my father's kit should be put in the great Erewhonian Museum. As regards my father's receipt, and the Professors' two depositions, he said he would have them carefully preserved in his secret archives. ' A document,' he said somewhat enigmatically, ' is a document–but, Professor Hanky, you can have this '–and as he spoke he handed him back his pocket-handkerchief.

" Hanky during the whole interview was furious, at having to play so undignified a part, but even more so, because the King while he paid marked attention to Dr. Downie, and even to myself, treated him with amused disdain. Nevertheless, angry though he was, he was impenitent, unabashed, and brazened it out at Bridgeford that the King had received him with open arms, and had snubbed Dr. Downie and myself. But for his (Hanky's) intercession, I should have been dismissed then and there from the Rangership. And so forth. Panky never opened his mouth.

"Returning to the King, his Majesty said to Dr. Downie, 'I am afraid I shall not be able to canonize any of you gentlemen just yet. We must let this affair blow over. Indeed I am in half a mind to have this Sunchild bubble pricked; I never liked it, and am getting tired of it; you Musical Bank gentlemen are overdoing it. I will talk it over with her Majesty. As for Professor Hanky, I do not see how I can keep one who has been so successfully hoodwinked, as my Professor of Worldly Wisdom; but I will consult her Majesty about this point also. Perhaps I can find another post for him. If I decide on having Sunchildism pricked, he shall apply the pin. You may go.'

"And glad enough," said George, "we all of us were to do so."

"But did he," I asked, "try to prick the bubble of Sunchildism?"

"Oh no. As soon as he said he would talk it over with her Majesty, I knew the whole thing would end in smoke, as indeed to all outward appearance it shortly did; for Dr. Downie advised him not to be in too great a hurry, and whatever he did to do it gradually. He therefore took no further action than to show marked favour to practical engineers and mechanicians. Moreover he started an aeronautical society, which made Bridgeford furious; but so far, I am afraid it has done us no good, for the first ascent was disastrous, involving the death of the poor fellow who made it, and since then no one has ventured to ascend. I am afraid we do not get on very fast."

"Did the King," I asked, "increase your salary?"

"Yes. He doubled it."

"And what do they say in Sunch'ston about our father's second visit?"

George laughed, and showed me the newspaper extract which I have already given. I asked who wrote it.

"I did," said he, with a demure smile; "I wrote it at night after I returned home, and before starting for the capital next morning. I called myself 'the deservedly popular Ranger,' to avert suspicion. No one found me out; you can keep the extract; I brought it here on purpose."

"It does you great credit. Was there ever any lunatic, and was he found?"

"Oh yes. That part was true, except that he had never been up our way."

"Then the poacher is still at large?"

"It is to be feared so."

"And were Dr. Downie and the Professors canonized after all?"

"Not yet; but the Professors will be next month–for Hanky is still Professor. Dr. Downie backed out of it. He said it was enough to be a Sunchildist without being a Sunchild Saint. He worships the jumping cat as much as the others, but he keeps his eye better on the cat, and sees sooner both when it will jump, and where it will jump to. Then, without disturbing any one, he insinuates himself into the place which will be best when the jump is over. Some say that the cat knows him and follows him; at all events when he makes a move the cat generally jumps towards him soon afterwards."

"You give him a very high character."

"Yes, but I have my doubts about his doing much

in this matter; he is getting old, and Hanky burrows like a mole night and day. There is no knowing how it will all end."

"And the people at Sunch'ston? Has it got well about among them, in spite of your admirable article, that it was the Sunchild himself who interrupted Hanky?"

"It has, and it has not. Many of us know the truth, but a story came down from Bridgeford that it was an evil spirit who had assumed the Sunchild's form, intending to make people sceptical about Sunchildism; Hanky and Panky cowed this spirit, otherwise it would never have recanted. Many people swallow this—"

"But Hanky and Panky swore that they knew the man."

"That does not matter."

"And now please, how long have you been married?"

"About ten months."

"Any family?"

"One boy about a fortnight old. Do come down to Sunch'ston and see him–he is your own nephew. You speak Erewhonian so perfectly that no human being would suspect you were a foreigner, and you look one of us from head to foot. I can smuggle you through quite easily, and my mother would so like to see you."

I should dearly have liked to have gone, but it was out of the question. I had nothing with me but the clothes I stood in; moreover I was longing to be back in England, and when once I was in Erewhon there was no knowing when I should be able to get away again; but George fought hard before he gave in.

It was now nearing the time when this strange meeting between two brothers–as strange a one as the statues can ever have looked down upon–must come to an end. I showed George what the repeater would do, and what it would expect of its possessor. I gave him six good photographs of my father and myself–three of each.

He had never seen a photograph, and could hardly believe his eyes as he looked at those I showed him. I also gave him three envelopes addressed to myself, care of Alfred Emery Cathie, Esq., 15 Clifford's Inn, London, and implored him to write to me if he could ever find means of getting a letter over the range as far as the shepherd's hut. At this he shook his head, but he promised to write if he could. I also told him that I had written a full account of my father's second visit to Erewhon, but that it should never be published till I heard from him–at which he again shook his head, but added, "And yet who can tell? For the King may have the country opened up to foreigners some day after all."

Then he thanked me a thousand times over, shouldered the knapsack, embraced me as he had my father, and caressed the dog, embraced me again, and made no attempt to hide the tears that ran down his cheeks.

"There," he said; "I shall wait here till you are out of sight."

I turned away, and did not look back till I reached the place at which I knew that I should lose the statues. I then turned round, waved my hand–as also did George, and went down the mountain side, full of sad thoughts, but thankful that my task had been so happily accomplished, and aware that my life henceforward had been enriched by something that I could never lose.

For I had never seen, and felt as though I never could see, George's equal. His absolute unconsciousness of self, the unhesitating way in which he took me to his heart, his fearless frankness, the happy genial expression that played on his face, and the extreme sweetness of his smile–these were the things that made me say to myself that the "blazon of beauty's best" could tell me nothing better than what I had found and lost within the last three hours. How small, too, I felt by comparison! If for no other cause, yet for this, that I, who had wept so bitterly over my own disappointment the day before, could meet this dear fellow's tears with no tear of my own.

But let this pass. I got back to Harris's hut without adventure. When there, in the course of the evening, I told Harris that I had a fancy for the rug he had found on the river-bed, and that if he would let me have it, I would give him my red one and ten shillings to boot. The exchange was so obviously to his advantage that he made no demur, and next morning I strapped Yram's rug on to my horse, and took it gladly home to England, where I keep it on my own bed next to the counterpane, so that with care it may last me out my life. I wanted him to take the dog and make a home for him, but he had two collies already, and said that a retriever would be of no use to him. So I took the poor beast on with me to the port, where I was glad to find that Mr. Baker liked him and accepted him from me, though he was not mine to give. He had been such an unspeakable comfort to me when I was alone, that he would have haunted me unless I had been able to provide for him where I knew he would be well cared for. As for Doctor, I was sorry to leave him, but I knew he was in good hands.

"I see you have not brought your knapsack back, sir," said Mr. Baker.

"No," said I, "and very thankful was I when I had handed it over to those for whom it was intended."

"I have no doubt you were, sir, for I could see it was a desperate heavy load for you."

"Indeed it was." But at this point I brought the discussion to a close.

Two days later I sailed, and reached home early in February 1892. I was married three weeks later, and when the honeymoon was over, set about making the necessary, and some, I fear, unnecessary additions to this book–by far the greater part of which had been written, as I have already said, many months earlier. I now leave it, at any rate for the present, 22nd April 1892.

*

Postscript.–On the last day of November 1900, I received a letter addressed in Mr. Alfred Cathie's familiar handwriting, and on opening it found that it contained another, addressed to me in my own, and unstamped. For the moment I was puzzled, but immediately knew that it must be from George. I tore it open, and found eight closely written pages, which I devoured as I have seldom indeed devoured so long a letter. It was dated XXIX. vii. 1, and, as nearly as I can translate it was as follows:

"Twice, my dearest brother, have I written to you, and twice on successive days in successive years, have I been up to the statues on the chance that you could meet me, as I proposed in my letters. Do not think I went all the way back to Sunch'ston–there is a ranger's shelter now only an hour and a half below the statues, and here I passed the night. I knew you had got neither of my letters, for if you had got them and could not come yourself, you would have sent some one whom you could trust with a letter. I know you would, though I do not know how you would have contrived to do it.

"I sent both letters through Bishop Kahabuka (or, as his inferior clergy call him, 'Chowbok'), head of the Christian Mission to Erĕwhēmos, which, as your father has doubtless told you, is the country adjoining Erewhon, but inhabited by a coloured race having no affinity with our own. Bishop Kahabuka has penetrated at times into Erewhon, and the King, wishing to be on good terms with his neighbours, has permitted him to establish two or three mission stations in the western parts of Erewhon. Among the missionaries are some few of your own countrymen. None of us like them, but one of them is teaching me English, which I find quite easy.

" As I wrote in the letters that have never reached you, I am no longer Ranger. The King, after some few years (in the course of which I told him of your visit, and what you had brought me), declared that I was the only one of his servants whom he could trust, and found high office for me, which kept me in close confidential communication with himself.

" About three years ago, on the death of his Prime Minister, he appointed me to fill his place; and it was on this, that so many possibilities occurred to me concerning which I dearly longed for your opinion, that I wrote and asked you, if you could, to meet me personally or by proxy at the statues, which I could reach on the occasion of my annual visit to my mother–yes–and father–at Sunch'ston.

" I sent both letters by way of Erewhemos, confiding them to Bishop Kahabuka, who is just such another as St. Hanky. He tells me that our father was a very old and dear friend of his–but of course I did not say anything about his being my own father. I only inquired about a Mr. Higgs, who was now worshipped in Erewhon as a supernatural being. The Bishop said it was, " Oh, so very dreadful," and he felt it all the more keenly for the reason that he had himself been the means of my father's going to Erewhon, by giving him the information that enabled him to find the pass over the range that bounded the country.

" I did not like the man, but I thought I could trust him with a letter, which it now seems I could not do. This third letter I have given him with a promise of a hundred pounds in silver for his new Cathedral, to be paid as soon as I get an answer from you.

" We are all well at Sunch'ston; so are my wife and eight children–five sons and three daughters–but the country is at sixes and sevens. St. Panky is dead, but his son Pocus is worse. Dr. Downie has become very lethargic. I can do less against St. Hankyism than when I was a private man. A little indiscretion on my part would plunge the country in civil war. Our engineers and so-called men of science are sturdily begging for endowments, and steadily claiming to have a hand in every pie that is baked from one end of the country to the other. The missionaries are buying up all our silver, and a change in the relative values of gold and silver is in progress of which none of us foresee the end.

"The King and I both think that annexation by England, or a British Protectorate, would be the saving of us, for we have no army worth the name, and if you do not take us over some one else soon will. The King has urged me to send for you. If you come (do! do! do!) you had better come by way of Erewhemos, which is now in monthly communication with Southampton. If you will write me that you are coming I will meet you at the port, and bring you with me to our own capital, where the King will be overjoyed to see you."

*

The rest of the letter was filled with all sorts of news which interested me, but would require chapters of explanation before it could become interesting to the reader.

The letter wound up:

"You may publish now whatever you like, whenever you like.

"Write to me by way of Erewhemos, care of the Right Reverend the Lord Bishop, and say which way you will come. If you prefer the old road, we are bound to be in the neighbourhood of the statues by the beginning of March. My next brother is now Ranger, and could meet you at the statues with permit and luncheon, and more of that white wine than ever you will be able to drink. Only let me know what you will do.

"I should tell you that the old railway which used to run from Clearwater to the capital, and which, as you know, was allowed to go to ruin, has been reconstructed at an outlay far less than might have been expected–for the bridges had been maintained for ordinary carriage traffic. The journey, therefore, from Sunch'ston to the capital can now be done in less than forty hours. On the whole, however, I recommend you to come by way of Erewhemos. If you start, as I think possible, without writing from England, Bishop Kahabuka's palace is only eight miles from the port, and he will give you every information about your further journey–a distance of less than a couple of hundred miles. But I should prefer to meet you myself.

"My dearest brother, I charge you by the memory of our common father, and even more by that of those three hours that linked you to me for ever, and which I would fain hope linked me also to yourself–come over, if by any means you can do so–come over and help us.

"GEORGE STRONG."

"My dear," said I to my wife who was at the other end of the breakfast table, "I shall have to translate this letter to you, and then you will have to help me to begin packing; for I have none too much time. I must see Alfred, and give him a power of attorney. He will arrange with some publisher about my book, and you can correct the press. Break the news gently to the children; and get along without me, my dear, for six months as well as you can."

*

I write this at Southampton, from which port I sail to-morrow–*i.e.* 15th November 1900–for Erewhemos.